"Daniel!"

Ellen Hall spun to face him, her blue eyes brilliant with azure sparks. His gut tensed. He always forgot, between her rare visits home to Pinewood, how beautiful she was. He held his place as she walked toward him, the fabric of her long skirts swishing, small bits of the clinging snow falling off her swaying cloak to dot the plank floor.

"I've *told* you not to call me that, Daniel." Her eyes flashed, high spots of color crept into her cheeks. "We're no longer children, lest you've forgotten."

As if that were possible. He looked away from her. "I remember. Though why you'd prefer to be called Muskrat makes no sense to me."

"Don't be boorish!" She sniffed and slanted a look up at him from beneath the fur-trimmed brim of her bonnet. "Would it destroy you to call me Ellen?"

Likely so, the way his heart jolted at that look—phony as it was.

Books by Dorothy Clark

Love Inspired Historical

Family of the Heart
The Law and Miss Mary
Prairie Courtship
Gold Rush Baby
Frontier Father
*Wooing the Schoolmarm
*Courting Miss Callie
*Falling for the Teacher
*A Season of the Heart

Love Inspired

Hosea's Bride
Lessons from the Heart

Steeple Hill Single Title

Beauty for Ashes
Joy for Mourning

*Pinewood Weddings

DOROTHY CLARK

Critically acclaimed, award-winning author Dorothy Clark lives in rural New York, in a home she designed and helped her husband build (she swings a mean hammer!) with the able assistance of their three children. When she is not writing, she and her husband enjoy traveling throughout the United States, doing research and gaining inspiration for future books. Dorothy believes in God, love, family and happy endings, which explains why she feels so at home writing stories for Love Inspired Books. Dorothy enjoys hearing from her readers and may be contacted at dorothyjclark@hotmail.com.

A Season of the Heart

DOROTHY CLARK

HARLEQUIN® LOVE INSPIRED® HISTORICAL

Recycling programs
for this product may
not exist in your area.

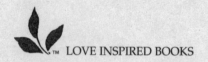

™ LOVE INSPIRED BOOKS

ISBN-13: 978-0-373-28291-3

A Season of the Heart

www.Harlequin.com

Printed in U.S.A.

Chapter One

December, 1841
Pinewood Village, New York

"Daniel Braynard, what brings you to town in this snowstorm?"

Daniel looped the reins over the hitching post, squinted up through the thick fall of snow and smiled. "Your husband's skills, Mrs. Dibble." He stepped forward and offered his hand to the older woman descending the steps from the wood walkway that ran in front of the block of stores. "He's doing some repair work on one of the stoves from camp. How have you been keeping?"

"I'm well. And busy helping Willa with Christmas preparations. Though I tend to hold the baby more than work. She's such a sweet little mite."

"She's little, all right. Not much bigger than my hand." He gave the proud grandmother a sheepish grin. "Truth is…she's sort of scary to hold."

"She won't break, Daniel."

"That's what Willa said when she handed her to me."

His grin widened. "Trouble was, my big, clumsy hands didn't believe it."

Helen Dibble laughed, gripped the hood of her green wool cape against a sudden gust of wind and stepped toward the road. "That tiny baby takes a lot of time and care, and with all Willa has taken upon herself as the pastor's wife—Christmas decorations for the church and all—I'm afraid it will be too much for her strength. And Matthew is too busy making calls on his sick parishioners to give her a hand. The grippe is bad this year." She pinned him with a glance. "Mayhap Willa could put your strong back and those big, clumsy hands of yours to good use."

That was not a suggestion. He grinned at the woman who had been like a second mother to him all his life, grabbed the empty burlap bag off the seat of the pung and tossed it over his shoulder. "I'll be glad to help any way I can. I've no time to go there today, but I'll stop by the parsonage next time I'm in town. Mind that slick spot." The brown paper package in her hand crackled as he took her elbow and guided her around the patch of ice in the frozen rut. He helped her across Main Street, then hurried back toward Cargrave's Mercantile.

The young boy shoveling the snow from in front of the stores stepped aside to let him pass.

"Looks like you're fighting a losing battle there, Jasper."

"Yes, sir, Mr. Braynard." The boy blinked flakes from his eyelashes and gave him a gap-toothed grin. "It's fallin' faster than I can scoop it for sure. I get down to the end of the walkway, turn around and come back and start all over again."

"Well, all that shoveling will make you good and

strong." He thumped the youngster's shoulder, then slanted a look up at the large flakes streaming from the sky and frowned. If it started blowing and drifting, it would be hard going on the way back to camp.

He hurried to Cargrave's Mercantile, stomped his boots in the store's recessed entrance and shoved open the door. The bell overhead jangled a welcome. The elderly men hunched over a checkerboard in front of the woodstove at the back of the store looked his way.

"Hey, Daniel. Game's almost over. You got time to play the winner?"

"You know you and Mr. Grant are too good for me, Mr. Fabrizio. I'd only lose." He grinned at the men, yanked off the burlap bag he'd slung over his shoulder and tossed it onto the counter. The heat from the stove stung his cold hands and made his cheeks prickle.

"Must be some dire needs at camp to bring you to town in this weather." Allan Cargrave pulled the bag toward him.

"*Dire* is right. One of the woodstoves needed repaired—" he pulled a list from his pocket and handed the paper to the proprietor "—the molasses is running low, the men's chew is about gone and I'll find the cook hanging by his toes from the ceiling if I don't get back with some coffee before suppertime—among other things."

He joined in the general chuckle, grabbed two shovels and an ax from the tools leaning against the back wall and carried them over to the long counter.

Allan Cargrave shoved four five-pound sacks of Old Java coffee beans into the bag and reached for the boxes of cut plug tobacco. "Looks like this cold snap has been hard on your tools."

"It's not the weather. We need more tools for the hicks."

"Townsend's lumber camps are still hiring?"

He nodded at Emil Grant and rubbed his cold hands together. "We're having a hard time downing enough timber to hold against the spring rafting *and* keep the sawmill satisfied since Manning bought that clapboard machine and Cole—"

The bell jangled. He blew on his hands, glanced toward the door and eyed the woman who entered. The fur that traced the brim of her snow-covered blue wool bonnet hid her face. More fur formed a collar and edged the elbow-length shoulder cape of the blue wool cloak that fell to within a few inches of the hem of her dress. A fur muff enfolded her hands. *Fancy.* The hunter in him took a closer look at the fur. *Rabbit.*

He turned his attention to the basket of leather gloves on the counter. His had split into useless pieces yesterday. He pulled out a couple pair that looked as if they might fit, tried one pair on and flexed his fingers, then stole another look at the woman. Must be one of the guests at the Sheffield House. No Pinewood woman wore anything as fancy as that gear. Not even Callie, though she surely could now that she'd married Ezra Ryder in spite of all his money. His lips slanted into a grin. Callie had sure led Ezra a merry chase, refusing—

"Good morning, madam. How may I help you?"

Allan Cargrave's voice drew him back to his task. He grabbed the top keg of molasses from the stack on the floor at the end of the counter.

"Good morning, Mr. Cargrave. I've come to see if there's any mail for Mother. And I'm not a madam—yet."

Ellen. The unexpected sound of her soft voice froze him with the keg hoisted halfway to his shoulder.

"My apologies, Miss Ellen. I didn't recognize you."

"Nor did I." He settled the keg in place and turned. "Hey, Musquash. When did you come back to town?"

"Daniel!"

Ellen Hall spun to face him, her blue eyes brilliant with azure sparks. His gut clenched. The memory of her beauty dimmed between her rare visits home to Pinewood. He held his place as she walked toward him, the fabric of her long skirts swishing, small bits of the clinging snow falling off her swaying cloak to dot the plank floor.

"I've *told* you not to call me that, Daniel." Her eyes flashed; high spots of color crept into her cheeks. "We're no longer children, lest you've forgotten."

As if that were possible. He adjusted the position of the keg and looked away from her. "I remember. Though why you'd prefer to be called Muskrat makes no sense to me."

"Don't be boorish!" She sniffed and slanted a look up at him from beneath the fur-trimmed brim of her bonnet. "Would it destroy you to call me Ellen?"

Likely so, the way his heart jolted at that look—phony as it was. Well, what of it? He was a man now, not a twelve-year-old boy with a first crush. He covered his agitation with a grin. "Is that what you have all your rich beaux in Buffalo call you?"

"Of course not!"

He reached down to the counter and grasped the neck of the filled burlap bag. "I must say, all those society doings in the big city agree with you." He lifted his gaze back to her face and strengthened the teasing note in his voice. "You're looking well…lots of color in your cheeks and all."

The spots of red spread across her cheekbones. The delicate nostrils on her narrow nose flared. "I don't know why I bother to talk to you, Daniel Braynard!" She tossed her head and turned toward the wall of glass mailboxes.

"For old times' sake, I guess." He kept his tone light, pasted a grin on his face. "It's for sure not because I compare favorably with your rich new society beaux."

"True indeed. My society friends have *manners*." She gave a huff, glanced over her shoulder at him. "They would never think of calling me by such names."

He chuckled, shoved the end of the burlap bag into his hand balancing the keg, then gathered the handles of the tools into his free hand. He'd had enough of this conversation. The words stung like salt rubbed into an old wound.

She whirled and glared up at him. "And they would *not* laugh at me. They are gentlemen. And they are devoted to me."

The leather of the new gloves strained across his tightened knuckles. He relaxed his grip on the bag and the tools and lifted his lips into another slow grin. "Now, Musquash, don't go all niminy-piminy on me. We go back too far for that. As for manners…" He leaned over and put his mouth close to the blue wool covering her ear so she alone would hear him. "I've never told anyone *why* I call you Musquash. How devoted would your fine gentlemen friends be if they'd seen you looking like a drowned muskrat?"

A sound, somewhere between a gasp and a growl, escaped her. He jerked his head up and barely missed getting his jaw clipped by the top of her head as she spun about and stormed to the waist-high shelf in the mailbox wall.

"Mother's mail please, Mr. Hubble."

"There's nothing today, Miss Ellen. That new *Godey's Lady's Magazine* your mama's waiting on didn't come in yet."

"Very well. I'll come back tomorrow. Good day." She gave a stiff little nod in the direction of the counter, turned and swept to the door. The bells jangled, then fell silent.

"Miss Ellen, so beautiful she is. Ahh, to be young again…" Ilari Fabrizio's deep, heavily accented voice sighed through the store.

There was a loud snort. A checker brushed across the wood game board. "Forget the dreaming and take your turn, Romeo."

Good advice, Mr. Grant. There's no one in this town good enough for Ellen. Not anymore. Daniel ducked his head and stole a look through the window. Ellen's fur-adorned blue cloak and bonnet blurred and disappeared into the rapidly falling snow. Another image to join the others he'd stored up through the years. A fitting one—Ellen walking away. He took a firmer grip on the tools and headed for the door.

Allan Cargrave came from behind the counter and reached to open the door. "You two scrap with each other the same as when you were growing up, Daniel. I guess some things don't change."

"I guess." He braced the keg on his shoulder and stepped outside. "Put the gloves on my account."

He ducked his head against a rising wind and headed for the pung. The new snow was already higher than his ankles. He frowned, stashed his burden in the back of the long box, freed the reins and turned the horse to face the road. Allan Cargrave was wrong. Everything changed with time. Ellen certainly had. And so had their old friendship and the childhood crush he'd once had for her. He didn't even *like* the woman she'd become.

Ellen turned into the shoveled walk that led to the parsonage, her boots crunching the newly fallen snow, her dragging hems leaving a wide swath behind her. A gust of wind flapped the front edges of her cloak and sneaked beneath the warm wool. She shivered and hurried to the porch. How she hated winter! Of course, the cold did give her a chance to wear her cape and bonnet, and the fur around her face was very flattering. Harold Lodge and Earl Cuthbert had both been lavish in their compliments of her beauty in the new garments. As had others.

The thought tugged her lips into a smile. She withdrew her gloved hand from her muff, fluffed the fur brushing against her cheeks and knocked. Daniel, of course, hadn't even noticed. Her smile faded.

The door opened a crack. She stared at the blank space, slid her gaze downward. A pair of brown eyes peered up at her from beneath a mop of blond curls. "Oh. Good morning, Joshua. Is—" The boy's head disappeared.

"It's Miss Ellen, Mama!"

"Ellen?"

There was delight in the muffled reply. She smiled, then sobered at the sight of a furry black muzzle poking through the crack, the black nose twitching. The dog barked, thrust his head and shoulders through the opening and jumped out onto the stoop.

The memory of the snarling dog that had leaped at her out of the woods behind Willa's home when they were children snapped into her mind. *Don't let him know you're afraid!* The words Daniel had shouted at her that day as he dropped from a tree and rushed between her and the dog held her in place. She stood perfectly still. There was no Daniel to save her from an attack today.

"Don't let Happy out, Joshua! Take him to your room." Hurrying footfalls sounded in the hallway.

Joshua leaned out and thumped his dog's shoulder. "C'mon in the house, Happy!"

The dog rose, shook and leaped back inside. Willa appeared in the doorway. "Ellen! Matthew heard you'd come home last night. I'm sorry about the dog. Come in."

She looked at Willa's smile, the welcoming warmth in her friend's blue-green eyes, and gathered her courage. "I didn't know the children were home. I'm afraid I've come at an inconvenient time, Willa. But I wanted to see you and your baby." She brushed off the snow as best she could and stepped into the small entrance, watched the boy thunder up the stairs with the dog at his heels and held back a sigh of relief.

"There was no school because of the storm, but I'm glad you came, Ellen. I was hoping to see you today. It's been months since you were home. My, what a lovely cloak and bonnet!" Willa held out her hands. "Let me hang it on the peg and we'll go into the sitting room and visit by the fire."

"That sounds delightful." She slipped off her gloves and tucked them inside the muff, then removed her cloak and untied her bonnet. "You're looking well. How are you feeling?"

"I'm fine, Ellen. My confinement went smoothly. Did you have a pleasant trip home?"

"Yes." She smiled and fluffed her curls, relieved at the change of subject. "Mr. Lodge insisted on accompanying me as far as Dunkirk. Then he sent me on in his enclosed sleigh while he tended to business there. With the wind blocked out, a warmed soapstone under my feet and the fur lap robe covering me, it was a comfortable ride."

"I heard about the enclosed sleigh. But then, of course, I would." Willa laughed and led the way to the chairs by the fire. "Tommy Burke and Kurt Finster saw your arrival last night and were very impressed by the odd-looking equipage. They spread the word."

"I'm sure they did. There's certainly nothing like Mr. Lodge's sleigh in Pinewood. Truth be told, there are very few in Buffalo. Of course, Mr. Lodge and Mr. Cuthbert both have one." She stopped and leaned over the baby sleeping in a cradle beside the hearth. "So this is Miss Mary Elizabeth Calvert." A smile curved her lips. "She has your auburn hair."

"Yes, though it curls like Matthew's."

The love in Willa's voice drew her gaze. Her friend's face was a picture of contentment and happiness. A twinge of envy curled around her heart. She sat and smoothed out her skirts, then fingered the layers of lace that formed a frothy V at her throat, taking comfort in the richness of her gown. She brushed back a curl and gestured toward the settee. "What is all that?"

"Several children are going to speak Scripture verses at church for Christmas and I thought it would be nice if they wore suitable costumes." Willa gave the cradle a gentle rock and went to stand beside the settee. "I asked for donations of material to make the costumes, and this pile is the result."

"You're going to make the costumes?" She lifted her skirt hems higher to warm her feet.

"Yes. Agnes was going to help me sew them, but her aunt took sick and she's gone to stay with her. Callie would help, of course, but she and Ezra have gone to visit his sister for the holiday—and Sadie has to watch over Grandfather and Grandmother Townsend. All the others I've asked have no time."

Ellen swept her gaze over the narrowed blue-green eyes and slightly pursed lips that Willa always wore when she was considering something. Surely she wasn't— No. She misunderstood Willa's intent. No one ever asked her for help. She laughed and stretched her feet out closer to the fire.

"There is something amusing?"

She shook her head and fluffed her curls. "Not really. It was only that, for a moment, I thought you were going to ask me to help you."

"Would you, Ellen?"

"Would I *help* you?" She frowned. "Stop teasing, Willa. I get enough of that from Daniel."

"I'm not teasing." Willa took a breath, gave her an odd look. "I hate to ask it of you…truly. I know you don't do such menial tasks, Ellen. But I have the costumes to make…and the church decorations. And our own Christmas to prepare for, as well. It's our first as a family, and I want it to be wonderful for Joshua and Sally and Matthew. Mother has offered to help, of course, but she tends to hold the baby more than work."

She stared at Willa, unable to fully believe that she was serious in her request. "Well, I—I'll give it some thought. I have plans to make for Mr. Lodge's and Mr. Cuthbert's visits."

"Oh, of course. Forgive me, I shouldn't even have asked."

A look of disappointment swept over Willa's face. Guilt smote her. Well, what did Willa expect? She didn't *sew.* Still, it was nice to be asked for help, she—

"Who is this Mr. Cuthbert you mentioned, Ellen?" Willa moved back to the fireplace, lifted a piece of split log out of the carrier on the hearth and put it on the fire. "I don't believe I've heard you mention his name before."

A soft sigh escaped her at the welcome question. She was back on safe ground now. "He's been paying me court since last August. He approached me at a soiree given by the Halseys, said he was quite taken by my beauty and asked if he might call on me."

"What of Mr. Lodge? I thought he was your beau?"

"He is." She glanced at Willa and sat a little straighter. "You needn't look disapproving. I've not given Mr. Lodge my promise. I'm still free to accept another suitor if one takes my fancy, and I find Mr. Cuthbert's maturity attractive."

"His maturity?" Willa's brows rose. She hung the poker she was using on its hook and looked at her. "As in steadfast character or years?"

She lifted her chin. "Both."

"I see." Willa's eyes narrowed on her. "If I remember correctly, Mr. Lodge is six years older than you, Ellen. How 'mature' is Mr. Cuthbert?"

"That is not important." She rose and held her hands out to the fire to avoid meeting that penetrating gaze. Willa was only two years older but she'd always had the ability to make her want to squirm. "Mr. Cuthbert is a man of great distinction and social eminence, and I'm flattered by his attentions."

"And he is as wealthy as Mr. Lodge."

Judged and found guilty. The indictment was in Willa's voice. She squared her shoulders. "Not quite."

"Ellen! You have true affection for this man?"

She took a breath and turned. "I have admiration for him and his accomplishments. He is a personal friend of the governor and may become the next secretary of state—if the Senate approves Mr. Seward's appointment of him. And then…who knows how far his abilities may take him? Perhaps even to our nation's capital." She smiled, waited for the gasp of disbelief, the look of envy that always accompanied her announcement.

"I see." Willa's gaze shifted to the cradle, then came back to rest on her. "And what of love, Ellen?"

The question brought the romantic young-girl dreams she had forsaken rushing back. A frisson of anger slipped through her, stiffened her spine. She should have guessed that would be Willa's reaction. Willa had been preaching to her about love in marriage ever since she'd wed Matthew Calvert. And Callie was as bad since her marriage to Ezra Ryder. No doubt Sadie would be the same. The fire crackled. Ellen took a breath and turned back to gaze down into the flickering fire. Seeing Daniel again made those romantic dreams all too real. But she was no longer a hero-worshipping child. She was a woman with a purpose. "What about love, Willa? You, of all people, know that love can be fickle."

"Not true love, Ellen."

Enough! She would not be belittled because she chose to follow her head instead of her heart. "And how does one know the difference?" She threw a challenging glance over her shoulder. "You and your mother were both deceived. I prefer not to take that chance." She looked back at the flames devouring the wood, the way poverty turned love into ashes. "Mother told me love is simply an emotion that will trap you in a log cabin with a husband who spends his time trying to earn enough to provide food and shelter for you and the children that come of such a union. She was not interested in that menial sort of life. That's why she married Father. And she's never regretted her decision."

She lifted her chin, turned and faced Willa again. "I'm not interested in that sort of drudgery either, Willa. I mean to have every advantage—and both Mr. Lodge and Mr. Cuthbert can provide them. And both have spoken for my hand. That's why I've come home. I have to decide which man will best serve my plans. As for love—" she gave an eloquent little shrug "—I'm certain a fondness between me and the man I choose to marry will develop over the years. And if not…" She looked at the happiness glowing in Willa's eyes and caught her breath at a sudden empty feeling inside. Daniel's crooked grin appeared before her, enticing her. *Foolishness.* Daniel was nothing but a friend from her childhood. A teamster with nothing to call his own. She blinked the image away and ran her hands over the rich fabric of her gown. "If not…I will have the finest of everything to take its place."

Chapter Two

"Whoa." Camp had never looked so good. Daniel draped the reins over the edge of the wood seat, jumped off and trudged to the back of the pung's low wood box. A quick swipe of his gloved hand cleared the mounded flakes off of the molasses keg and he hoisted it to his shoulder. Bits of clinging snow fell off the keg against his neck, sent a shiver chasing down his back. He ignored the chill and searched for the neck of the burlap bag, took hold and pulled it free.

The pigs milling around the kitchen door waiting for the cook to throw out the leavings from his supper preparations came snorting and grunting, pressing against his legs as they fought for position. "Give over!" He kneed them aside, stomped his way to the log building and gave the door a swift kick.

Irregular footsteps thumped against the puncheons of the kitchen floor. The door was yanked open. "Ain't ya got a hand?"

"Not an empty one." He thrust the burlap bag at the scowling cook. "Here are the things you ordered."

"'Bout time." The cook folded a meaty fist around

the neck of the bag, kicked the door shut and limped his way over to the worktable.

"What are you grumbling about, Smiley? You're still alive, aren't you?" He grinned and shrugged the keg of molasses off his shoulder onto a long plank shelf on the wall. Heavy boots thumped against the floor in the other room. "You'd better get the coffee going if you plan to stay that way. The men are coming in."

"I'm lame, not deaf. I hear 'em." The cook tugged open the strings on one of the sacks of coffee beans, dumped some in the grinder and turned the crank. The beans popped and crackled, the fragments whispering down the chute into a bowl and releasing their tantalizing fragrance to blend with the smell of the beef stew simmering in the iron pots hanging in the fireplace. Loaves of fresh-baked bread piled on a table by the dining room door added their tangy sourdough aroma.

Daniel tugged the shoulder of his coat back in place, turned and took a deep sniff. "Smells good in here, Smiley. Feels good, too. It's turning nasty outside. The temperature's dropping fast."

"Then, was I you, I'd stop jawing and get some heat in the dining room."

"My exact intentions." He grinned and clapped the scowling cook on the shoulder, strode by the table loaded with bread and into the dining room. "Irish, come help me carry the woodstove in from the pung."

A roar of approval rose from the snow-covered loggers stomping in from outside to find a place on the plank benches alongside the sawbuck tables.

"*Ja. Und* be quick about it, Irish!" A ham-sized fist landed on the thin Irishman's shoulder as he turned back toward the door. "Get those jigging feet moving so ve can have some heat in here, *ja?* It's bad enough ve freeze—"

"Thump me again, Hans, an' you'll not be warmin' yourself by any fire." Irish scowled and pulled his coat collar up around his neck. "'Tis eatin' an' sleepin' in a snowbank you'll be doin'."

The stocky German wobbled his knees and shook his arms, pretending to quake in his boots. A burst of laughter filled the room.

"An' that—" Irish yanked the rolled brim of Hans's hat down over the German's face "—will get you the joy of helpin' me fetch in an' set up the stove, while Danny-boy-o tends to his horses."

The crowd of laughing loggers parted, making a pathway to the door. Irish gave Hans a friendly shove and followed him outside.

Daniel grinned at their antics and stepped back into the kitchen. "Save me some supper, Smiley. I'll be back when I've stabled Big Girl."

"I ain't yer servant. Come before the victuals are gone, or feel yer stomach pressing against yer backbone all night." The cook grabbed a pair of gloves off the table and waved them in his direction. "What am I supposed to do with these—add 'em to the stew?"

"It might improve it some." He laughed at the cook's growl, took the leather gloves from his meaty hand and stuffed them into his jacket pocket. "Guess those got tossed in the bag by mistake. I'll take them back next time I go to town." He tugged his collar tight around his neck and headed for the door. "Don't forget to save me some supper—a crust of bread will do. As long as it's followed by some of that dried apple pie I see on the warming shelf." He yanked open the door and hurried to the pung to unhitch. There didn't look to be an abundance of those pies, and Smiley was only one man against all those hungry loggers.

"C'mon, Big Girl, that's enough." Daniel tugged on the reins and the mare obligingly lifted her muzzle from the creek and followed him to the stable. Soft whickers from her barn mates greeted them. The Belgian's hoofs thudded against the puncheons, the vibrations quivering beneath his feet. He opened the stall door and led the mare inside, slipped her bridle off and stroked the white race that flowed from her poll to her muzzle. "Good job, pulling the pung through those deep drifts, Big Girl." The Belgian lowered her head and nudged him in the chest.

"So you want food instead of praise, huh? All right, don't push. I'll get out of your way." He stepped aside, and the chestnut stretched out her thick neck and grabbed a mouthful of the clean hay in the rack. He patted her shoulder, hung the bridle on a peg and grabbed a grooming cloth. The mare's contented munching accompanied his long sweeping strokes as he dried her huge body.

Being a teamster wasn't a bad life. He worked hard hauling logs and caring for the horses—not as hard as when he'd been a logger, of course. Still, he was tired enough at day's end to sleep without dreaming most nights. The tightness in his gut told him this wasn't likely to be one of them. His unexpected meeting with Ellen was too fresh, the images of her too strong, the sound of her voice too recent, for him to block them from his mind. It was always that way when she came home. A residue of his childhood love for her.

He frowned, swapped the wet cloth for a dry one,

smacked the mare's hip to let her know he was going behind her and crossed over to wipe down her other side.

He disliked teasing Ellen to the point of anger. Not that it took much teasing with her flash temper. But when he was face-to-face with the spoiled, selfish woman she'd become, disappointment stung him like a slap to the cheek and sharpened his tongue. She'd been so sweet, so kind and loving— He sucked in a deep breath, tugged his thoughts from what had once been. It was good for him she had changed. A grown man would look mighty foolish carrying around the sort of crush he'd had on her when they were kids. Especially since she wouldn't give him a passing thought as a beau. Not with his life. And she was right not to. He had nothing to offer any woman, let alone a woman like Ellen who lived a life of ease.

The mare nickered, swung her head around and butted his shoulder. He shot out his right leg to brace himself. "Sorry, Big Girl. I didn't mean to ignore you." He tossed the wet rag over the stall wall beside the other one and picked up the comb to take any tangles out of the chestnut's flaxen mane and tail. One thing about working with horses—you couldn't waste time feeling sorry for yourself too long.

"You're all set, girl." Daniel tossed her blanket over the Belgian's back, pulled the hold strap snug against her broad chest so it wouldn't slide askew through the night, fastened the buckle, then strode to the feed bin. He shoved a pail beneath the hopper chute, lifted the door and let the grain flow until it was full. "Here's supper, Big Girl."

The gelding in the stall on his left whickered, tossed his massive head and thudded his front hoof against the floor.

"I'm coming, Big Boy." He dumped the oats and bran into the mare's manger, closed the stall door and returned to the feed bin for another pail of grain.

Ellen turned back a page and studied the dress in the picture. "Mother, have you any shaded velvet material at your shop?"

"Why, yes, I do." Her mother glanced up from the feathers she was sorting. "I don't recall any velvet dresses in that magazine. Why do you ask, Ellen?"

"I need a new gown for when Mr. Lodge and Mr. Cuthbert come to visit over the holiday, and I think this one may suit." She pulled her fringe-trimmed silk wrap close around her, rose from the chair in front of the fire and walked over to sit beside her mother on the settee. "It's this coatdress, with the high neck, moderate cape and tight sleeves." She indicated the dress she was considering. "See how the narrow belt above the long full skirt shows off the model's small waist."

Her mother glanced at the magazine she held out, then leaned forward and placed a black feather in a pile with other black ones. "It's a lovely dress, dear. But it's made of silk."

"Yes, but you know how I hate to be cold." She gave her mother a hopeful glance. "Could you make me this dress in velvet? It would be so lovely and warm."

"Well…" Her mother laid the remaining handful of feathers in her lap, took the magazine into her hands and tilted it so the candle on the stand beside her illuminated the picture. "Yes. This design is simple but elegant. It can be made of velvet."

"Wonderful!" She rose and hurried back to the stand

by the fire. "And with velvet in the shop, you can start—" She stopped, frowned. "What color is the velvet?"

"It's a beautiful shade of plum."

"Oh, Mother—*plum?* With my fair skin?" She put on a pout.

"That will not be a problem." Her mother went back to sorting feathers. "I have a length of dark green velvet left from the cape we made for Rebecca Cargrave. I can use that for the high collar and add a wide band of it around the hem of the shoulder cape. It will look lovely against your skin and make your eyes seem bluer."

"Plum with dark green trim…" Her lips curved in a smile. "That's a wonderful idea, Mother. I'll need the dress—"

"Before your beaux arrive—I know. Polly and Hanna are both engaged with other orders, but you've no need to be concerned. I'll make it myself. I shall start cutting the pattern promptly." Her mother looked up and smiled. "As soon as I finish attaching the trimming to the blue merino gown I made you for the holiday."

"Oh, Mother…truly?" She laughed and moved a little closer to the fire. "I should have known you would think of my need for a new gown."

"Indeed." Her father raised his head from his reading. "You must look your very best when your gentlemen friends come to call. Have you made your decision as to which one's hand you will accept?"

"Not yet." Daniel's grinning face flashed before her. She frowned and pushed at the curls dangling at her temples. "It's difficult to know what is the wisest thing for me to do as each man has his own recommendations. That's why I've come home to decide. I need your counsel, Father. And yours, too, Mother."

"My choice is Mr. Lodge." Her mother placed the last white feather on its pile, then folded the piece of fabric they rested on over them to make a neat package. "You did say he is the wealthier of the two, did you not?"

"Yes. But—"

"Don't be hasty with your advice, Frieda."

"Whatever do you mean, Conrad?" Her mother glanced at her father, then finished folding the fabric over the pile of black feathers and started wrapping the brown ones. "You've always said Ellen should marry a man of means and prestige."

"I have indeed. And I stand by that opinion. I meant only that you are, perhaps, judging these men too quickly."

"Well, I don't see how that can be." Her mother's voice held a hint of irritation. "Ellen has told us that both Mr. Lodge and Mr. Cuthbert are men of wealth and prestige. And that there are no personal considerations involved. Therefore, I choose Mr. Lodge as the wealthiest."

"He is the wealthiest at the moment, my dear. But Ellen is wise to consider the future."

"Thank you, Father." Her heart warmed at her father's smile. His approval was seldom given.

"I don't understand. Ellen can't know the future, Conrad. No one can. It's chancy at best." Her mother frowned, stacked the small packages of feathers into a pile and secured it with a ribbon.

"Very true, my dear—in most cases. But Mr. Cuthbert is a politician of some renown." Her father laid down his book, looked up at her and again smiled. "If, as Mr. Cuthbert has implied to Ellen, his appointment to the position of secretary of state, by his friend the governor, is approved by the Senate, he will be a man of great influence in the entire state." His smile widened. "That opens the path to greater wealth as there will be those who wish to curry his favor. And, of course, should this come to pass, there would also be the possibility of a national political future for him. And great prestige for members of his family."

"Oh, my! I hadn't thought—" Her mother gazed up at her, a speculative look in her eyes that morphed into one of admiration. "Why, Ellen…you could attend dinner parties and soirees with our governor and…and perhaps, someday, with the president! Oh, daughter—" her mother rose, rushed to her side and wrapped her in an enthusiastic hug "—you have exceeded our plans and expectations. I'm so very proud of you!"

Ellen strolled around her bedroom, reflections of the flames from the fireplace dancing on the flowing silk of her dressing gown. Which man should she choose? Her father had given her a great deal to think about. She hadn't considered that a highly placed politician would be in a position to make wealth from those who curried his favor for one reason or another.

A twinge of unease rippled through her. Was that lawful? To sell your political influence? Oh, of course it was. Her father wouldn't have been so approving if it were not. And anyway, what did it matter? If she chose to marry Mr. Cuthbert, his actions would have nothing to do with her.

The uneasiness rippled through her again. She pushed it aside, stepped out of her slippers and removed her dressing gown. The softness of the mattress and warmth of the covers enfolded her. She stretched out her legs, searching with her toes for the towel-wrapped, heated soapstone the housekeeper would have placed at the foot of the bed. Ah, there it was! She placed her feet against the warmth, snuggled into a comfortable position on the down-filled mattress and yawned.

She had been favoring Mr. Lodge as her future husband. He was much younger and better looking than the stout, balding Mr. Cuthbert. And Mr. Lodge's dark hair and beard were a handsome contrast to her blond curls and fair skin. And he was the wealthier of the two. Still, the prestige of being a prominent politician's wife was not to be overlooked....

She tucked the quilt more closely beneath her chin and smiled. Imagine dining with the governor! Her mother and father would be so proud of her. And if what her father had said was true—and it surely was—Mr. Cuthbert might soon be wealthier than even Mr. Lodge. He would surely be more powerful. And there was another reason to give preference to Mr. Cuthbert. His age. He was a widower with grown children older than she. He would not demand an heir, as would Mr. Lodge. Yes, she would have to reconsider.

What of love?

Her face tightened. She turned onto her side and stared at the flames devouring the wood on the hearth. Willa had no right to challenge her decision to follow her parents' advice and marry for comfort and prestige. Her friend was only jealous. Willa would be forever stuck in this small village, serving the people as their pastor's wife, while she would be living a life of ease and social prominence in Buffalo—or attending parties with the governor and other high officials in Albany. Oh, what an entrance she would make into that social scene!

She smiled and closed her eyes, imagining her first

attendance at a governor's ball. The men would all be in handsome evening wear, and the women would all be richly gowned. But her gown would be more lavish and beautiful than all the rest, and every eye would be on her as she entered on Mr. Cuth—*Daniel.*

Her breath caught.

She jerked her eyes open to rid herself of the image of him standing in the midst of all that finery in his logger clothes with his green eyes laughing, his mouth slanted in that teasing, heart-stealing grin and his hand held out to her.

Daniel shivered and tugged the covers closer around his neck. The temperature had to be below zero and falling to make the boards creak like that. Even with the drafts adjusted wide and the coals burning hot, the woodstove couldn't warm the small lean-to attached to the stable. The cold emanated from the sawn-wood wall behind his cot and chilled his back, even through his blankets. Nights like this, he almost wished he slept in the common room of the camp house with the loggers, snores, smells and all. At least the log building held the cold out and the heat in. He frowned and flopped over so his back was toward the stove.

Ellen hated to be cold.

The thought came unbidden and unwanted along with a memory of her looking up at him from beneath her fur-trimmed bonnet. He scowled and opened his eyes to replace her image with the sight of the moonlight-washed rough board only inches from his face. Why didn't she stay in Buffalo? When she came home, when he'd seen her again, all the old memories resurrected in spite of his good sense.

He stared at the board, at the grain that looked like flowing water. He'd loved Ellen when he pulled her, pale and struggling for breath, out of the flood-swollen waters of Stony Creek twelve years ago, and a remnant of that boyhood love was buried beneath all that had transpired since that time. It lingered with the stubbornness of a burr in a horse's tail. He'd given up thinking the memory of that childhood love would someday die. If his dislike of the uppity, citified, stuck-up *fidfad* Ellen had grown up to be hadn't killed it by now, nothing would.

He blew out a cloud of breath. At least his pride was intact. Only Willa knew how he'd once felt about Ellen—and she'd promised to keep his secret. Callie and Sadie suspected, but they didn't know. And Ellen, for sure, didn't know. As long as that was true, he could live through her rare visits home. He just came out of them feeling like the boor she accused him of being.

He pulled in a lungful of the cold air, coughed and burrowed his head beneath the blanket to block the aching cold on his forehead. The memories had brought the familiar knots to his stomach. He pressed his lips into a thin line and forced himself to stop remembering that it could all have been different, if only his father hadn't died.

Chapter Three

It was still snowing. Ellen tossed the magazine onto the settee, rose and went to the window. Snow clung to the wood grids that separated the glass, leaving only the center section of each small pane clear. She caught a glimpse of movement, leaned close and looked to the side. Asa was shoveling their slate walk. For what purpose? There would certainly be no callers today.

She glanced at the road, at the snow rutted by the runners on pungs and sleighs and trampled by the hoofs of the horses that pulled them. Not that many were passing. The blizzard had slowed village life to a crawl. Her warm breath fogged the glass. She shivered at the draft of cold air coming off the small panes, pulled her lace-trimmed silk wrap more closely about her shoulders and went to stand by the fire.

A log popped. Cinders dropped to the shimmering coals and the flames flared. She pulled her long full skirt back away from the edge of the hearth, smiled and ran her hand over the smooth Turkish satin material. She loved the way the skirt was caught up at random intervals with a silk knot securing the resulting puff. She was the only one she knew who had a dress of this design. Of course, the other women in the social set would have copied it by the time she returned to Buffalo.

Her smile faded. Her women acquaintances in the city would not be standing in an empty room wishing for something to do. They would be at the dressmaker's being fitted for a new gown, or paying calls on others of their set and enjoying a gossip over tea this afternoon, before hurrying home to prepare for the evening's entertainment. What would it be for tonight? A dinner party? A musical? Or the theater? There was always something important to attend. One had to be seen at the right places. Had she erred in coming home for the holiday?

She sighed and ran her fingers over the silk knot that secured the narrow band at her waist. What good was a stylish gown if there was no one to admire or envy it? The silence pressed in upon her, increased her restlessness. Her mother and father had gone to their shops. There was no one to talk to and nothing to do. Her mother didn't even need her for a fitting for her new gowns. And she certainly wasn't going to walk to town in this weather.

She shivered at the thought, walked back to the window and looked out. There was nothing to see but the road, the empty field across the way and the parsonage, barely visible through the rapidly falling snow. She huffed out a breath, turned away, then turned back. The parsonage wasn't that far. And Willa was there. Of course, there was that open field to cross.

The wind gusted, drove the falling snow sideways and moaned around the window, dashing her hope. It was foolishness to even think of going outside. Still, her cloak was warm....

The lure of tea and conversation with her old friend pulled at her. She whirled from the window and hurried up the stairs to her bedroom. Wading through that deep snow in the field would ruin her silk gown. She would wear one of her old dresses.

"Give me twenty minutes or so, Daniel. That wound is going to take some cleaning before I stitch it up."

"All right, Doc. I'll be back to get him." Daniel led Big Boy to a spot beside Doc's stable where he'd be out of the wind, fastened the blanket on him, then trudged his way across lots to the parsonage.

"Woof!"

"Hey, Happy…" He bent down and scratched behind the ears of the dog standing watch at the top of the back porch steps. "Waiting for Josh, are you?" The dog let out a whine, lay down with his muzzle resting on his crossed front paws and stared toward the road. He grinned and thumped the dog's solid, furry shoulder. "I wish I'd had a dog like you to roam the woods with me when I was a kid. We'd have had ourselves a time."

He brushed the snow from his shoulders and pant legs, stomped it from his boots crossing the porch, rapped three times and opened the kitchen door. "Hey, Bertha." He hooked his hat and jacket over one of the pegs on the wall. "Those cookies sure smell good."

"I've never had no complaints." The housekeeper dropped small mounds of dough onto the emptied tin and slid it in the oven, then swatted at his hand as he helped himself. "You might ask first."

"Why waste time? We both know you always say yes." He grinned, took a bite of the warm cookie and smacked his lips in approval. "Where's Willa?"

"In the sitting room. And leave some of them for Joshua and Sally."

He waved the second cookie he'd snatched in the air and headed down the hallway to the sitting room devouring his treat. "Hey, Pest, what's that you've got?"

"Daniel! I thought I heard your knock." Willa dumped the load in her arms onto the settee and smiled up at him. "I might ask you the same question."

He popped the last bite of cookie into his mouth. "Nothing."

Her lips twitched. "You're not very imaginative, Daniel. That's the same answer you always gave Mama, Grandmother Townsend and Sophia."

"It was always true."

"After you swallowed."

He gave a loud gulp, and they both burst into laughter. A cry came from the cradle sitting by the hearth. He stepped over to it and squatted on his heels, his chest tightening at the sight of the sweet baby face topped by downy auburn curls. He'd hoped to have children one day. He shoved the thought away and rocked the cradle. "Sorry, tiny one, I didn't mean to disturb your rest." The cries grew louder. He shot to his feet and sent a panicked look to Willa. "What's wrong? I only rocked her."

"Our laughter startled her. She wants comforting." Willa leaned down and wrapped the baby in her blanket, cuddled her close for a moment, then held her out to him. "You hold her while I sort through those clothes."

"Me!" He shoved his palms out toward her and backed away. "She's too little. I don't want to hurt her."

"You won't. You only need to keep her head supported."

His heart lurched as Willa placed the baby in his

arms. He cuddled the infant close, rocked her gently. The cries turned to a whimper, then stopped. He lifted his gaze to Willa and grinned.

"She feels safe." She smiled and turned toward the settee. "Mama said you were going to come see me, but I didn't expect you to come to town in this blizzard."

He stayed rooted in place, afraid to move lest the baby begin crying again. "A hick slipped with his ax and sliced open his leg. I had to bring him to Doc to get the wound sewed up, so I came on over. I'll need to take him back to camp shortly."

"I hope the man heals well. What was it you wanted?"

"Your mother said you needed help with Christmas decorations or something."

Willa lifted a shirt that had seen better days off the top of the pile she'd dropped on the settee and grinned at him. "You needn't whisper. Mary won't waken." She set the shirt aside. "So you are obeying Mama's orders to come help me?"

He matched her grin. "Something like that."

"Good! I accept your help. But I'm not ready yet. I need—" She stopped at a knock on the front door. "Someone must need Matthew, to come out in this weather. The grippe is hitting people hard...." She hurried toward the entrance hall.

"Ellen! Is something wrong?"

Ellen? What was she doing out in the storm? He glanced down at the baby, wished he dared put her down and leave.

"No, everything is fine. I only came to visit."

He took a long breath and braced himself to see her again so soon.

"I can't believe you braved this snowstorm, but I'm

so glad you did. Here, let me take your cloak and bonnet. You go in by the fire and warm yourself."

"Thank you, Willa. I'm chilled through and through. The wind is terrible."

Soft footsteps crossed the small entrance toward the sitting room. Ellen swept through the doorway, stopped and stared at him, her azure eyes looking bluer than ever above her rosy cheeks. Her blond curls had been blown into disarray around her forehead and temples, and one dangled from behind her ear to lie against the high collar of her dark green gown. She'd never looked more beautiful. But he always seemed to think that. He slanted his lips in a teasing grin. "Hey, Musquash. What are you doing out in the cold?"

Her eyes flashed. She tossed her head, lifted her snow-rimmed hems and came toward the fireplace. "What are you doing here? Shouldn't you be hauling logs or something?"

The words cut deep. He broadened his grin. "Shouldn't you be home writing to your rich beaux in Buffalo? You don't want them to forget you."

Her chin jutted into the air. "There is no danger of that. And no need for letters. I'm to be betrothed. I've come home to decide which of two men I shall accept as my husband—Mr. Lodge or Mr. Cuthbert."

There was a soft gasp from the doorway. He shot Willa a look, then dipped his head to Ellen. "My felicitations. It must be hard to choose, with all that wealth involved."

She gave him a cool smile with anger shadowing its edge. "And *prestige*. One mustn't forget that." She gave her skirts a sharp shake and bits of clinging snow fell off onto the warm stone hearth and melted into small dark blotches.

"Oh, I'm certain you won't. Prestige *and* wealth. My, my, however will you choose?" He shook his head in mock gravity and watched the pools of moisture shrivel and dry up like the dream of marrying her he'd had years ago.

"That's none of *your* concern." She looked down at the infant in his arms. "Aren't babies supposed to cry a lot?"

"Mary Elizabeth knows she's safe with Daniel. Babies are very intuitive. And smart enough to follow what their hearts tell them."

How could the swish of a skirt sound angry? Or maybe it was the decided edge in Willa's voice. He jerked his gaze to Willa's blue-green eyes—dark and shooting sparks. She had her dander up all right. "You are a proud mama, Pest." He chuckled and stepped forward to stand between Willa and Ellen, blocking their view of one another. "Take the tiny one, Pest. I have to go. Doc will be through with his stitching by now." He put his mouth close to Willa's ear and hissed, "You don't have to protect me, Pest. I was over her long ago. Remember your promise." A quick glance in her eyes told him she would say no more; her tight-pressed lips said she didn't like it. He winked, turned toward Ellen and made an exaggerated bow. "If you'll excuse me, Musquash, some of us don't have the luxury of sitting around idle."

"Stop calling me that name!"

He grinned, turned his back on her furious face and headed for the kitchen to get his jacket and hat.

* * *

Ellen looked away from the unsettling expression on Willa's face and watched Daniel stride from the room, irritated by the uncomfortable notion that she had missed something. Willa considered Daniel the brother she'd never had, which was understandable as they'd lived next door to one another all their lives, but it had bred a closeness between the two of them that was annoying at times.

The pile of worn clothes and pieces of fabric on the settee looked higher. She seized on the opportunity to talk about a neutral subject. "It looks as if you've gathered more material for making the costumes." She lifted her skirt hems and stuck her right foot out closer to the fire to dry her damp stocking.

"Yes. Matthew brought more offerings home with him after his round of visits to sick parishioners yesterday."

A long sigh followed Willa's words. Ellen glanced over her shoulder. Willa was fingering the top garment, a look of frustration on her face.

Some of us don't have the luxury of sitting around idle.

"Willa." Her friend looked over at her. "You are always so efficient, I can't believe you can't manage to make the costumes, but if you need me—"

"I do, Ellen. Truly, I do."

She lowered her gaze from Willa to the pile of fabric and tried to remember the last time she'd done any sewing. "All right, then. I'll help you." Doubt over her ability to do so rose with the declaration. Her face tightened. She shouldn't have allowed Daniel's words to goad her into offering to help.

"Oh, Ellen, truly? What of your preparations for your suitors' visits?"

The perfect opportunity to back away from her offer without losing face! She drew breath to explain she wouldn't be able to help after all and glanced up—there was such a hopeful look in Willa's eyes. The recantation died unspoken. "Mr. Lodge and Mr. Cuthbert will be staying at the Sheffield House when they come. And Mother will arrange any entertainments. I have only to look fetching and be charming while they are here." She brushed her hand down her skirt. "Not that I can manage that in this old green wool dress."

"You don't need fancy gowns to look beautiful, Ellen."

She looked down at her dress, eyed the plain bodice and the long full skirt devoid of tucks or ruffles. "Thank you, my dear friend. But I'm afraid Mr. Lodge and Mr. Cuthbert would not share your opinion."

"Then they do not deserve you." Willa sank onto the settee next to the pile of old clothes. "I can't thank you enough for offering to help me, Ellen. I'm sure I don't know how I would have managed the costumes and the decorations and— The *decorations.*"

She stared at Willa's aghast expression. "What decorations?"

"I forgot...." Willa rose, crossed the room and stood looking out of a snow-encrusted window.

"What have you forgotten?"

"To ask Daniel to make arrangements for the pine boughs. I'll never have time to get the wreaths and swags finished now." Her shoulders slumped. "I can't leave the baby, and I can't take her out in this weather to go and ask Grandfather Townsend if he will donate the branches. And Matthew is too busy to help me make the decorations even if he does."

"Why, Willa! I've never heard you speak in such a discouraged way." She stared at her friend's dejected posture, uncomfortable in the position of comforter. She was always the one being cosseted. "Of course you will manage. You always do."

"I've never been the wife of a pastor with two children and a new baby at Christmastime before."

Willa's defeated tone tugged at her heart. "Even so, everything will be all right. I'll help with the decorations, as well." *Had she lost her mind?*

Willa turned and looked at her, hope in her eyes. "Are you certain, Ellen? With your beaux coming—"

"We'll make the decorations before they arrive. I'll take Father's cutter out to Butternut Hill to ask about the pine boughs today. I've been wanting to see Sadie anyway."

"But the snow, Ellen… You can't—"

"Of course not. I'll have Asa drive me. I'll leave as soon as I'm warmed. Meanwhile…" She stepped to the settee and lifted a threadbare brown wool dress from the pile to distract herself from the panic building at her rash offers. "This would serve for a shepherd's robe." She glanced up as Willa joined her, reading relief and something more in her friend's blue-green eyes—satisfaction? Willa truly needed her. It was an odd sensation. She had always been pampered and taken care of. No one had ever *needed* her. She tilted her head and smiled. "I assume there *is* a shepherd?"

"Yes. And the Three Wise Men. And Joseph and Mary, of course."

"Of course. Is there anything green in this pile? I

think green would be lovely for Mary—it's the color of life."

"A wonderful suggestion, Ellen." Willa smiled and scooped the pile into her arms. "Let me put these on the chair by the hearth while we make our choices. That way you'll get nice and warm before you leave for Butternut Hill."

"A good idea. Perhaps we can— Oh, my..."

"What?"

She laid aside the brown wool dress she held and touched a bit of white lace peeking out of the pile. "Look at this." A tattered lace-trimmed tablecloth unfolded as she pulled it from the pile. "Is there an angel?"

"Certainly. We can't have the Christmas story without including the angel that brought the good tidings." Willa smiled at her, then leaned down and riffled through the pile. "What have we to use for Joseph? Perhaps dark blue? Ah..."

"What?"

"Here is something green." Willa tugged a dress from the pile and held it up. "Is this the color you had in mind for Mary?"

She stared at the deep green color of the dress—the color Daniel's eyes turned when he was angry. The color they were whenever he looked at her. Her pleasure in their quest for the right fabrics dulled. "It's perfect." She draped the white tablecloth over the chair back and moved closer to the fire to warm herself. Daniel was on his way back to camp, and soon she would be following his path on the sleigh ride to Butternut Hill. He was leading the way, cutting a trail as he always had. A bittersweet smile touched her lips, then turned to a frown. She had to stop remembering. Thankfully, Daniel would be busy at work hauling logs during her time home and would not be around to remind her of her silly, childish dreams.

Chapter Four

"Ease up, Big Girl. Whoa, Big Boy." Daniel hopped off the sledge and tromped forward as yard workers, peaveys and steel rods in hand, swarmed onto the pile of logs he'd hauled in.

"Daniel!"

He turned at the hail, spotted Cole Aylward and trudged through the trampled snow of the log yard to the sawmill. "You wanted me?"

"Yes. Come into the office while the men unload your sledge."

He glanced up at the smoke rising from the chimney. "With pleasure." He stomped up the log slide to the sawmill deck and followed Cole into the attached room. Warmth from the woodstove greeted him. He tugged off his hat and stayed close to the door, lest he get chilled when he went back outside. "Is there a problem?"

"Yes. Mine, not yours...yet."

He lifted a brow, stared at Cole's grin. "I'm not sure I like the word you tacked onto the end of that sentence."

His boss's grin widened. "Ellen Hall came to see Sadie today. She passed on a request from Willa. She needs pine boughs for decorating the church and asked if Townsend Timber would provide them."

He stuffed his hat into his pocket and rubbed his gloved hands together to create some warmth. "We're behind in our lumbering because of the snow."

"Yes. I mentioned that."

He studied Cole's face, let a grin tug his lips aslant. "Sadie cajoled you into it, did she?" He chuckled and shook his head. "I'm thinking it didn't take much coaxing on her part."

Cole's grin matched his. "I collapsed like a felled tree. As did Manning. We've donated a wagonload of boughs. And more if needed."

There was something in Cole's voice.... Daniel tugged off a glove to scrub his hand across the back of his neck. "Ah, yes. The 'yet.' Let me guess.... I'm elected to deliver the boughs?"

"That would be correct." Cole's face sobered. "After you've cut them."

He raised his brows.

"I know." Cole settled into his chair. "I'd like to give you a man to help you, Daniel, but I can't spare a logger while we're so far behind."

He nodded, tugged his glove back on and pulled his hat from his pocket. "You can't spare your teamster either. It won't help any to cut logs if you've no one to haul them here to the mill. Fortunately, there's a full moon at present, and with it shining on the snow, it's as bright as day. I'll down a couple of small pine and hemlock tonight, fill the pung with the boughs and deliver them after I'm through hauling logs tomorrow."

"That's a lot of extra work for no pay, Daniel. Thank you."

"Don't thank me—thank your wife." He grinned and pulled his hat on, tugged the rolled brim down to cover the tops of his ears. "I never could withstand Quick Stuff's coaxing either."

Ellen glanced at her mother studying the fashions in the new *Godey's Lady's Magazine* she'd received, drew breath to speak, then exhaled and turned back to the fire. She'd started to ask her mother if she would donate trims left over from dress orders at least a dozen times since dinner and then stopped. It would be best to wait a few days, until the costumes were finished but for the final touches. *Coward.* She frowned at her lack of will and pulled her wrap closer about her bare shoulders. The silk gown she'd donned before her parents came home was stylish but chilly.

"You seem restless tonight, Ellen. I hope you're not feeling adrift because of the lack of suitable society in Pinewood."

"No, Mother, I've been spending time visiting with Willa. And I had Asa drive me out to see Sadie today. I'm only…thinking."

"You took the cutter out to Butternut Hill in this weather?" Her mother gave her an astounded look. "Whatever for?"

She drew breath to explain about the pine boughs for the church, then swallowed back her words. "I wanted to see Sadie."

Her father lowered his book and peered up at her. She held still, determined not to fidget beneath his penetrating gaze. Her answer had been the truth—as far as it went.

"Are you any closer to a decision as to which gentleman you will accept as your husband?"

"No, Father." She'd been so busy she hadn't even thought about her beaux today. Only Daniel. But that was natural, since he'd been present—and annoying. She leaned down and added a piece of log to the fire lest her father read the truth in her expression, and she read disapproval in his as a consequence.

"Well, you tend to what your mother and I say. Don't allow your old friends to talk you into accepting less than you can achieve in life by a good marriage."

"Indeed." Her mother looked up at her, a hint of a frown on her face. "Willa, Callie and Sadie have done quite well for themselves considering they have settled for village life. But we have groomed you for the greater, more important things of high society, Ellen. You mustn't forget that. Now go and cream your hands. And don't handle any more rough wood, dear. You want your appearance to be perfect when Mr. Lodge and Mr. Cuthbert arrive."

Suitable society. Ellen rubbed cream into her face and hands, swirled her silk-and-lace dressing gown on over her nightdress and stepped to her bedroom window. Cold air seeped from beneath the hems of the winter drapes her mother had fashioned from a woven bed coverlet and chilled her slippered feet. She drew her dressing gown close and pushed one drape aside far enough to look out. Large snowflakes fell through the moonlight that shone on the rutted ribbon of Oak Street and glistened on the snow-covered ground across the way.

Beyond the park stood the new parsonage, but the snowfall was so thick all she could distinguish was a small glow of lamplight from a window. Had she made a mistake by offering to help Willa? Performing such mundane tasks would lessen her worth in Mr. Lodge's and Mr. Cuthbert's opinions. *If* she could even do them. And her mother was right. What about her hands? What if she suffered needle pricks? Or if her skin became roughened and dry from handling the pine boughs? Oh, why had she let Daniel's words prod her into saying she would help? It would, of a certainty, displease her parents as well as her beaux. Still...

Cold coming off the window chilled her. She let the drape fall back into place and crossed the room to her bed. She'd felt odd but nice all afternoon. The truth was, she had enjoyed helping Willa. Still, there was no possible way she could do the work without it becoming known. There were no secrets in Pinewood.

A wry smile tugged at her lips. That was one thing she and her friends had learned while very young. No matter what secret adventure they set off on, it was always already known by the time they returned home. Or soon confessed. Especially if they faced Callie's aunt Sophia. The woman was formidable! She laughed and shook her head. The truth was, she'd always been a little frightened of Sophia Sheffield in spite of her kindness. What a timid child she'd been....

The silk of her dressing gown whispered softly as she shrugged it off her shoulders and down her arms. A chill slithered down her spine in spite of the fire as she stepped out of her slippers. She slid beneath the covers searching out the heated, towel-wrapped soapstone at the foot of the mattress with her cold feet. "Ahh." Warmth caressed her toes as she tucked them in a fold of the warm cloth. Did Willa enjoy even such a small luxury as this? Likely not, even though she was married to Reverend Calvert and had Bertha Franklin for their housekeeper.

Suitable society.

A twinge of apprehension tingled through her. How would she entertain her beaux? Reverend Calvert and Willa would qualify as suitable society, but neither Mr. Lodge nor Mr. Cuthbert cared about church—except for appearances' sake. Callie and her husband would qualify—Ezra Ryder was wealthier than either Mr. Lodge or Mr. Cuthbert. Unfortunately, Callie and Ezra were away visiting Ezra's sister for the Christmas season. Sadie and Cole? No. Sadie spent her time looking after her grandmother and grandfather, and Cole—well, Cole was too straightforward to get on well with her beaux.

That thought gave her pause. She frowned, closed her eyes and directed her thoughts away from the unflattering comparison. Her parents would simply have to entertain her beaux—there was no one else who would be... compatible. She would keep her word and help Willa, but she must finish the tasks quickly. It would not do for her beaux to come and find her working like one of their servants. That would not do at all.

How long would it take to make the children's costumes? She was certainly not skilled at sewing, and Willa had the baby and Joshua and Sally, as well as her husband and home to care for. A smile curved her lips. Sally was a sweet little girl. And she would make a beautiful angel with her fair skin and her golden curls. The white lace tablecloth would make her a lovely flowing gown. But what of a halo? Or— Her old gowns! Perhaps she wouldn't have to ask her mother for leftover dress trimmings after all.

She threw the covers aside, pulled on her dressing gown and slippers and hurried across the bedroom to open the large chest that held some of her old dresses. There was a yellow watered silk with a narrow band of gold braid that tied around the waist....

Firelight flickered on the various fabrics as she dropped to her knees and looked through the piles. Rose...green... silver—she'd always liked that dress—blue...copper... yellow. Ah! There it was. She slipped the yellow dress out of the pile and sat back on her heels to free the band of gold braid. It was stiff enough to hold a circular shape. A perfect halo. Wait until she showed Willa. A tiny twinge of excitement wiggled through her. She smiled and set the gold braid aside, put the dress back in the trunk.

Some of us don't have the luxury of sitting around idle.

The words grated. She shoved her curls back over her shoulders and tossed her head. She'd show Daniel Braynard. He'd have to swallow those words when he saw the work she did with Willa on the costumes and the decorations—and she hoped he *choked* on them!

She leaned forward onto her knees and plowed through the pile of dresses again. The lace-edged net of the overskirt on the silver gown would make lovely wings. She yanked the gown from the pile, dropped it on the floor beside her and dove back into her search. There had to be other things she could find that would be helpful in making the costumes. She'd show Daniel! She'd make the best costumes Pinewood had ever seen!

Silence reigned, the only sounds the soft, muted thud of the Belgian's hoofs and the whisper of the pung's runners over the deep snow. It was as if the forest were holding its breath. Daniel smiled at the whimsical thought, looked up at the snowflakes shimmering in the moonlight that lit the forest track and wished he had a wife beside him to witness the beauty.

Ellen.

His imagination placed her beside him, their shoulders touching, their laps covered by a thick, warm blanket. He frowned and glanced at the folded, snow-covered horse blanket on the seat to disperse the yearning. That dream had died years ago. There would be no wife, only grim reality. He would not subject any woman to the sort of life his mother had known—most certainly not the spoiled Ellen Hall with her fancy gowns and fur-trimmed bonnet and cloak.

"Hup, Big Boy, hup!" He snapped his wrists and rippled the lines, and the huge Belgian dragged the pung off the track into a small clearing, his great muscles rippling as he plodded through the knee-high snow. He reined the gelding to the right, around the edge of the clearing to a spot a short way beyond a small thickly branched hemlock. "That's far enough. Whoa, Big Boy."

The Belgian stopped, tossed his head and snorted. Hot breath puffed from his nostrils, forming small gray clouds. He pawed the snow with his right front hoof and snorted again.

"I know. You don't like having to work tonight. But orders are orders. And it's to help Willa." He grabbed the horse blanket beside him, jumped from his seat, then tossed it up over Big Boy's back and tugged it into place. The buckle on the hold strap glinted against the gelding's massive chest. "There you are, fellow." He patted the thick neck and went back for the feedbag. "This will keep you content while I work." He slipped the bag on, adjusted it and left Big Boy munching on his oats and bran while he lifted his ax out of the pung and trudged through the snow toward the hemlock.

The moonlight gleamed on the snow-covered ground and reflected off of the snow-burdened branches of the trees that circled the small clearing, protecting it from the worst of the winter storm. Wind rose, tossed the tops of the towering pines and whistled softly through their lower limbs, its power diminished by the thickness of the forest.

At least he could see. He smacked the hemlock's branches with the flat side of the blade to knock off the snow and grimaced at the shower of white that rained down on him as the limbs flew up to their normal position. He yanked off a glove and swiped the cold, moist flakes from his face and neck. The things he did in the name of friendship! No. It was more than that. He tugged his glove back on, took hold of the ax and lopped off the lower limbs. Willa and Callie and Sadie and Ellen had pestered him mercilessly when they were kids, but he'd grown to love them like sisters. All except Ellen. What he had felt for her had nothing to do with brotherly affection. Would that it had.

He scowled, dragged the branches he'd cut off to the pung, tossed them into the box and returned to the tree. His first hefty swing buried the blade deep into the exposed trunk. He yanked it free and swung again, the power of his strong shoulders behind the stroke. Thunk! A chip flew from the trunk and buried itself in the snow. More chips followed in rapid succession. There was a creaking, cracking, splintering sound.

He leaped aside, watched the small tree wobble, then fall with a soft thud across the track made by the pung.

Perfect! He hurried to the downed tree and lopped off the smaller top branches with one stroke each. In five minutes he had denuded the top of the tree. He buried the blade of his ax in the bared trunk and used both arms to scoop up the small branches. Snow packed in between his gloves and the sleeves of his jacket, chilled his flesh. He pulled off his gloves, shook the snow out of his sleeves, then tugged his gloves back on and picked up the ax.

Willa and Sadie were going to pay for this. It would cost Sadie a batch of those good molasses cookies she made, and Willa would have to let him take Joshua and Sally skating on his next weekend in town. It was as close as he'd ever get to being a father. He pressed his lips together against the pain of the thought and went back to work.

The snow came faster. It piled on his shoulders, hat and collar of his jacket, found the bare spot between them and melted against his neck. He ignored the shivers it caused and looked around for a small pine. None offered.

He trudged through the snow to the smallest pine standing on the edge of the clearing, eyed the snow-laden branches and frowned. He'd really get a snow shower this time.

The quick, sharp blows of his ax shook the tree. Snow cascaded from the upper branches, fell in large clumps that plopped against the ground and broke into pieces against his head and shoulders. That was two batches of cookies for Sadie! And an added afternoon of sledding with Willa's children. No penalty for Ellen, though he knew the one he'd like to claim. He'd like to send her back to Buffalo! As much as she hated the cold weather, how had Willa talked her into going out to Butternut Hill to ask Manning Townsend to donate boughs, anyway? He swung again and the large limb split from the trunk and fell at his feet. He dragged it out of the way and took his frustration out on the next one. Snow showered down on him as he chopped it off.

He dragged it over beside the other one. It was dangerous to fell a tree this large alone using only one notch. When the trunk got thin enough, the tree could twist and fall in the wrong spot. He frowned and swept his gaze over the area at the tree's base. The snow was too deep and the branches of the trees too tangled together for him to get behind it to make a second notch. He eyed the branches on the back side of the tree. They were half-buried by the snow. It was possible they would hold the tree from twisting or kicking out and toppling before he could get out of the way.

"I'm going to need Your help with this one, Lord. Please let the trunk hold until I can get free." He shot a look toward the sky, took a firm grip on his ax and swung it again and again, watching the trunk as the chips flew off into the snow, listening to the sound as each stroke hit. There was a creak. The trunk trembled. The far edge of the thin remaining piece of trunk splintered. The tree lurched and twisted, the buried back branches bursting out of the snow into the air.

He threw his ax through the branches of the neighboring pine and dove after it, hit the snow and rolled toward the massive trunk.

Craaack! The hewed tree slammed against the pine. A shudder traveled down the trunk. He curled tighter, covered his head. Snow and sheared-off branches rained down. "Lord Jesus, be with me!" The falling tree slid down the pine's trunk and crashed onto the limb over him, its large branches driving deep into the snow, cracking and splintering when they hit the frozen ground.

Silence. Nothing but the whisper of the pine needles on the quivering branches, the soft plop of bits of snow sliding off to hit the ground. The snapping and shattering of wood had stopped.

He pulled his hands away, raised his head and opened his eyes. Pieces of broken branches, pine needles and shreds of bark littered the snow, while larger boughs formed a tangled tent over him. A weight pressed against his back, pushed down on his shoulders. He craned his neck around, eyed the deep crack in the broken limb above him and the trunk of the fallen tree that rested across it, its branches buried in white. "Thank You, Lord, for the deep snow."

His words were swallowed by the night. A cautious sweep of his arm cleared away the debris between him and the pine's trunk. He said another quick prayer for the cracked branch to hold, pawed the snow from beneath his chest and slithered out from under the damaged limb. *Free!*

The end of his ax handle was sticking up out of the snow at the base of the sheltering pine. He grasped it in his trembling hand and pushed through the snarl of broken branches, then looked up at the sky. "Thank You, Lord, for Your protection. I'll take You for my partner over any other, anytime."

His hat was dangling from the nub of one of the small offshoot limbs he'd broken when he dove for safety. He shook it free of snow and debris, tugged it on, then hacked his way clear and went back to work, tossing the branches into a pile.

The snow came thicker and faster, closing out the moonlight. Time to quit. He shouldered his ax, tromped through the snow to the pung, removed Big Boy's feed-bag and led him toward the downed pine's skeleton. There would be another five or six inches by morning, and it was already too deep for safely logging and haul-ing out timber—as he'd just proved.

He frowned and started throwing the branches in the pung. It was likely the jobber would call off operations until the storm stopped. If so, he would stay in town and help Willa. And there was another blessing to the wors-ening storm. Ellen would stay at home in front of a nice warm fire, sip hot tea brought to her by the housekeeper and ponder which of her two wealthy beaux she should marry. There would be no chance he would accidentally meet her when he delivered the boughs to the parson-age tomorrow evening or while he worked with Willa on the decorations. "Thank You, Lord, for the storm."

Chapter Five

The horse's nicker stilled her hands. Ellen shot a curious glance toward the dining room window. Who would be paying a call on Willa in this weather? Or perhaps it was someone needing the reverend. She dropped Willa's scissors on top of the skirt she was cutting from the old brown wool dress and hurried to the window. A man, head lowered against the blowing snow, halted a team of huge horses, jumped to the ground and headed up the shoveled pathway for the back porch. *Daniel.*

She didn't need the pung heaped with pine boughs to identify him. She would know those broad shoulders and that confident stride anywhere. What was he doing here this time of day? Why wasn't he at the camp hauling logs or something? She stepped to the side, lest he look up and find her watching as he passed the window. He had always been—

"There! Joshua and Sally are on their way to visit Mama. Now I can— What are you looking at, Ellen? There's nothing outside but snow."

She started and whirled from the window to face Willa, heat rushing into her cheeks as if she were guilty of a misdeed—which was ridiculous. "I heard horses. Daniel has brought the boughs." She fluffed the curls at her temples, walked to the table and picked up the scissors.

"Already? That's wonderful! I didn't expect them until this evening." Willa rushed to the window and peered through the frost-rimmed panes. "Oh, look! The branches are *heaped*. We shall have enough boughs to decorate the gazebo, too. May God bless Grandfather Townsend for—"

"The *gazebo?*"

The growled word jerked her gaze from Willa to the doorway. Daniel stepped into the room wearing a mock scowl.

"Are you planning to decorate the whole town, Pest? And what about a blessing for me? I cut and hauled those branches—near killed myself, too. It's going to cost you."

Willa laughed and left the window. "Not me, Daniel. It's Grandfather Townsend you work for."

"Not alone and in the moonlight, I don't. And not when I'm cutting branches for your husband's church."

A chill traveled up Ellen's spine. Daniel had downed the trees *alone?* At *night?* How could he make light of the danger? Or had he made it up to tease Willa? She lifted her gaze to his face. Light from the candelabra glinted on his green eyes and played over his uncovered head, making his hair look more red than brown—the way it was when he was young. Memories surged. She frowned, breathed in the scent emanating from him. He had always smelled of the outdoors—and now a bit like horse. She resisted the urge to sniff and instead lowered her gaze to rest on the knit hat he clutched in his gloved hand. He had big hands. And strong. Even when he was—

"All right, you win. What is it to cost me?"

Willa's laughter cut into her reverie. She looked up, caught her breath at the warm smile curving Daniel's lips. He'd once smiled at her that way.

"Two afternoons of skating and sledding with Josh and Sally." He turned slightly and his gaze fell on her, hardened. "Hey, Musquash. I didn't see you there at the table. What are you— Scissors?" His gaze dropped to the table, and his brows shot toward the ceiling. "You're *sewing?*"

His shocked tone stiffened her spine. She jutted her chin into the air. "You needn't be so—"

"Ellen is helping me make costumes for the children who will be speaking in church at Christmas, Daniel. Isn't that kind of her?"

Willa's voice drowned out hers—which was probably for the best. She took a calming breath, then made the mistake of meeting Daniel's gaze. His green eyes were dark, his expression dubious. She lifted her chin another notch and glared at him. "There's no reason for disbelief, Daniel. I *am* capable of performing an act of kindness on occasion."

A grin slanted across his lips, showed his teeth white against his red beard. "No doubt you are, Musquash... on occasion. But, *sewing?*"

"You know full well mother is a seamstress! Even *I* was bound to learn something of the skill from watching her over the years." She tossed her head and resumed her cutting, praying there was at least a modicum of truth in her words so she could make Daniel Braynard swallow his.

"Did you need something in town, Daniel? Is that why you were able to deliver the boughs so early?"

A sigh rose to her throat at Willa's less-than-subtle change of subject. She glanced up through her lashes, caught the easy smile Daniel gave Willa as she moved toward the table. The sigh turned to a painful pressure. All he ever gave her now was that mocking grin.

"No, it's because of the storm. The jobber has stopped logging operations until this blizzard passes and the temperature warms a bit. So I'll leave the pung here at the parsonage until it's time to go back to camp—if that's all right."

He would be in town! She frowned and placed the cut-off skirt on the growing pile of ready-to-work material.

"Yes, of course it is, Daniel. It will save you having to unload all those boughs into the back room of the church."

"Is that where w—"

"Oh!" Willa lurched, bumped against Daniel.

"Careful, Pest…." Daniel gripped Willa's arm and steadied her.

"I'm sorry. That was clumsy of me." Willa brushed back a lock of hair that had fallen onto her forehead. "What were we— Oh, yes…. What of the horses? We haven't stalls for them."

Her frown deepened. What was wrong with Willa? She sounded flustered.

"I know. I'll stable them at Dibble's, then get settled in at home. Do you want me to com—"

Willa broke into a coughing fit.

Alarm tingled along her nerves. Willa had said Matthew was busy visiting those sick with the grippe. Had he brought the illness home? Was that why Willa looked a bit flushed? She took a step back. Willa glanced her way, and understanding flashed in her eyes.

"There's no cause for alarm, Ellen. I'm not ill. It's only a tickle in my throat. I'll be fine when I get a drink." Willa spun toward the door. "Come with me, Daniel. We'll finish our discussion in the kitchen."

She stared agape as Willa all but shoved Daniel out the door ahead of her. She'd never known Willa to act so…strange. So…undone. She really *did* need her help. That odd sense of satisfaction she'd felt the other day returned. She smiled, picked up the scissors and began cutting the sleeves from the old green overdress they'd chosen to make Mary's garment.

Daniel would be in town. Her stomach flopped. She would have to be watchful to not run into him. If he called her *Musquash* one more time— Oh, no! She froze, then took a breath and slanted a glance up at the ceiling. "Please, Lord, make the storm stop so Daniel will be back at camp working soon. Please don't let him be in town when Mr. Lodge or Mr. Cuthbert arrive. *Please.*" She clenched her teeth and cut off the other sleeve. It would be bad enough if her beaux came and found her helping Willa with the sewing or decorations, but if Daniel were to—

"Steady, Big Boy. Back, Big Girl…back."

Daniel's muted voice came from outside. Chains rattled. He was leaving. Good. She glanced at the window, pressed her lips together and cut along a side seam to turn the green dress into a flat piece of material. Where was Willa? They had to get this work done!

She rose and started for the doorway, paused as the chains rattled again, then gave in to her urge and crossed to the window. The pung now sat behind the church.

She wrapped her arms about herself and watched Daniel unhitch the team, his movements confident and sure. She couldn't even imagine Mr. Lodge or Mr. Cuthbert attempting such a feat. What a disaster that would be. And how disloyal was she to even think such thoughts?

She whirled from the window and hurried back to the table, picked up the green dress she'd finished cutting and folded it. What did it matter if Mr. Lodge and Mr. Cuthbert knew nothing of hitching and unhitching horses? They had money enough to hire others to do it for them.

"I'm sorry for my delay in returning, Ellen. The baby was fussing."

Ellen pulled her thoughts back to the task at hand, looked up and smiled as Willa entered. "No matter— you're here now." Her fingertip poked through a threadbare spot as she shook out a piece of what was once a blanket. "I have the fabric ready for Mary's cloak. That leaves only Joseph's garment. Do you think there will be enough of this blanket left when I've cut around the holes?"

"More gingerbread?"

Daniel shook his head and grinned. "There's no place for any more, Ma. I ate too much pork pie. Smiley's food is good, but he can't cook like you."

"Well, if you're certain, I'll clear this mess away." His mother beamed a smile at him, rose and began stacking the dirty dishes. Her long skirts swayed from her plump hips as she carried the dishes to the sink cupboard, scraped the scraps into a bucket and slipped the plates into the water in the wash pan. "I hope we don't have a storm like this over Christmas. It'll delay my trip to Syracuse to care for your aunt Ruth. I'm plannin' on leavin' when you go back to camp. Ruth's rheumatiz is bad with the cold, and I was figurin' to go and stay with her till the weather warms. She's no one to do for her since Asel passed."

"You're a good woman to make that long trip during the cold weather, Ma."

"Bein' good or not ain't got nothin' to do with it." She lifted the steaming kettle off its trivet over the coals in the fireplace and tossed him a look over her shoulder. "She's a need, and you do for family."

He rose and put his arm about her soft shoulders. "And *you* do for any others that need help, as well, Ma. Even if it costs you time or discomfort."

"Well, it's the Christian thing to do, helpin' others." Steam rose in a cloud as she poured the water into the pan. "I'm strong and able, and you share the blessings God gives you with them less fortunate. Don't you forget that, son."

"I won't, Ma. How could I, with you for my example?" He leaned down and kissed her pink cheek. Her green eyes shone up at him, warm with pleasure.

"You're a good man, Daniel. You put me more in mind of your pa every day. It's good to have you home." She set the kettle aside, tossed a bar of soap into the water and picked up a cloth. "What will you be doin' to help Willa with the Christmas decorations?"

"She hasn't told me. But I know it will take longer than I figured." He crossed to the door, took his jacket off the peg and shrugged into it. "She's decorating the gazebo, too. Says it will make it more festive for the carol sing."

"The gazebo..." A smile touched his mother's mouth,

then disappeared. She ducked her head and soaped the cloth. "Seems like you'll be spendin' a lot of time at the parsonage."

"Seems like you're probably right." He pulled his hat from his pocket. "Maybe that's why we're having this storm. Maybe Willa took her need for help to her Abba, Father. He seems to pay close mind to her prayers."

"And mine."

"What? I didn't hear, Ma. I was putting on my hat."

"Nothin' important." She swished a plate through the rinse pan and set it on the towel on the wood drainboard. "It gonna bother you, havin' Ellen so close by while you're there workin'?" She flashed a look in his direction. "Her bein' across the street, I mean."

There was no sense pretending he didn't understand her. "That's an old dream that died long ago, Ma." He pulled up a grin and shot her a teasing look. "Surely *you* know Ellen's come home to decide which of her rich beaux she'll marry."

"I heard. But she ain't betrothed yet."

There was a determined note in his mother's voice that said clearly she wasn't letting up on her prayers. Twelve years she'd been at it. He tugged his hat down over his ears, exposed by his newly trimmed hair, frowned and ran his hand over his clean-shaven face. Did she think… "Look, Ma, Ellen will be at home sitting cozy and warm in front of their fire while Willa and I are working on the decorations in the back room of the church. She won't even see me. I stopped at Fabrizio's for a haircut and shave to get rid of the itching, not to change Ellen's goal. Besides, I'm not *that* good-looking—except maybe to you." He chuckled and put on his gloves.

She looked at him.

He wished for the hundredth time he'd never told her that making himself an acceptable suitor in the eyes of Ellen's parents when he was old enough to court Ellen was the reason he'd apprenticed himself to the counting house in Olville when he was twelve. She knew that had all come to a halt when his father died. And she still felt guilty that he'd had to give up his dream and become a logger in order to keep the cabin and provide a home for her. "Look, Ma, I was only a kid with a crush that lasted longer than it should have. It's over. You can stop praying for me."

"And what makes you think it's you alone I'm prayin' for?" His mother looked down, swished the cloth over another plate.

What did *that* mean? He stared at her, shook his head and walked over to pick up the bucket. "I'll throw these scraps out back for Millers' pigs on my way to Willa's. See you at supper, Ma."

Snow was still falling, though it had eased up. He tossed the scraps onto the trampled-down area where the neighbor's pigs rooted, set the bucket back inside the kitchen door and tromped out to the road. The wind picked up, blew cold against his bare cheeks. He tucked his chin down into his collar and wished it were as easy to bury his scruples. He hadn't exactly lied to his mother, but he hadn't told her the truth either. He hoped Ellen *would* see him around town, all clean-shaven and with his hair trimmed just like those rich beaux of hers. Not to try to change her mind, though. That part was true. It was a pride thing.

A wry smile tugged at his lips. He sure couldn't tell his Ma that. He knew exactly what she would say—*Pride goeth before destruction, Daniel.* But in his case, there was nothing for pride to destroy but the memory of his childhood love for Ellen—and he'd sure welcome that. He'd been carrying it around for too many years. It was time to be done with it.

Ellen snipped the thread and stuck the needle in the pincushion that was fastened to the arm of Willa's chair. That was the last seam. She caught her breath, turned the garment and held it up. Nothing was crooked or puckered. A smile tugged at her lips, but she refused it possession. It was silly to feel such a sense of accomplishment. Sewing straight seams required no real talent with a needle.

"You've finished the shepherd's robe."

She glanced at Willa, her heart warming at her friend's smile. "Well, I've sewn it together. But I'm afraid my ability with a needle is unequal to the hemming required around the neck and armholes."

"That's not needed, Ellen. That wool won't ravel. And it need last only one day. Which is a very good thing because my finger keeps poking through this cotton!" Willa wiggled the exposed fingertip of her hand tucked beneath the fabric on her lap. "I'm afraid one of the Wise Men is going to look quite tattered."

"Well, he *has* been on a very long journey."

Willa laughed, real, genuine laughter, not the polite titter of the elite women in Buffalo. The sound of it brought her own laughter bubbling up. It felt wonderful. How long had it been since she'd really laughed? She shoved the thought aside, carried the folded robe to the table and eyed the costumes waiting to be sewn. She *so* wanted to make the angel's costume, but she was simply not that capable with needle and thread. She picked up the pieces for Joseph's robe and turned back toward her chair. Willa was looking out of the window—again. "Are you expecting a caller?"

Willa started, sat back in her chair and resumed sewing. "What put that notion in your head?"

"That's the third time I've seen you looking out of the window."

"Well, that doesn't mean— Bother! I've poked another hole." Willa cut her thread, stuck her needle in the shared pincushion and jumped to her feet. "I'd best find different fabric and cut another Wise Man's costume. This cloth will fall apart if Tommy moves."

She watched Willa hurry to what remained of the old clothes and start sorting through the pile, pursed her lips and crossed to the window to see for herself what was so interesting. If there was one thing she easily recognized, it was evasion—the elite were masters at it. There was no horse and buggy, not even the tracks of one, only undisturbed snow. And more falling. Would it never stop? She sighed and lifted her gaze toward the sky. *Ah.* "So *that* is what you were watching for—a glimpse of your husband as he walked over to the church."

"What are you talking about, Ellen? Matthew went to Olville directly after dinner, and—" Willa jerked upright, a faded red garment in her hands. "Is someone out there?"

"No, but a fire has been started at the church. Smoke is beginning to rise from one of the chimneys—the rear one."

"Are you certain? It's hard to tell with the snow." Willa tossed the dress back onto the pile, hurried to her side and peered out the window. "Yes, you're right—there is smoke. He's here."

She stared, taken aback by the flash of satisfaction in Willa's blue-green eyes. "So you *were* expecting someone?"

"Not exactly. Daniel only said *perhaps* he—"

"Daniel?"

"Why, yes." Willa looked down, brushed at the front of her skirt. "Didn't I tell you he is going to help us with the decorations?"

"Daniel is going to—" She squared her shoulders and lifted her chin. "No, Willa Jean, you did *not*. And if—"

"Well, I meant to. It must have slipped my mind while I was caring for Mary." Willa sighed, slanted a glance up at her and sighed again. "Babies take *so* much time, Ellen. I simply don't know how I would manage all I have to do without your help."

Her protest died. It was plain she would have to endure Daniel's presence for Willa's sake. She had given her word. And he would be going back to the lumber camp soon. *Please, Lord!* Meanwhile, she would avoid him as much as possible. The parsonage wasn't a large house, but it was big enough to—

"Come along, Ellen." Willa lifted her hems and hurried toward the doorway.

"Come along where?"

"To get our cloaks and go to the church. We will make the decorations in the back room, and I want to get started while Mary is napping and Bertha can watch over her."

Her stomach sank. She took a breath and offered the only excuse she could think of that might delay the inevitable. "What of the sewing? I'll stay here and—"

Willa didn't even pause, merely glanced back over her shoulder. "I'll work on the costumes in the evenings after the children are abed. It's the decorations I'm most concerned about—or was, until your kind offer of help. And Daniel's, too, of course."

Willa's smile stole her resistance. "Very well." She laid the costume pieces she held on the table and frowned down at her old green wool dress. If she had known about having to work with Daniel, she would have worn one of her lovely gowns. Not that he would notice. But, even so, they gave her confidence. And she needed that around him. Daniel was the only man she knew who could undermine her self-assurance with merely a look. She blew out a breath, fluffed her curls and followed Willa into the hall. At least her old dress would be hidden from Daniel's view by her lovely new cloak.

Chapter Six

Daniel dumped his armful of branches on top of the growing pile in the corner. That would be the last load until they were used up. Any more and he and Willa would be crowded right out of the small room.

He brushed his jacket free of bits of bark and pine needles while he took inventory. His small hand ax lay on the upended piece of log he would use for lopping the offshoots from the branches, the coil of twine Willa had requested was on the table, the woodbox was full and the stove was going. It was time to let Willa know he was here and they could start working. He slapped his gloves together over the pile to rid them of snow and tugged them back on. The latch clicked. He jerked his head around as the door swung open, hit the heel of his boot and stopped.

"Daniel, the door is stuck!" The door was drawn back, shoved forward again with more force.

"Whoa! Hold on, Pest." He turned and pulled the door open. "That's my foot you're—" The words froze on his tongue. He stared at the blue wool visible between Willa and the doorframe, scowled and shifted his gaze to Willa's face. She gave him a sweet smile. *Asked and answered.* His scowl deepened. Willa stepped into the room and his vision filled with blue wool and rabbit fur.

Ellen looked up and stopped dead in her tracks. Her blue eyes widened.

"Don't look so surprised, Musquash. Your rich beaux aren't the only ones who enjoy a shave and a haircut. Even we lowly loggers like to get one now and then—when we come to town and all."

"I thought you were a *teamster*."

The rejoinder was not a compliment. He dipped his head. "True. But I figure we're all one and the same to you and your friends—common laborers."

Those blue eyes flashed. "You said it, not I." She tossed her head and swept by him.

Nor do I intend to ever give you the opportunity. If there's any belittling of me to be done, I'll do it. He clenched his jaw and closed the door, peeled off his jacket and hung it on a peg. It was going to be a long afternoon—unless he could make Ellen so angry with his teasing she went home in a huff.

"My, we'll be toasty warm while we're working, Ellen." Willa shoved her hood back and stepped close to the table in front of the stove. "I do believe it's warmer in here than in my dining room."

My mistake. He eyed the stove chimney, entertained the thought of turning the damper down. Spoiled as Ellen was, she would run home fast enough if it got chilly. She'd always hated to be cold. His gaze shifted to her, pulled by a force he couldn't resist. How many times had he given her his coat to wear? Too many to recall. He yanked his thoughts from the past, swept a glance over her fancy fur-trimmed cloak and bonnet and pulled in a breath. For sure she didn't need his coat now. She needed nothing from him, which was perfect, for he had nothing to give. Yesterday was gone forever.

He tugged off his gloves and hat, shoved them into his jacket pockets and rubbed his palms together. "All right, Pest, let's get this work done. Tell me what to do."

"I think it would be easiest if I show you how I want to decorate the church. So if you would both come with me into the sanctuary?"

His brows pulled down. Willa gave him another sweet smile and hurried toward the door, which was wise of her, because if she gave him that smile one more time, she was going to *need* sanctuary! He stifled the growl pushing at his throat and motioned Ellen through the door ahead of him. She was none too happy with Willa's request either, if her stiff movements were any indication. Not that that was surprising. She was never happy when their paths crossed. He slowed his steps, stopped at the first box pew and watched the women continue up the aisle—the more space between them, the better.

"First, of course, we'll need a large wreath for the front door. Then a cluster of boughs to adorn each pew door and—" Willa stopped halfway up the aisle and swept her gloved hand through the air "—garlands to drape around the windows."

Ellen halted, glanced left and right. "All *eight* of them?"

Her aghast tone would have been amusing if he didn't share her feelings. They'd never finish all of that in one afternoon. He stiffened, fastened his gaze on Willa's face. Perhaps that was what she… No. Willa knew how he felt about—

"It won't look right unless we do them all, Ellen."

Willa sighed, bowed her head and ran her hand along the waxed wood of a pew wall. "And I so want to do a good job. This is my first Christmas as a pastor's wife and, well…I want Matthew to be proud of me. But if you feel it's too much work for you to help me with…"

"No, of course not, Willa." Ellen stepped forward and placed her hand on Willa's arm. "I only wanted to be sure I understood your intent."

He studied Willa's bowed head, ashamed of his suspicion. He'd become far too self-absorbed since Ellen's return. Her haughtiness had that effect on him. It was time to put some enthusiasm into helping Willa, Ellen or no Ellen. He pushed away from the pew and grinned. "You're sure that's *all* you need, Pest?"

"For the church." Willa looked directly into his eyes and smiled. "We'll discuss the parsonage when we're finished here."

"The *parsonage!*"

"Why, yes." Willa started back down the aisle toward him, Ellen, who was making a poor job of hiding her displeasure, in her wake. "It should look festive and welcoming for any parishioners who come calling over the holiday. And, of course, I want it wonderful and special for Joshua and Sally."

The names of the children struck deep—and Willa knew it. That was obvious in the way she avoided meeting his gaze. His suspicion came roaring back. Nonetheless, he had given his word. And he could bear the discomfort of being around Ellen for the children's sake. But for how long? He moved forward to open the door, scowled when Ellen's arm brushed against him as she glided by and glanced toward the window—still snowing. He wouldn't be returning to the camp anytime soon.

"Well, I believe we're ready to begin working now. And I think the wreath for the door should be made first." Willa removed her cape and hung it over one of the chairs at the table. "Daniel, if you will lop the off-shoots from the branches, then lay the greenery here on the table, Ellen and I will tie the sprigs in small bunches and then— Oh, bother! I've forgotten to bring scissors to cut pieces of twine. I'll have to go get them."

Oh, no, you don't, Pest! You're not leaving me here alone with Ellen. He snatched up the coil of twine. "There's no need for scissors, Pest. Tell me how long you want the pieces, and I'll chop them off." He carried the twine to the upended log, looked back at her standing with her cloak in her hands and smiled. The look of annoyance she gave him confirmed his suspicion better than words—Willa was playing matchmaker. He frowned and gave a small shake of his head to warn her to stop.

"A clever solution." Willa shrugged and hung her cape back on the chair. "Eight inches long will be fine, Daniel. And when you have stripped a limb that is long and supple enough, if you would bend it into a large circle and bind the ends together, we will attach bundles of pine to it to make the wreath."

He nodded, draped the coil over the end of a log sticking up out of the wood box, snaked out the twine and chopped off eight-inch pieces as he dragged it over the upended log. That shrug meant Willa wasn't going to give up. Sly woman! She knew he wouldn't confront her about her matchmaking efforts in front of Ellen. He tossed the fistful of twine pieces onto the table, grabbed a branch, hacked off the greenery and grabbed another. Small sprigs of pine littered the floor around his boots. He gathered them into a pile and scooped them up, kicked aside a few pinecones that had fallen off the branches and carried the greens to the table. Ellen stood there, still wearing her fancy cloak and bonnet. She might as well have waved a flag announcing his inadequacy. But there was a blessing in it, as well.

He dumped his armload of greens in the middle of the table where they could be easily reached from either side. "I hope you aren't thinking of working with this pine in that fancy cloak of yours, Musquash. Your fine beaux won't be so admiring when it's all dotted and smeared with pine sap. Come to think of it, you'll likely ruin your fancy dress, too. Perhaps you'd best forget about helping."

Ellen's finely molded nostrils flared. "I'll do no such thing, Daniel Braynard!" She shot him a haughty glance, undid the bow beneath her chin with a sharp yank and tossed her bonnet onto a chair. "I gave my word to help Willa and that is exactly what I intend to do. If I ruin my garments it's none of your affair. *Nothing* I do is of your concern!"

More salt rubbed in old wounds. She used to look to him for advice in everything. He gave a lazy shrug. "True enough. Ruin your cloak if you're of a mind to."

Her cheeks flamed. The heel of her boot clacked against the floor, the sound muted by her long skirts. "I am *not* going to ruin my cloak! Or my dress. I wore one of my old ones." She whipped the blue wool off of her shoulders, tossed it over the chair back and jutted her chin at him. "I'm not a child, and I'd appreciate it if you would stop treating me like one."

"Then stop stomping your foot." He forced a grin and turned away, snatched up a branch and his ax to keep from grabbing Willa and demanding to know what kind of torture she was putting him through. The sight of Ellen in that plain green gown with her face tipped up toward his was enough to make him dream for weeks! Any man would! He swung the ax so hard the blade buried itself in the log. He gritted his teeth, yanked it free and lopped greens from the branch so fast the blade blurred. From the corner of his eye he saw Ellen pull the kid gloves from her hands and toss them onto the chair atop her bonnet.

"You'll have to show me what to do, Willa. I've never made decorations."

He shot a quick glance at her face at the odd sound of the words—she was gritting her teeth, all right. It wouldn't be long before she'd be so mad she'd head for home. He relaxed his own jaw and grabbed another branch.

"It's not hard, Ellen. You simply gather the greens one at a time until you have a nice full bunch, like this—" Willa picked up some greens, holding the stems in her left hand "—then wrap a piece of twine about the twigs good and tight, cross the ends over and tie a knot. See?" Willa held up the tied bunch and smiled. "When we have made enough bunches, we will use the dangling ends of the twine to tie them to the branch ring Daniel will make for us. Now you try it."

He turned his head slightly to watch as Ellen gathered and tied pine sprigs into a bunch.

"Is this right?"

Ellen held the bouquet of sprigs out for Willa's approval, then glanced his way. He jerked his head down.

"Perfect. Keep making them exactly like that."

"All right, I— What are you doing?"

That sounded a little panicked. He slid his gaze back toward the table, stiffened at the sight of Willa putting on her cloak. He lifted his head and cleared his throat, but she ignored him and smiled at Ellen.

"I have to go to the house and check on the baby. She's probably awake and crying to be fed. I'll be back when I get her settled again."

The words held him mute. How could you argue against a baby? Willa tugged her hood in place and headed for the door. He scowled and opened it for her. She gave him another of those sweet smiles, stepped outside and hurried down the steps to the pathway. And there was nothing he could do about it. He stifled another growl and went back to work, the thunk of his ax and the whisper of the falling offshoots loud in the sudden heavy silence in the small room.

Ellen tied the small bunch of pine twigs, placed it with the others at the end of the table and stole a glance at Daniel from under her lowered lashes. The muscles along his shoulder and arm rippled beneath his wool shirt as he wielded his hatchet. The steady thud grated on her nerves. Why didn't he say something? Even his mocking and teasing would be better than this weighted silence.

The heaviness settled in her chest, pushed a sigh into her throat. They used to talk so easily with one another, the way he talked with Willa and Callie and Sadie now, only…different somehow. He'd been so thoughtful of her, so protective during those years when they'd all followed him wherever he went—probably because she was the youngest. Whatever the reason, she'd thought then that their friendship was special, especially after he dove into the flood-swollen Stony Creek to save her. Now he couldn't bear the sight of her, and he certainly didn't want to talk with her.

Tears stung her eyes. Well, that was what she got for remembering when she was a silly, impressionable young girl, and Daniel was her hero. She blinked the watery film away, gathered pine sprigs from the pile on the table and formed them into a small cluster. Thankfully, her mother and father had told her the true way of things and set her on the right path to achieve a life of ease among the wealthy and influential people of society. She could so easily have erred....

She fought an urge to look again at Daniel, tucked a rough piece of twine between her thumb and the pine cluster, careful to leave the end dangling as Willa had shown her, then wrapped the twine twice around the stems and tied it off. He looked so different without the bushy beard and long hair. Handsome and more like... well, Daniel.

The urge strengthened. She stole another look at him from under her lowered lashes, yielded and raised her head to study his profile showing clean and clear against the plastered wall. There was no need for her to hide her perusal; he was paying her no mind. It was as if their friendship had never existed.

She swept her gaze from his brown crisply waving hair with its lingering hue of boyhood red to his pronounced cheekbone and on to the shadowed area beneath his strong square jaw. How well she remembered that jaw. He always clenched it when he set his mind to something, and that little muscle at the joint jumped. It was a sure sign that he was determined about something. She stared at his jaw. That muscle was twitching now. What—

"We'll never get this work finished if you stand there looking holes through me. Do you need something?"

She jumped. Hot blood rushed into her cheeks. "No, nothing. I was only thinking about Willa and...things." She jerked her gaze from his face, threw the finished bunch onto the pile and snatched up more pine sprigs. "Ouch!" She dropped the pine and shoved the tip of her finger into her mouth, then yanked it out again. "Ugh!"

"I guess how pine sap tastes wasn't one of those 'things.'" He buried the edge of his hatchet in the log and held out his hand. "Let me see your finger. Slivers can get painful if you don't take them out."

She stared at his big, calloused, sap-dotted hand and swallowed hard against the sudden lump in her throat. His touch had always made her feel so safe, so...*cared* about, and it wasn't that way any longer—his stiff posture and the hard edge to his voice made that clear. She took a breath and shook her head. His long fingers curled into his palm, and his hand jerked back.

"Sorry. I forgot. Perhaps one of your beaux with clean, soft hands will remove the sliver when they arrive."

Her beaux! The thought jolted her from the past. She squared her shoulders and lifted her chin. "I'm certain they would." *Not true. They would be appalled at the way her hands looked—and by the old plain gown she wore.* "However, as you can see, there *is* no sliver. It was only a prick." He didn't even glance at the extended index finger she held forward, merely grunted, stepped back to the log and picked up his ax.

How could she have forgotten what an insufferable

man he'd become? She batted her long skirts out of the way of the chair leg, stepped around the table so her back was toward him and shot a look at the door. Where was Willa? How long did it take to feed and settle a baby, anyway? She frowned and snatched up a sprig of pine, put it in her left hand and snatched up another. Did an infant go right back to sleep or remain awake after being fed? She had no idea. But one thing was certain—her mother was right. A woman's life was much easier with a wet nurse and nanny to care for any babies. Her wealthy lady friends in Buffalo never missed any activities because of their children.

She looked down at the spot of blood among the sticky dabs of sap on her fingers and scowled. And those women didn't ruin their hands making costumes or Christmas decorations either. It had been a mistake to offer. How was she to get the pine sap off?

Daniel would know. No! She'd swallow her tongue before she'd ask his advice about anything! She pressed her lips together, thrust more pine sprigs into her hand and reached for the twine to bind them. The quicker this job was finished, the better!

That was the last branch, and he'd no reason for going outside to get more. Daniel scowled down at the lopped-off greens so deep they brushed against his ankles, buried the edge of his hatchet in the chopping log and turned to sort through the heap of denuded branches. He'd put off making the circle for the wreath as long as he could. Where was Willa, anyway? He'd agreed to help *her* make Christmas decorations, not to work with Ellen. He snatched up one of the longer branches, tested its flexibility, threw it down and snatched up another.

The third one he tried curved easily into a large circle. He held the overlapping ends together, carried it to the table and bound the juncture with a piece of twine.

"What's that?"

"The circle Willa asked me to make for the wreath."

"Oh."

Ellen's sigh pierced his determination. He braced and looked at her. She was staring at the rounded branch in his hand and tugging at the corner of her lower lip with her teeth the way she did when she was unsure of what to do. Her head lifted, and her blue eyes fastened on his. He gritted his teeth as the old urge to help her, to take care of her, rose. He jerked his gaze down to the table before his emotions became more entangled. The pile of pine bunches she'd made was pitifully small. "I'll put more wood in the stove, then give you some help. There's no sense in my going outside to get more pine until what I've already cut is used up."

More's the pity! He could use a good dose of cold air to clear his head—memories were powerful things. And the room was too small. He couldn't get a decent breath. He hunched his shoulders forward to make them as narrow as possible when he stepped around the table, but his arm still brushed against Ellen's. Warmth tingled along its length. *You'd better get back here soon, Pest, or I'm leaving—promise or not!* He opened the draft, tossed two small pieces of split log into the firebox, then adjusted the draft for a slow burn and stepped over to the chopping log. He bent and scooped his arms full of pine sprigs, dumped them in the center of the table, then snatched up a handful and tied the stems together.

Silence, taut and uncomfortable, stretched between them. He made another bunch, threw it on the pile and grabbed more sprigs. Ellen reached for more at the same moment and his hand brushed against hers. His fingers twitched.

"Am I doing this wrong?"

He shook his head and snatched up a piece of twine.

"Then why are you scowling?"

The stubborn tilt of her chin told him she would not stop until she had an answer. But he for sure wasn't going to tell her the real reason—only the one behind it. "I'm wondering what's keeping Willa so long. It seems as if she should be back by now."

She studied his face for a moment, then nodded and brushed at a lock of hair that fell loose with the movement. "I was wondering the same thing. I've no idea how long it takes to feed and settle a baby, but it's been a long while."

It feels that way for certain! He dragged his gaze from the blond curl now nestled cozily behind her ear and fought the desire to fall into their old, comfortable way with one another. That would lead to disaster—his. "No doubt you'll soon find out. After you're married to one of your beaux, that is." The ends of the sprigs he was tying into a bunch snapped off. He blew out a breath, eased the pressure of his grip and unwound the too-tight loops of twine. "Have you decided which one you're going to accept yet?" He forced his lips into a grin and looked over at her. "Will it be Mr. Money or Mr. Prestige?"

"That is not the basis for my decision! They *both* have money and prestige." Ellen threw the bunch she held onto the finished pile and glared at him. "And their names are Mr. Lodge and Mr. Cuthbert."

He dipped his head in a mocking bow, and if the flash

in her eyes was any indication, he no longer had to be concerned about a return to their childhood ease with one another. He tossed the sprigs he'd ruined onto the pile of denuded branches and gathered up more.

Wind moaned around the stovepipe. Driven snow plastered against the remaining bare spots on the small window and closed off the outside world. Light from the sconces played among the golden curls atop Ellen's bowed head and created a shadow beneath the one dangling behind her ear. He gritted his teeth, set his mind against the soft candle glow on Ellen's smooth cheeks and focused on the conversation he was going to have with Willa as soon as he got her alone.

The door latch clicked. Cold air rushed into the room and the candle flames flickered behind their protective globes. He swiveled his head toward the door and watched in silence as Willa stepped inside, stamped her booted feet and shoved back her cloak's snow-covered hood.

"Glory be, I don't believe I've ever seen a storm as ferocious as this one."

Wait until we're alone, Pest. He let his eyes telegraph the message.

"Oh, dear...." The worry in Ellen's voice drew his gaze. She was staring at the snow-clogged window and nibbling at the corner of her lower lip. "I hope the storm hasn't caused Mother and Father to return home early." The nibbling increased. "Perhaps I'd better go."

An excellent idea. He jerked his gaze from the assault her teeth were inflicting on her lip and cleared his throat to tell her so.

"There's no need. Your parents haven't come home."

His brows zoomed skyward. *She'd been watching?* He shot Willa a look.

"How can you know that?"

Indeed. Answer Ellen's question, Willa. He quirked his lips into a challenging smile.

"I…er…glanced out the window a time or two while I was gone."

"Tending the baby?" The comment earned him a look. He tried to emulate one of those sweet smiles she'd been giving him earlier.

"It's possible to hold an infant and look out a window at the same time, Daniel."

He raised a brow and dipped his head.

Willa lifted her chin and sniffed.

"You *are* taking ill, Willa." Ellen backed up.

"Careful!" He shot out his hand and grabbed her arm.

"Oh!" Ellen glanced over her shoulder, then looked up at him. "I forgot about the stove being so close."

He stared down into the azure depths of her eyes and all the feelings he'd been holding at bay flooded through him. He gave a curt nod, let go of her arm and straightened, the muscle along his jaw jumping in time with his racing pulse.

Willa swooped into view. "I'm not sick, Ellen. It's only the heat of the room after the cold." She gave him a look, then snatched up one of the sprig bouquets. "My, you've done a lovely job with these! And, Daniel, this wreath circle is the perfect size." Her hand touched his arm. "Why don't you carry out those bare branches and bring in more. Ellen and I will have these sprigs used up in no time."

He looked at the greenery still littering the floor but was in no mood to argue the point. All he wanted was to get out of that room. "You're the boss." He shrugged into his jacket and pulled on his hat and gloves, then stooped and filled his arms with the useless branches. There was the soft swish of a woman's skirts behind him. The door latch clicked. His lips twisted into a sour grin. *It's going to take more than your opening the door for me to forgive you for this, Pest.* He straightened and turned. Ellen peered at him over the tangle of branches he held, then pulled the door wide. He cleared the tightness from his throat and moved forward. "Thank you."

"It's little enough. You saved me from harm…again."

Like old times. He stepped outside, the bitterness he kept under tight control swelling with the snick of the latch as she closed the door behind him. "Except nothing is the same. I'm a nobody you look down on now." The wind whipped the words away. Good. There was nothing worse than self-pity. All the same, it was too bad the wind couldn't carry off memories. He had a heartful he'd like to be rid of.

Have faith, Daniel.

He grimaced and plowed through the snow to the pung. How many times had his mother admonished him to have faith? More than he could count. But how could you have something that had died? His faith, hope and dreams had all been buried along with his father in a grave twelve years ago. His life was what it was—what it had to be. And by God's grace, he'd make the best of it. It wasn't so bad. At least, it hadn't been until today when Willa started stirring things up. He'd put a stop to that, and things would settle back to normal. As soon as they were through with this decorating, that was.

How did Willa ever get Ellen to agree to help her? No matter. After tasting of the work and learning what all

Willa had in mind, it was certain Ellen would not return tomorrow. He dropped his load onto the snow at the back of the pung, then filled his arms with new green boughs to take inside. Only one afternoon. He could manage that.

Chapter Seven

"It's beautiful, Mother!" Ellen lifted the skirt of the new dress her mother held up for her inspection. "The blue color is a perfect match for my eyes."

"Do you think Mr. Lodge and Mr. Cuthbert will find it compares favorably with your gowns made by the modiste in Buffalo?"

"Of course they will, Mother." She smiled and touched the fancy needlework that decorated the bodice. "Your stitching is—" She stopped, taken aback by a sudden frown on her mother's face. "What is it? What's wrong?"

"You've been tending the fire again. There's sap on your hand."

She twisted her wrist and stared at the small dark smudge on the outside edge of her right hand. She'd been so thorough scrubbing and creaming her hands. How had she missed it?

Her mother draped the new dress over the hoop-backed chair beside the window and returned to stand beside her. "I understand you were visiting Willa again today."

She stopped rubbing at the spot and looked up, grateful for the change of subject but leery at the cool tone. "Yes, I was."

Her mother nodded, glanced down.

Had she inadvertently gotten sap from her hands on the lavender silk gown she'd changed into when she came home? She squared her shoulders and resisted the urge to look down and check.

"It's thoughtful of you to wear one of your old gowns when you call on Willa. I'm sure she would be quite envious of these costly, stylish ones."

"I see Isobel has been reporting on my activities." She raised a brow and arranged her features in the pout that always won her her way. "Really, Mother, I'm no longer a *child*." She huffed out a breath and ran her hands down over her gown. "And you know Willa is more than generous. She would not envy my gowns." The responding flicker in her mother's eyes tightened her stomach and sent a warning tingle up her spine.

"You're right, of course, dear. I should not have spoken so of Willa. But now I'm puzzled." Her mother gathered her skirts, sat in the chair at the edge of the hearth and smiled up at her. "If not to spare Willa's feelings… why *did* you wear your old gown for your visit? Obviously, it's not because you prefer it, since you changed into the lovely one you're wearing as soon as you came home."

Isobel and her tattling! She looked at the glint in her mother's eyes and pasted a faux smile on her face. "Why, Mother, you know walking through the deep snow would ruin this silk. And my old wool gown is much warmer. Besides, I was helping Willa." Her mother's nose flared like a dog's that had caught the scent of its prey at her last words. *So her mother had heard.* She braced herself for the discomfort of a confrontation.

"I understand that you are bored until your beaux arrive, Ellen. But if you must visit with your old friends, please remember you are not a servant, and do not do mundane tasks. I'm shocked Willa would ask such a thing of you."

Disapproval frosted her mother's voice. She lifted her chin. "Truly, Mother, I'm surprised that you, of all people, would call sewing costumes mundane. I understand you speaking so of making decorations, but not of sewing."

Her mother gaped, recovered. "You are helping Willa make costumes for the children that will be speaking verses at Christmas?"

Is it so inconceivable to you? She nodded. "Yes. I thought you—"

"What decorations?"

She looked at her father, squared her shoulders at the sight of his scowling face. "Willa is making decorations for the church and parsonage."

His eyes narrowed. He pulled his pipe from his mouth and stared at her. "So that is where Daniel Braynard took that load of pine boughs I saw in the pung when he drove by the store this morning." He rose, crossed to the hearth and knocked the side of his pipe against the end of a burning log. The dottle fell onto the shimmering coals and burst into flame. "I should have guessed." The fire shadowed his face as he straightened and slowly nodded his head. "Manning Townsend is a generous man, and it only makes sense that Willa would ask Sadie if her grandfather would donate pine branches to trim the church."

"And that Daniel Braynard would deliver them." Her

mother gave an eloquent sniff. "After all, Daniel is one of Manning's loggers—and Willa and Sadie, and Callie for that matter, have always remained close with him."

As I once was, until you and Father stopped it. Her face drew taut. She turned and looked into the flickering flames to drive away the useless memories. "Daniel is a *teamster.*" She snagged her lower lip with her teeth, but it was too late—she'd spoken the correction aloud. From the corner of her eye, she saw her father glance her way, then pull the pewter pipe holder on the mantel toward him.

"I heard the logging camps have shut down until this blizzard passes. That means most of the loggers have come home for the time being." He lifted his pipe and blew through the stem. "I would suppose Daniel is among them." He turned his head and fastened his gaze on her. "Did he say what he'd be doing while he's home when you saw him at Willa's?"

She shook her head, then tucked back a curl that fell free. "No. We spoke very little." The words left a sour taste in her mouth and the memory of the uncomfortable, strained silence between them filling her thoughts. She tugged her silk wrap closer over her bare shoulders and turned to warm her other side, unable to make herself comment further. They would hear soon enough that Daniel was also helping to make the decorations.

"I see. Well, all the same, perhaps it would be best if you forget your little philanthropy."

It was an order couched in soft words. She turned her head and looked into her father's eyes.

"Your beaux may not understand why you would do such…work."

"Then I shall explain." She lifted her chin, startled

by her unaccustomed defiance. "I have given Willa my word, Father. And I intend to keep my promise."

"And risk your future of ease?"

Mine, or yours and Mother's, Father? The thought shamed her. She'd never considered it before. Still, what did it matter that her father might be thinking of what he would gain by her marriage to a wealthy man? It was the way of things in society. She shrugged her shoulders. "There is little danger of that. Mr. Lodge and Mr. Cuthbert, as well as the other men of the Buffalo elite, are always in competition. This time it is for my hand. Neither of them would let the matter cause them to lose to the other." Another sobering thought. Did either man truly care for her? Oh, what did any of it matter? She would have what she wanted.

Her father's brows lowered. A chill touched her that had nothing to do with the temperature of the room.

"Perhaps *you* have judged too hastily this time, Conrad."

Her father stiffened and shot a frosty look at her mother. "Explain yourself, Frieda."

"Isn't it possible that Mr. Lodge, and even more Mr. Cuthbert, would consider it an advantage to have a wife who does charitable works? Or, at least, oversees them? It could be beneficial to a politician."

Her father's eyes narrowed. He set his pipe in its holder, pushed it back in place, then stood looking into the fire and stroking his beard. She watched him and waited, tensed when he lifted his head and looked at her. "Presented in the right way, the help you're giving Willa can be turned to your advantage, Ellen. We'll discuss it further, when I've given it more thought. Meanwhile, continue on."

The discomfort of her parents' displeasure was gone. And so was some of the good feeling she'd had about helping Willa.

No steam drifted from the spout. Daniel crossed to the fireplace and felt of the iron kettle—it was barely warm. He picked up the small shovel, carefully raked the covering ashes off of the coals and blew gently. The embers shimmered, began to glow red at the breath of life-giving air. There was a soft rustle behind him.

He rose and turned, held back a frown at the sight of his mother's old, worn wrapper with its frayed ties and tattered hems on the sleeves. The faded blue fabric fell unrestrained from her shoulders and swayed at her stocking-clad feet as she came to stand in front of him. Warmth filled his chest. She'd never have to wear the ragged dressing gown again after Christmas.

"Can't sleep?"

"I felt the need for a cup of coffee. Sorry I woke you, Ma. I tried to be quiet." He lifted his foot and wiggled his toes inside his thick wool sock as proof.

"Goin' without your boots don't do no good." She smiled, gave his foot a gentle swat. "I'm your ma. When you're up and stirrin', I don't hear it—I feel it."

He leaned down and kissed her soft cheek, all pink, creased and warm where it had been resting against her pillow. "I know, Ma. It's a heart thing."

She tilted her head back and gave him a look. "Don't you make game of it, Daniel Braynard. God puts it there. You'll know when you have young'uns of your own."

The words cut deep. He wanted children, but that dream had died along with the others. This afternoon had made him more certain of that than ever. He pulled up a smile and nodded—not that it would fool his ma. She had an uncanny ability to look straight into his heart.

"How about some hot chocolate, 'stead of coffee?"

He looked down at her small pudgy hand she'd rested on his forearm. That was his ma, always trying to make the hurt go away, to make everything better for him. But there were some things not even a mother could fix. He was a teamster—and a teamster he would stay. "No, Ma, coffee's fine. I bought that chocolate as a treat for you."

"Tastes better when it's shared." She lifted a small pan off a nail driven into the log mantel and waved it toward the flickering coals. "You get that fire goin', whilst I fetch the cream."

His protest died. If he wanted his mother to enjoy that chocolate, he'd have to drink it with her. She'd save it until he did. He lifted two small pieces of dried pine branch out of the kindling box, then stood and watched her hurrying to the small cupboard he'd made for her birthday the year his father died. The thick braid of her long gray-streaked dark hair dangled against the faded blue cotton between her shoulders. Her new dressing gown was dark green. She was partial to green.

His lips tugged into a smile at the thought of her pleasure when she saw the new wrapper and the moccasin slippers he'd had Bowing Fern make for her. It wasn't what he'd planned. He'd hoped to buy her a stove so she wouldn't have to keep the fire going summers and bend over the hearth to cook, but losing work when his shoulder was injured set him back in his saving. Maybe by spring he'd have enough set aside, if it stopped snowing so he could go back to work.

He shot a glance at the window by the door at the opposite end of the kitchen. The small panes, visible between the curtains made from a burlap bag dyed red, were coated with frost. He'd put the stove down at that end of the room. With fires going in the stove and on the hearth, the whole kitchen would be warm even on the coldest winter day. And in the summer heat, she could open the door and catch the cool breezes that flowed off the forested hill behind the row of company-owned cabins while she cooked.

"You plannin' on rubbin' those together to make a fire?"

He started from his thoughts, saw the slight twitch of her lips, remembered and grinned. "Something like that. Barking Fox taught me how."

"Well, I know! What were you—nine? Ten?" His mother's eyes, a more pronounced green than his own, brightened with laughter. "You almost burnt the house down practicin'."

"Now, Ma…it was only the kindling pile that caught fire." His grin widened at her teasing, faded when he saw her shiver. That wrapper was worn too thin to keep her warm. He laid the pieces of branch on the fire and gave a couple of puffs to encourage them to burn. Tongues of flame leaped up from the fire and wrapped around them. He added a couple small chunks of ash, then waited for them to catch fire.

"'Less I disremember, Sadie missed out on that adventure. But Willa, Callie and Ellen were all here that day." His mother set the crock she carried on the table and took a ladle off a shelf. "You scared 'em for certain."

"No more than I scared myself." He chuckled and rocked back on his heels. "They were sore impressed when I demonstrated my new skill, but I'll never forget all the running around and squealing those girls did when I accidentally caught that kindling afire."

"For all that, they helped you. They're good friends."

Message received. But you're wrong this time, Ma. "Not Ellen. Not anymore." He stared into the flames, seeing Ellen as she'd looked on that long-ago day with her golden curls dancing around her pale face and her blue eyes wide with fear as sparks flew from the burning wood. Still, frightened as she'd been, and worried, as always, of getting into trouble if she soiled or tore her dress, she'd helped Willa and Callie pull the burning kindling away from the pile stacked against the cabin while he pumped a bucket of water. He'd tried to stop her to protect her from her parents' displeasure, but she'd pressed her mouth together so tight her lips had disappeared, shook her head and gone back to work. She'd had that same look of determination this afternoon. Only this time it was him she was defying. His gut tightened. He blew out a breath, dusted off his hands and rose.

"Bad workin' with her today, was it?"

He glanced his mother's way. Firelight glinted off the knife in her hand as she shaved chocolate into a small pile on the table. He grabbed a candlestick off the mantel, held the candle's wick to the fire, then shielded the flame with his cupped hand and carried the candle to the table. Golden light flickered into the room, gleamed on the pan and what remained of a sugar cone and shimmered on the bowl of cream his mother had skimmed from a crock of milk. She looked up and smiled her thanks, but the question was still in her eyes. He scrubbed his hand across the back of his neck and gave an evasive answer. "Willa was gone tending her baby a good part of the time."

"Umm." She leaned down and picked up the teapot. "Babies take a sight of care."

"Seems so."

The wood crackled. A wisp of smoke drifted up the chimney. His mother poured warm water into the sugar in the bottom of the pan, added the shaved chocolate, carried it to the fireplace and set it on a trivet. "Fire feels good."

"You stay there and get warm. I'll take care of the milk." He picked up the crock and carried it to the cupboard at the other end of the kitchen. The cold chilled him, even through his wool shirt. He started back toward his mother and caught a glimpse of her rubbing her arms for warmth before she spotted him coming, dropped her hands to her sides and smiled. His face tightened. He couldn't provide for a wife—certainly not one like Ellen. But he could keep his mother warm. "I'll be right back, Ma."

He strode to his bedroom, grabbed the paper-wrapped parcel he'd brought home and carried it back to the kitchen. His mother was pouring steaming creamy brown liquid into their cups.

"The chocolate's ready." She set the pan on the sink cupboard, turned and stared. "What's that?"

He held the parcel out to her. "Merry Christmas, Ma."

"But it's not—"

"I want you to have this now." He couldn't quite hold the anger from his voice. It took him that way sometimes when he thought too much about how things were. He pasted on a smile. It didn't fool her, but she pretended it did, and that was good enough. He held his breath as she placed the parcel on the table, untied the string and set it aside to save. Steam from her cup rose and twined itself among the wisps of gray hair on her forehead as she bent forward to unfold the paper. He clenched his hands, watched her face.

"Daniel!" She gasped, touched the green fabric showing in the package, then drew her hands back and looked up at him.

"It's a wrapper, Ma. One that'll keep you warm." She ducked her head. He glanced at the small dark splotch that spread on the green fabric, saw another form and swallowed hard when she covered them with her small pudgy hand. "Put it on, Ma. I'll get us some bread and butter." He strode to the cupboard, then kept his back turned until the rustling sounds of fabric stopped.

"It's so fine…so warm and pretty…and green…."

He turned. His mother stood by the fireplace, murmuring to herself, her small hands touching the dressing gown's stand-up collar, patting the quilted sleeves and bodice, then smoothing the fabric that fell free from beneath it.

"Fit's you fair. I was worried it might be too long." He glanced down. "Do the moccasins fit?"

She blinked and took a breath. "They fit, and they're fine, Daniel—mighty fine. And the wrapper is so warm and pretty. Mayhap the prettiest thing I've ever owned…." She blinked and shook her head. "I thank you, son. I truly thank you. But you—"

"Don't say it, Ma."

She stopped, looked at him.

He clamped his jaw to keep from saying more—from spilling out his frustration. His life was what it was. And most of the time he could accept it without rancor. But being forced to spend time with Ellen today had brought back all his old dreams and the memory of all that his father's death had cost him. He'd spend all of his life alone. He set the bread and the crock of butter on the table, yanked off the towel that covered the loaf and picked up his mother's knife.

A long soft sigh floated over his shoulder. Plates clinked together. "So, will you be goin' to Willa's early in the mornin', or—"

"I haven't made up my mind." The words came out as sharp as the cuts he made with the knife. He sucked in a long breath. "Sorry, Ma. I didn't mean to bark at you. I'm feeling growly."

"I know." She patted his arm, then took hold of a table knife and started buttering the bread.

He sank into a chair, stretched his legs out toward the fire and lifted his cup to his mouth. The sweet taste of hot chocolate flowed over his tongue, left a hint of bitterness behind when he swallowed. "Willa plans on decorating the parsonage and the gazebo after we finish the church. I didn't know that—or that the baby would take so much of her time. And I, for sure, wasn't planning on Ellen being involved when I said I would help."

"Things don't always turn out the way we figure they will."

He was no stranger to that truth. He held back a snort, took another swallow of chocolate so he didn't have to answer. At the moment he didn't have anything good to say. He was trying not to hear the voice inside, reminding him that somewhere in the Bible it mentioned that an honorable man "swears to his own hurt and changeth not."

"Still…"

"I know, Ma. God works all things for the good, for those that love Him." It was one of her favorite verses.

He eyed the plate holding bread slathered with butter she slid toward him as if it were an enemy. He'd lost his appetite.

She settled into her chair and blew on her hot drink. "You don't sound very believin'."

"It's a small room we work in." His face flushed at what he'd admitted. He set down his cup and shoved to his feet, gave a couple of hops when the heated soles of his socks pressed against his flesh.

"That could be a mite uncomfortable."

He let the snort free. "It's the memories that make it so hard, Ma. But I'm not twelve years old now. I was only grousing—I'll be going back in the morning. I gave Willa my word." He scrubbed his hand over the tense muscles at the back of his neck and gave her a rueful smile. "And if God does work all things out for good, Ellen will stay home."

"You're a good man, Daniel. Don't you ever forget that." She stared up at him over the rim of her cup, her eyes dark with that look of determination he'd seen so often over the years. "I'll pray."

He'd said more than he'd intended. He kept forgetting how easily she read his heart. "Good." He grinned, resumed his seat and picked up his cup. "Between you and God, Ellen doesn't stand a chance."

A smile was her only answer.

Chapter Eight

The bell on the mercantile's door jangled its welcome. Ellen glanced toward the front of the store and froze. *Daniel.* Her stomach tensed. She hadn't thought to see him until this afternoon. She frowned and edged behind a display of wooden buckets atop a center table, feeling too weary, after her restless night, to spar with him. Perhaps if she turned her back and pretended not to see him, he would follow her lead and ignore her. Else—

"Hey, Daniel! We heard timbering had stopped. Got time for a game?"

No! She shot a disgusted glance at the men bent over the checker game atop the barrel in front of the heating stove. There would be no pretending ignorance of Daniel's presence possible now.

"Not today, Mr. Green. I'm headed for the parsonage."

"So is true, what we hear? You make the *decoration!*"

Ilari Fabrizio sounded outraged at the very idea. Ellen blew out a breath and held herself from stamping her foot. Now there would be an exchange, and she was in no mood to stand there and listen.

"No, gentlemen, I do *not.* For which we must all be

grateful." Daniel chuckled, stomped his boots free of snow and started forward. "*Willa* makes the decorations. I cut the greens for her and such." He stepped past the table with the stacked buckets, stopped short when he spotted her. Something flashed deep in his eyes but disappeared so quickly she might have imagined it—except for the warmth creeping into her cheeks.

"Sort of early for you to be up and about, isn't it, Musquash? Especially in this weather." That cool, teasing grin she hated slanted across his lips. "Must be you're expecting a letter from one of your rich beaux and couldn't wait to read their words of adoration."

And you thought he was admiring you? Foolish woman. It was simply a trick of the lamplight. "That's no business of yours." She turned her back to him, thankful he couldn't see the letter tucked in her muff, and sorted through the packets of buttons on a shelf, furious at the tears stinging her eyes. She had dozens of admirers—what did Daniel's opinion matter? Nothing. It was only that encountering him unexpectedly jolted her, made her remember their friendship and the way it had been between them. Important or not, his disapproval hurt. Not that she'd ever let him know.

"Something I can do for you, Daniel?"

Yes. Please... A breath escaped her as he turned and stepped to the counter.

"I stopped in to return this pair of gloves. They were put in the company's bag, by mistake, the last time I was here."

She stopped fingering through the buttons and glanced at the door. She had to get to Willa's and gather herself together before Daniel arrived. She moved slowly along the bolts of fabric toward the front of the store, watching him from the corner of her eye, ready to stop if he looked her way. She'd not give him the satisfaction of knowing he was the cause of her leaving.

"No, they're yours. I wrote it down." Allan Cargrave reached for his account book. "Yes…here it is—Daniel Braynard, one pair of leather gloves."

"These." Daniel lifted his gloved hands and wiggled his fingers. His head dipped toward the counter. "Those are yours."

That was Daniel, always honest. She glared at the bell that would toll her retreat and hurried outside, stopped and stared in dismay at the snow being swooped up off of the ground and swirled through the air. The wind had come up while she was in the store. Was the storm returning? She felt of the letter beneath her hands in the muff and shot a look toward the gray, overcast sky. *Please don't let it start snowing again, Lord. Please let Daniel be able to go back to work at the camp.*

The fur edging her bonnet fluttered against her face. She ducked her head and stepped out of the protected entrance, staggered as her cloak and long skirts plastered back against her legs, the hems flapping wildly behind her. The brim of her bonnet flipped backward. A shiver raced through her. She yanked her gloved hands from her muff, tugged the brim of her bonnet back in place and fought her way across the raised walkway, struggling to keep her balance, watching her footing lest she slip and fall.

A strong hand gripped her elbow, steadied her. A pair of scarred calf-high logger boots with gray wool socks folded down over the tops and brown twill pants tucked into them came into view. The force of the wind was blocked from her by a tall, broad-shouldered body.

Daniel. She straightened, the top of her head coming level with his shoulder. Someone had mended a rip in his green wool jacket. She had a sudden fervent hope that it was his mother.

He spoke, his words snatched away by the roaring wind so all that she heard was the rumble of his deep voice. She looked up. His eyes were shadowed, unreadable.

"Careful of the steps. The wind's too strong for you." He lifted his arm and crooked his elbow. "Hold on, and I'll get you across the street."

She glanced up Main Street at the church, barely visible through the blowing snow, nodded and slipped her hand through his arm. The texture of his wool jacket was rough beneath the soft kid leather of her glove.

She moved forward with him, ducking her head behind his shoulder for protection. Gusts buffeted them as they descended the steps and crossed the road, stepping over frozen ruts and around ice patches. The cold stung her nose, made her eyes water. She moved closer to his side, felt his arm flex beneath the wool.

"It'll be faster going in the front." He kicked a path through a patch of drifted snow, ushered her along the walkway to the church stoop and up the steps. Hinges squeaked as he opened the door and held it with his shoulder.

She followed his glance down to where her gloved hand was gripping his arm, withdrew it and stepped over the threshold. The room was silent but for the muted moan of the wind coming down the stovepipe in the sanctuary. He closed the door, and darkness settled in the small entrance. She blinked and turned to face him. "Th-thank you for h-helping me."

"You're shivering." He stomped his feet free of snow and started down the center aisle of the sanctuary. "I'll get a fire going."

Dim light filtered through the snow-rimmed panes of the windows they would decorate today. She watched him hurry to the back room, gathered her cloak close and followed, wishing he would talk to her, wishing they were still friends, wishing she'd never taken hold of his arm. Letting go of it made her feel…lonely.

She shivered, tucked her chin into the soft velvet ties on her bonnet and shoved her cold hands into her muff. The letter crackled against her fingers. She pulled it out and looked at the direction written in a heavy, bold hand. What was she thinking? Of course she was feeling lonely. But it had nothing to do with Daniel. She simply missed her beaux and the parties and entertainments she attended on their arms. She would be fine once Mr. Lodge and Mr. Cuthbert arrived.

Fool! You had to rush out to help her. Daniel shoved another chunk of oak in the firebox and closed the door. *What did that gain you, beyond misery?* He stole a side-long look at Ellen, huddled close to the stove. She was so beautiful with her eyes shining and her cheeks all pink from the cold. All these years, whenever she'd come home, he'd been careful to maintain his distance, to never touch her. And now… *I need to get back to camp!*

The stovepipe crackled with the rising heat. He adjusted the dampers, shot a glance toward the door. He'd wait until the room warmed, and then he was going to march over to the parsonage and bring Willa back—baby and all if necessary. He'd had enough.

"The fire feels wonderful."

He grunted and was immediately ashamed of the response but let it stand. He was in no mood for polite conversation—for any interaction with Ellen. He could still feel the place on his side where her arm had pressed against him, the spot on his arm where her hand had clung. "Now that the fire's started, I'll go let Willa know we're here." He shoved his hands in his pockets and yanked out his gloves.

The door opened and Matthew Calvert stepped inside. "Ah, Daniel, I was hoping you'd be here—Willa sent me to see. She—" He stopped, smiled and gave a polite nod of his head. "Ellen, I didn't see you there by the stove. Good morning."

"Good morning, Pastor Calvert. Willa is delayed?"

Ellen's smile looked a little forced. Not surprising. He was having trouble with his own. He gave up the effort and shoved his gloves back in his pockets, his suspicions of yesterday returning. *If Willa thought—*

"No, not delayed. She sent me to tell you she will not be able to come and work on the decorations today. The baby was fussy and fretful last night, and Willa doesn't want to leave her."

"The baby is ill?"

He shot a look at Ellen, noted the hand she'd pressed to her chest, the small involuntary step she took backward. *She's remembering Walker.*

"Willa thinks it's only colic—not this flu that is laying people low. Speaking of which…" Matthew smiled, gave another polite nod. "I must take my leave. I have sick calls to make. Thank you both for volunteering to help Willa make the decorations. May the Lord bless you for your kindness." He cracked open the door and slipped out into the howling wind.

Another day alone with Ellen. His stomach knotted. *It's no blessing, Reverend.* He turned to Ellen and forgot his discomfort at the sight of her pale face. She'd been terrified of being around illness since her brother, Walker, died of the measles when she was four years old. For the rest of them, their friend's death had brought sadness—in Ellen it had instilled fear. He fought down his old instinct to reassure and comfort her and waved his hand toward the table. "Well, it seems it's up to us to get these decorations finished now."

"Yes."

Her gaze fastened on his. He shed his coat and cleared his throat. "I'm no decorator, only a worker. That makes you the boss, Musquash. Tell me what you want me to do." His use of the name worked. She jerked her gaze from his and lifted her chin.

"I want you to stop calling me *Musquash*." She flung her muff onto a chair, then removed her bonnet and cloak, hung them over the chair back and stepped to the table.

He tried not to notice the way she looked as she stood there in her old green wool gown, her hands fisted on her hips, her teeth nibbling at the corner of her mouth while she stared down at the work they'd already done, but he knew he'd never forget. His heart kept storing up memories in spite of him.

"I don't know what Willa had planned for the pews and the windows, but making these bunches of pine takes a lot of time, and with only the two of us to do the work it will take forever. And we've the parsonage and gazebo yet to do. So—"

Her tone warned him. He rearranged his features into

an expression of polite interest in the instant before she looked up.

"—I think we should make sprays."

Sprays? His brow furrowed. "What are sprays?"

"You look so perplexed!"

Laughter rippled from her—the laughter he remembered, not that phony titter she used now. It sounded so good he didn't even care it was at his expense. At least she'd forgotten about the baby's illness.

"If you will carry in more branches, I'll explain. Meanwhile, I'll work on making a second wreath for the parsonage."

"As you wish." He pulled his gloves on and turned toward the door. "I'll try not to let more cold in than necessary." He reached for the latch.

"I'm sorry to make you go out in that wind again, Daniel."

The sincerity in her voice played havoc with his determination to not return to their old closeness. He turned back, looked straight into her beautiful azure-blue eyes and gave himself the gift of this one moment. He gave her a smile that came straight from his heart the way he had once done. "I could finish the wreath while *you* carry in the branches."

Her eyes widened, searched his and warmed. A smile touched her lovely mouth, tentative, then sure when he didn't look away. "I'm not *that* sorry."

It was the fun way they used to be with each other, an affectionate teasing born out of closeness and understanding. And it was dangerous. Far too dangerous for him. "I was fairly certain of that." He bit off further reference to his memories of her and let his smile die. The moment was over. And he had his pride to protect.

He stepped outside, lowered his head into the wind and trudged through the drifted snow to the pung.

"So Mr. Lodge is in Dunkirk and will be in Pinewood on Saturday?"

"That's what he wrote in his letter, Father. I suppose the weather could delay him, but it's not likely with his enclosed sleigh." Ellen laid down her fork, dabbed her mouth with her napkin and took a sip of tea. "He says it will be too late to call when he arrives on Saturday but asks permission to accompany us to church Sunday morning."

"Of course, of course." Her father crossed his knife and fork on his empty plate, leaned back in his chair and smiled at her. "You must be eager for Sunday to come, Ellen. It's not every day one gets to show clear vindication for their decisions."

"Vindication, Father?"

"Yes, indeed. Mr. Lodge is proof that you were correct to abandon the rough ways of your friends and learn to be a lady of leisure—to choose to live with your aunt Berdena in Buffalo and mingle with the elite."

Her mind flashed back to the morning twelve years ago when he had told her she would no longer be permitted to see Willa, Callie, Sadie or Daniel except at school or church. She had been sitting in this very chair, eating bacon and pancakes with maple syrup. And her throat had been so tight with her effort to hold back her sobs, she had almost choked while trying to swallow her food. It had been the worst day of her life. Her stomach tightened. She placed her cup on its saucer, looked at her father sitting in his place of authority at the end of the table and forced a smile. "Then Mr. Lodge is *your* proof of vindication, Father, not mine. I merely obeyed your orders."

"And when you enter the church on Mr. Lodge's arm, everyone will see that you were wise to do so."

She shook her head and gave him another forced smile. "No, Father. Wisdom infers a choice, and a ten-year-old has no choice. The approbation will be yours alone."

"And the compliments will be yours, Ellen." Her mother smiled and rang the small bell beside her plate. "You look so lovely in your new blue dress, dear, I'm certain Mr. Lodge will be smitten anew."

Her new dress. She ran her hand over the smooth silk of the long full skirt of the fancy silver gown she wore. Her stylish clothes and the pampering she'd received had become her refuge against the hurt and loneliness of being without her friends. And the clothes and her beauty guaranteed her acceptance—

"Thank you, Nellie. The cake looks delicious."

She looked up, saw the cook coming toward her and shook her head. Her appetite was gone. "I don't care for cake tonight, Nellie." She rose and glanced from her mother to her father. "If you will excuse me, I'm going to my room now. I have work to finish before tomorrow."

"Ellen! Surely, you do not intend to continue helping Willa with those decorations." Her mother looked aghast. "Why, Mr. Lodge—"

"I will not be seeing Mr. Lodge until Sunday morning, Mother. And the bows for the decorations need to be finished." A twinge of satisfaction rippled through her. "Willa is depending on me. Her baby has taken ill, and she can no longer do the work."

"That is not your concern, Ellen."

She stiffened, looked at her father. His gaze was cool, direct.

"Your mother is right. It is important that you stay home tomorrow and prepare yourself for Mr. Lodge's arrival. Willa can find someone else to do the work. You are not her servant."

And I am no longer ten years old. "No, Father, I'm not. I'm her friend." She dipped her head, pulled her wrap higher around her shoulders and walked to the door, the rich silk of her long three-tiered skirt whispering softly in the dead silence of the room.

"It sounds as if Aunt Ruth's having a real hard time, Ma." Daniel frowned down at the signature on the letter in his hand. "Who is Lillian Morton?"

"Ruth's neighbor. She's got seven children."

His mother's knitting needles clicked out a steady accompaniment to the whisper of the rockers on her chair—a comforting sound he'd listened to all his life. He watched her small hands manipulating the needles, one pudgy finger extended as she guided the red yarn between them. "Remember how I used to sit by your feet and watch you knit when I was a youngster?"

She glanced up at him, a soft smile on her lips. "I remember."

"I never could figure out how you could take a string of yarn, put it through those needles and have it come out a pair of socks or a hat or something. I still can't." He grinned down at her. "Remember that time you tried to show me how, and my fingers kept getting in each other's way until I was all tangled up in the yarn?"

She nodded and laughed. "You finally gave up, said, 'It must be a woman thing,' and went outside."

"At least I was smart enough to know when I was licked."

"Yes. You always knew...." She lowered her hands to her lap and looked up at him. "I'm sorry you had to give up your dreams when your pa died, Daniel. I tried to think of another—"

He raised his hand, palm out, and cut off her words. It was one subject he didn't discuss with her. There was no point. She felt guilty, and he felt cheated. But it was just the way of things. And it couldn't be changed. He was too old for an apprenticeship now. And he'd quit one again to take care of her. "There wasn't any other way, Ma. These cabins are for Mr. Townsend's loggers. The only way we could stay was for me to go to work for him." The sadness in her eyes made his heart ache. He pulled up another grin, chuckled. "I sure couldn't have provided us a home by knitting."

"No. But, all the same, it cost you the good life you could have had. And your hope of courting Ellen. And I see how—"

"Don't, Ma! It's over and done. And there's no way of knowing what would have been. We'll finish with the decorations tomorrow. Then Ellen will choose her husband, and I'll go back to camp." He pasted on a smile. "And aren't you the one that always tells me 'God works things out for the best'?"

She stared up at him, took a breath and nodded. "I guess my heart got in the way of my rememberin' that." Her voice choked.

He hurried to her chair, leaned down and kissed her cheek, tasted the salt of a tear. "No cryin', Ma. I'm fine. Besides, my ma doesn't cry—she prays." That won him a smile. It was wobbly, but it was still a smile. She returned to her knitting.

He went back to stand by the fire and looked down at the letter he still held. "This woman is kind to care for Aunt Ruth, but doing so, on top of caring for her own family, is working a hardship on her. I know you were planning to go and take care of Aunt Ruth after Christmas, Ma, but her need seems more urgent than ever."

"I'll go when you go back to camp."

That was his ma—always thinking of him. He shook his head. "I'd like that, but you didn't raise me to be selfish, Ma. You need to go tomorrow, while the weather is favorable. It's quit snowing this evening, and the wind has died off, which means the stage will get through to Olville all right tomorrow. But the weather can change faster than a blink." He slapped the letter against his palm, thinking. "You'll need some money for your needs while you're in Syracuse…and to get you through any emergency stops should the weather turn bad. I've some set aside. We'll stop at the bank and pick it up when I walk you to the trolley in the morning."

Silence. He looked over at his mother, met her gaze on him warm with love and shining with pride. "'Thy father and thy mother shall be glad, and she that bare thee shall rejoice.'"

Her whispered Bible quote filled his heart, tightened his throat.

"You're right, Daniel. I'll go tomorrow." A smile warmed her eyes. "And I have my new warm wrapper and slippers to take with me." The smile died. "But I won't be here with you on Christmas Day." She lifted a pile of knitting from her basket, rose and came to him. "Merry Christmas, son. I hope these keep you warm."

She handed him a pair of socks and a hat, then lifted a matching scarf into the air. He ducked down and she draped it around his neck and kissed his cheek.

He cleared his throat, tugged the hat on, slipped his hands into the socks and gave her a big hug. "Thanks, Ma. I'll sure appreciate these when the wind's howling and the snow's flying."

She nodded, blinked and started across the room toward her bedroom. "I'll get packed and I'll go tomorrow, Daniel. But I don't like leaving you…now."

Now. That last word was a mere whisper, not meant for him to hear. She didn't believe him about Ellen. He should have known she would sense the emotional tug-of-war going on inside him. *I'll make it, Ma.* He pulled his gifts off, folded them and strode to his bedroom to put them with his other gear. He'd be going back to camp as soon as his work for Willa was done—storm or no storm. He wasn't going to stay in town and watch Ellen with her beaux. A man could only take so much.

Chapter Nine

Both stoves were pouring out heat. The sanctuary and the back room were warm. The lamps were lit. Everything was ready. Daniel tugged his new hat and gloves on, left the church and headed for the parsonage.

Happy, busy sniffing out the news of the previous night, gave a welcoming bark and came bounding up the path from the stable to greet him at the porch steps. "Hey, fellow. How are you doing this nice sunny day?" He rubbed behind the dog's ears, thumped him on the shoulder and got peppered with snow sent flying by the dog's thick furry tail for his trouble.

"Is that the reward I get for being nice to you?" He laughed, brushed the snow off of his sleeves and climbed the steps. The dog jumped ahead to the door, gave a vigorous shake, then tilted his head to the side and peered up at him, tail wagging.

"All right, there's no need to beg. I'll let you in." He stomped his boots clean, knocked and opened the door. The smell of hot coffee tinged with a remaining hint of breakfast bacon greeted him. "Smells good in here." He reached up and tugged off his hat.

"Good morning, Daniel." Willa smiled and came toward him, patting the swaddled baby on her shoulder. "Did you come for a cup of coffee before you start working on the decorations?"

"No. I came for you."

"Oh? Is there a problem?"

"You might say that." Daniel looked around, didn't see anyone else in sight and lowered his voice. "Where's Bertha?"

"She took advantage of the break in the weather and went to visit her niece. Why? What's wrong?"

"I know what you're doing, Pest, and it stops now."

"I don't know what you're—"

He snorted.

"Oh, all right!" She tipped her head and looked up at him, gave him another of those sweet smiles. "Is it working?"

"Of course not!"

The baby whimpered.

"Shhh…" Willa patted harder, frowned up at him. "Stop snarling. You're frightening Mary."

He scowled and moderated his voice. "You know how I feel, Pest—there is no 'working' going to happen. I'm over my childhood love for Ellen, and I intend that it will stay that way. She doesn't know how I felt about her, and she's never going to. She deserves better than me, and she knows it. *I* know it. Now—"

"Daniel Braynard, I could shake you!" Willa's blue-green eyes flashed. She stopped patting the baby and poked her finger against the jacket covering his chest. "You are one of the finest men I know. And any woman would be blessed to have you for her husband!"

He gave another snort.

"Yes, they would! Even Ellen. *Especially* Ellen." She jabbed him again, so hard he had to take a step back. "You think you are so wise and gallant because when your pa died and you had to give up your apprenticeship at the counting house to provide a home for your ma, you decided you would never be good enough to be accepted by Ellen's parents as a suitor and gave her up."

He opened his mouth to respond, but she sucked in air and launched into him again before he got a word out.

"Well, you were *right* about Mr. and Mrs. Hall. But, that doesn't mean Ellen felt the same way. And *you*—" another jab landed on his chest "—never gave her a chance to decide for herself when she was old enough to think things through. And *she* has the right to choose. Open your *eyes,* Daniel, and you will see that Ellen's values are not the same as those of her parents—though she has been so swayed and led astray by them, she *thinks* they are." She narrowed her eyes, peered up at him. "Tell me you haven't seen a change in Ellen these last few days. Tell me you haven't seen traces of the old Ellen—"

"That's enough, Pest!" He held his voice quiet, reasonable, but what he wanted was to turn and drive his fist into the door to distract him from the pain rising in his heart. He'd buried his dream along with his father, and he didn't want it resurrected—there was no hope for it. Bitterness rose, crept into his voice. "I have nothing of worldly goods to offer Ellen, or any woman, Willa. You know that. And I'll not be the cause of a woman living the hard life my ma has endured."

"Oh, you are such a…a *man,* Daniel! Your ma *loved* your pa. And he loved her. Don't you make that small. Love and respect are worth more than all the worldly goods a man can heap on a woman." Her eyes darkened, challenged him. "Name me one time your ma has said she wished she'd never married your pa. Name me one memory she talks about that isn't a happy one."

He glowered down at her, tried to think of an answer. "Well?"

"Ma isn't a complainer."

"Because she's always been happy!"

"Happy!" He shook his head, huffed out a breath. "Ma doesn't even have a stove to cook on, Willa. And I can't get her one. And she's had to wear that old tattered and worn wrapper for years, until I saved up enough to get her a new one for this Christmas. She was *cold,* Willa."

"Not when she was in her husband's arms or holding her child close, Daniel. And never, *never* in her heart. Love warms a heart."

This was getting him nowhere. He yanked his hat back on, took a calming breath. "Are you coming back to the church with me, or not?"

"Or not." Willa heaved a sigh and shook her head. "I can't leave the house. I told you, Bertha is gone. And Mary can't be taken out into this cold weather." She straightened her shoulders and met his gaze full on. "But I wouldn't go with you even if I could, Daniel. You're as bad as Mr. and Mrs. Hall. You all think you know what's best for her. Well, Ellen deserves a chance to make her own choice about her future, and if you won't give her that chance, I will. At least, I'm going to try."

"It won't work, Willa." He set his jaw and reached for the door latch. "I don't care *how* long I'm alone with Ellen—I'm *not* going to tell her how I *feel!*"

"Felt."

He glowered down at her. "You know that's what I meant to say!"

"Yes. But you didn't. 'Out of the abundance of the heart, the mouth speaketh.'" She gave him another of those sweet smiles. "Give Ellen my regards. And you have a lovely day, Daniel. Oh, and don't worry about telling Ellen how you feel about her. You won't have to say a word. Ellen's a woman. She'll know."

The hinges on the door withstood his slam.

Trapped? Betrayed? He didn't know what he felt beyond the anger twisting his gut. Hoisted on his own gallows, that's what he was! He never should have offered to help Willa with the decorations—wouldn't have, had he known she planned to involve Ellen. He'd been *ambushed,* that's what. Thrown into the lion's den by his closest friend. "Swear to your own hurt and change not… Hah! Swear to your own *torture!*" Daniel stomped back to the church, filled his arms with wood for the stoves, stomped up the steps and shoved open the door to the back room muttering to himself.

"Oh!"

He froze, drank in the sight of Ellen standing at the table staring at him with a startled expression on her beautiful face and wanted to turn around and march right back out again. He gritted his teeth, gave a backward kick to close the door and bit out an apology. "Sorry. I didn't know you were here. I thought you would go to the parsonage first."

She looked away, shook her head. "I waited until I saw smoke coming from the chimney."

Selfish, insensitive oaf! So concerned about yourself you forgot about her fear of sickness. He moved to the woodbox and dumped his load. "The baby is well, but Bertha is gone visiting, so Willa won't be coming." *The traitor.* He cleared his throat in an effort to stop sounding as if he were ready to bite nails. "We'd better get to work. There's a lot to be done before church tomorrow. Unless you'd rather go home, since Willa won't be making an appearance and we'll be working alone without a chaperone?" He put the suggestion to her, but he didn't have much hope she'd leave, not the way his life was going these past few days.

She shook her head and her blond curls danced in the lamplight. "That won't matter. Everyone in the village knows—"

She broke off, leaving him wondering what she'd been about to say. He drew breath to ask, then let it go. Some things were better left unsaid.

"I'll stay. We haven't long now."

The words struck hard. Though why they should was beyond him. It was what he wanted—to have this time alone with her over. He looked down at the wreath she was holding. "What's that you're doing?"

"Well…" She motioned toward the pinecones he'd kicked into the corner to get them out from under his feet. "I was looking at that pile of pinecones while I was waiting for—" Her lips pressed together. Her lashes swept down, hid her eyes.

Him? His heart lurched at the thought. *Fool.*

She made a small dismissive gesture. "Anyway, I tied some cones to this wreath with twine and then added a bow from some strips I cut out of an old red dress last night. I thought it would help to hide this spot where we finished and the bunches come together." She tipped the wreath in his direction, caught her lower lip in her teeth and looked up at him.

He shifted his gaze to the wreath to keep from staring at her mouth. She'd always caught her lip like that when she was unsure of herself. It was only a habit now, no doubt. Still, none of that mattered. Her hard work deserved recognition. "It looks good. A lot better than those first bunches you made, for sure. And the bow looks good on it. Brightens it up."

"Thank you." She gave him a cool smile and laid the wreath down. "But a gentleman would not refer to a lady's mistakes."

Being found wanting in comparison to her beaux rasped on his already-raw ego. The muscle along his jaw twitched. He returned her smile in kind. "I meant no insult. It was only my clumsy way of saying that you've developed a talent for this, and your work is much improved."

"Truly?"

The word and the disbelieving tone in which she spoke it grated. Willa was wrong. There was little, beyond physical appearance, of the Ellen he remembered in the haughty woman across from him. And he'd be hewed down and debarked before he'd let her attack his character unchallenged. Somewhere deep inside, she knew better. "I may not be wealthy or have the polished speech of your beaux, Musquash. But have you ever known me to lie?"

Her eyes flashed at his use of the name. Her nose raised into the air. "No, indeed. You are unfailingly honest, Daniel—even when it would be *better* to be less so."

He clenched his hands, disgusted by the supercilious ways she'd adopted. "I guess you can blame that on my unworldly small-town ways. I was raised to honor the truth, not slide my tongue around it and pretend to be what I'm not."

"Oh! *Oh!* How dare you!" Color flamed in her cheeks. She stiffened like a pry rod and gave him a look that could have frozen the river, had the weather not already done so. "You, sir, are…are—"

"Busy. I've got a wreath to hang on the church door." *Bother with manners! She didn't appreciate them from him anyway.* He jammed his hat back on his head, then gestured at the different-length pine boughs bound into small clusters that were piled on the table. "You want more pinecones to fix up those decorations before I go outside?"

"You needn't bother about the pinecones. *I* will get them." She flounced over to the door, picked up the empty bucket kept there to carry water in case of fire and carried it to the pile of cones in the corner.

Her haughty posture had come a little undone. "As you wish." He reached for the wreath, paused. "Looks like you're running low on twine. I'll cut you some." His offer was met with a frosty silence. He looked over at her throwing pinecones into the bucket and couldn't resist prodding her to a response. "Unless you want to do that yourself also, of course."

"Humph!"

It wasn't quite a snort, but it was mighty close.

"I suppose that was meant to be amusing." She tossed a few more cones into the bucket, gripped the handle and headed back to the table, her swirling skirts scattering pinecones in all directions.

There was nothing cool about her now. She was angry. Their gazes clashed, and his chest tightened.

That haughty look he hated was gone, all right—but at what cost? There was a shadow of hurt mingling with the anger in her eyes. He clamped the hatchet handle in a choke hold, stepped to the chopping log and glanced back over his shoulder. "Do you want these cut the same length as before?"

Her gaze lifted, touched his a moment before she nodded, then looked down and began to work. Everything in him strained to go to her, to apologize for his oafish behavior and tell her how much he cared for her—which would only devastate his pride and gain him nothing.

Oh, and don't worry about telling Ellen how you feel about her. You won't have to say a word. Ellen's a woman. She'll know.

How could she, when he seesawed back and forth between dislike and…and an ardent attraction! He pressed his lips into a hard, thin line, raised his hatchet and chopped the twine. *Get me back to camp, Lord, I pray. Melt this snow, and get me back to camp before my resolve collapses and I destroy everything.*

"It's not quite in the center. A little more to the right." Ellen stood at the foot of the ladder, pine bough clusters and a red bow in hand, and waited for Daniel to pound in the nail at the top of the window. In spite of the tension between them, she was enjoying the work. She'd never felt so useful. She glanced, yet again, at the other windows they'd already decorated. The pine looked so pretty against the white plaster—

"I'm ready."

She turned her attention back to the work, took the hatchet Daniel handed down to her, leaned it against the ladder, then lifted the cluster up to him. He looked so confident standing on the ladder pounding in nails. Of course, he looked confident no matter what he was doing. He always had. Even as a boy. That was simply...Daniel. It was why she'd always felt safe with him. If only— She broke off the thought, but the wish still tugged at her, stealing the pleasure from the moment.

She watched him pull off one of the pieces of twine he had draped over his shoulder and bind the stem end of the cluster, his movements economical and sure. When he looked down, she had the other cluster waiting for him. He nodded his thanks, held the stem ends against those of the first, bound them together, then tied the whole to the nail. The uneven lengths of the boughs stretched in both directions over the top of the window to caress the corners of the frame, the offshoots drooping in random splendor, the brown cones a solid contrast to the feathery green needles.

"Here's the bow." She smoothed the last of the big red bows she'd carried into the sanctuary and lifted it to him, the long ties trailing down her raised arm. He reached for it and his fingertips brushed against hers, their touch rough and warm and...*different*. She lifted her gaze to his face.

He jerked upright and faced the wall, placed the bow over the bare stems where the sprays of pine joined, secured it to the nail and tugged the ties free to dangle down in front of the window panes. "That straight?"

The muscle along his jaw was twitching. Something had made him angry. This man was not the good-humored boy she remembered. She moved to the side for a better look. "Yes. It's fine."

"Then that's it for the windows." He started backing down the ladder.

She snatched the hatchet she'd leaned against it out of his way and watched the muscles along his shoulders and arms ripple beneath his wool shirt as he descended then folded the ladder. The lamplight played over his hair, shadowing the valleys and gleaming red on the crests of its crisp, neatly trimmed waves. Disappointment squiggled through her. It was an excellent haircut, as good as those of Mr. Lodge and Mr. Cuthbert, but, again, not what she remembered. Daniel's hair had been curly when they were kids. Her fingers twitched with a sudden urge to muss those neat waves and set his curls free.

"I'll take that."

She jumped, looked down at his outstretched hand and handed him the hatchet. "I'm sorry. I was…thinking…." Her cheeks warmed. She whirled and hurried toward the front to get the decorations for the box pews.

"We haven't time to do anything more, if that's what you were thinking." His deep voice blended with the thud of his boots on the floor as he followed her. "We have the gazebo to do when we finish in here."

"I know." She stopped short, stared at the pew beside her.

He halted and grounded the ladder. "What's wrong?"

"I suddenly realized there's no way to fasten the greenery to the pew doors."

"Sure there is." He lifted the hatchet he held. "I'll pound in a nail."

She gasped, shot him a horrified look. "You *can't*—"

He chuckled, and the boy's giggle she knew so well echoed in his deep male laughter, woke her memories. She smiled and looked up. His eyes darkened. Tiny flames shone golden in their smoky-green depths. His jaw muscle twitched. She heard him take a long breath, released her own when he turned away.

He laid the ladder down, then picked up a canvas bag lying on the floor beside the decorations they'd carried in. When he straightened, his eyes were their normal green. How odd that the lamplight could change them like that.

She looked down at the bag. "What's in there?"

"Hooks. David Dibble made them for me last night, while I was caring for the horses." He withdrew a flat, narrow, oddly bent piece of iron from the bag and held it out for her to see. "I'll show you how it works." He slipped the odd contrivance down over the top of the pew door. The longer piece of iron that formed one side of the hook stretched six inches down the front of the door and tipped up on the end.

"They're to hold the greens! Daniel, how clever!" She whirled about, picked up a cluster and handed it to him, watched closely as he tied it to the hook. The random-length boughs hung against the door, their feathery needles splayed out against the wood. "Oh, that looks lovely!" She tied on a bow and freed a snared tie to hang down. "Doesn't Mr. Dibble care for the horses he stables?"

"Of course." He pulled another hook from the bag and moved on to the next pew. "But Big Boy and Big Girl are my responsibility." He slid the hook in place, squatted and tied on the cluster of greens she handed him. "They're used to being pampered."

"Those huge horses need pampering?" She attached a bow and fluffed it, smiled at the way it dressed up the pew door. Her red dress had never looked lovelier.

"Absolutely. If they get sick, or a small wound goes unnoticed and untended and worsens, they can't haul logs to the mill—" he hung the greens "—the mill closes, and all the workers lose wages." He stood and slipped a hook over the next door. "Those horses are important to the company."

"I hadn't thought about it that way." She tied on the bow, straightened it and hurried to get him another cluster.

"No reason why you should." He fastened on the greens and moved across the aisle to decorate the pews on the other side.

She stared after him, an odd feeling in her chest. He was right. There was no reason why she should have thought of any of it. She never thought about anything but clothes and parties and pampering herself. Until now. And helping Willa with the decorations would end soon. She sighed, adjusted a twisted bough and hurried across the aisle to hand Daniel another cluster. She was being ridiculous. This strange lost feeling would go away once Mr. Lodge and Mr. Cuthbert arrived.

Another hour should do it. Daniel laid the long festoons of greens he carried on the gazebo floor, leaned his hatchet against the railing and stepped back and studied the structure as if he couldn't close his eyes and draw it. Anything was better than looking at Ellen. The hours they'd been together and their forced cooperation as they worked had worn the sharp edges off of them both. His determination to stay aloof from her was about ready to topple like a hewed tree. He needed distance, lots and lots of distance, between them.

"Well, at least we have good weather for doing this." The words came out more gruff than he intended.

"Yes. It's a blessing the wind isn't blowing the way it did yesterday."

"For sure." He took a couple of steps to the side but could still see her from the corner of his eye. He watched her graceful movements as she laid the bows she carried beside the decorations, tensed when she straightened and came toward him.

"I'm sure you have planned how you are going to hang these greens, but don't you need the ladder?"

The winter sun shining on her upturned face created shadows beneath her long, thick lashes that darkened the azure-blue of her eyes, heightened the delicacy of her fine-boned features and added depth to the small hollow beneath her lower lip. He shook his head, the power of speech stolen from him by her closeness and beauty.

"Then how—"

"Like this." He strode forward and snatched up his hatchet. One quick leap and he was balanced on the banister of the railing. He grasped hold of the pillar beside him, swung his body around to the outside, wrapped his left leg around the pillar and pulled a nail from his pocket. A few powerful hits from the butt end of the hatchet drove the nail into place at the top of the pillar.

"I should have known!"

He looked down. The hood of the old brown cloak Ellen was wearing had fallen back to rest on her shoulders. He clamped his jaw and locked his gaze on the festoons on the floor. She draped one over her arms and hurried toward him.

"Here you are."

He shoved the hatchet between his body and the pillar, leaned down and took hold of the end she held up to him, almost lost his balance when she smiled.

"I'd forgotten that you used to practically live in trees."

"You climbed a few yourself." He batted a long bough out of his way and grabbed a length of twine from his shoulder.

"With you coaching me. Or standing below to catch me if I fell."

It wasn't you that fell. "Well, you were too young to know better then."

And you never gave her a chance to decide for herself when she was old enough to think things through.

His face went taut. True or not, Willa's words didn't matter. He'd fallen far below what Ellen deserved and expected in a husband. And he had no business yielding to emotions he had no right to harbor. "How's that?"

She tipped her head to the side, narrowed her eyes. "Let some of the garland dangle down the pillar."

He took a breath and pulled the garland toward him.

"Perfect."

He nodded and tied it to the nail, then loosened his leg's grip on the pillar and swung back to the railing. She moved with him, playing out the garland as he walked the banister to the next pillar, took up his position and pounded in the nail. She handed him the end of the garland and stepped back.

"Don't pull it so tight, Daniel. Let it droop down between the pillars." He relaxed his hold.

"Oh, my! That looks wonderful!"

He peered over his shoulder and pulled up a smile for the woman standing on the shoveled walkway with a shopping basket over one arm and her other hand raised to shield her eyes from the sun. "Hey, Mrs. Finster. You out taking advantage of the good weather?"

"I am. And it looks as if you two are doing the same. How are you, Ellen? What with the storm and all, I haven't had the opportunity to see you since you came home. It looks as if you're keeping busy this visit."

He stiffened as Ellen stepped close to the railing and her shoulder brushed against his braced leg. He released his grip on the pillar and eased around to stand on the railing on the other side.

"I'm fine, Mrs. Finster. How are you and Mr. Finster and the children?"

"We're all well, outside of some sniffles." The older woman came down the sidewalk and squinted up at the pine boughs dangling down the top half of the pillar. "My, that is lovely!" A smile warmed her face. "I'd heard the gazebo was going to be decorated for the carol sing, but I figured with the storm and Willa's new baby and all, it would be left undone." She beamed a smile his direction. "It's too bad your mother won't be here to see this, Daniel. If you write her, give her my regards and tell her I said you're doing a fine thing for the church." Her gaze shifted. "And you, too, Ellen. Thank you both. Now, I'll let you get back to work. I've got to run and tell Gladys about this."

He leaned around the pillar where Mrs. Finster could not see him and whispered, "And Esther Price and Ormella Belson and…"

Ellen whipped around and pressed her fingers against her pursed lips, her eyes laughing up at him. He jerked back behind the pillar, his pulse pounding. Returning to camp was looking better and better. *Let the clear weather hold, Lord. Please, let the clear weather hold.* He took a breath and swung back into position. "Hand me the next one, or we'll never get done."

The gruffness in his voice stole the laughter from her eyes. He took hold of the next garland she held up to him and set his mind to the task at hand. *Only five more to do.*

Chapter Ten

"What draws your interest, Miss Hall?"

Ellen jerked her gaze from her parents, who had walked by the gazebo without so much as a glance, looked up at Harold Lodge through her long lashes and gave him her most winning smile. "I was admiring the lovely day and being thankful the storm has stopped, Mr. Lodge. Else it might have prevented your visit."

He smiled and covered her gloved hand that rested on his arm with his. "No storm could keep me from calling upon you, Miss Hall. My booby hut sleigh makes any journey comfortable no matter the weather."

"It does indeed." She gave him another smile, wondering if the compliment had been for her or his sleigh— or if they were equal in his eyes. "I thank you, again, for offering your conveyance for my journey home. I was most comfortable the entire way from Dunkirk, even though the weather was cold and blustery."

"It was my pleasure, Miss Hall." He glanced to the side as they turned the corner onto Main Street and gave a disdainful shake of his head. "What paltry decorations on that gazebo. You would think whoever did them would have used more opulent bows."

Her smile slipped. She tugged it back in place. "The church does not have funds for—"

Her father coughed and looked over his shoulder. "I've not seen an enclosed sleigh, Mr. Lodge, and I confess to a strong curiosity. Perhaps I might trouble you for a demonstration ride while you are in town?"

An obvious change of subject. She read the warning in her father's quick glance. Her work on the decorations was not to be mentioned.

"I'd be delighted, Mr. Hall." The shadow of Harold Lodge's top hat fell across her face as he dipped his head, which was just as well. Her phony smile had faded. She stole another look at the gazebo from the corner of her eye. It *would* look better with larger bows. Still...

"Excellent. I shall look forward to it." Her father gave her a sharp glance, faced forward again and led them up the shoveled walk to the church.

The wreath hung on the door, the dark green pine accentuated by the brown pinecones and the red bow. A *paltry* bow in Mr. Lodge's opinion. The word rankled. She arranged her features into a pleasant expression, lifted her hems with her free hand and walked up the steps holding to Harold Lodge's arm, hoping he would say nothing that further disparaged her decorating efforts.

Her father opened the door, and the moment passed. She followed her mother into the small entrance with only a few minutes to spare until the service began, and her good humor returned. Trust her father to make certain everyone noticed them as they entered. Or was it that he wanted no time for people to mention the decorations?

She glanced through the open door at the trimmed windows and pews, their beauty now tinged by her parents' attitude. How foolish of her to hope that when they saw the decorations, they might be proud of the work she'd done and find it worthwhile enough to mention—at least her mother.

She shook off her disappointment and fluffed the fur around her bonnet brim, straightened its wide ties. Mr. Lodge removed his hat and stepped to her side. She took hold of his offered arm, and they followed her parents through the door into the sanctuary. The murmur of people quietly chatting stopped. Fabric rustled as parishioners shifted in their seats to get a better look at the stranger in their midst. She curved her lips into a small smile, acutely aware of the striking picture the two of them made—she in her lovely fur-trimmed blue cloak and bonnet, and Mr. Lodge stylish in his black double-breasted chesterfield coat, gray-striped trousers, and gray scarf and gloves.

She smiled and dipped her head at the people she'd known all her life as they passed the open pews, lifted her chin higher as they came to the box pews filled with the town's elite. None of them could compare with Mr. Lodge's wealth and prestige. An indisputable fact displayed by his bearing and the richness of his clothing.

Movement caught her eye and she glanced left, met Sophia Sheffield's gaze. There was affection in Callie's aunt's eyes. "A moment, Mr. Lodge." She stepped across the aisle to the Sheffield pew, placed her hand on the door, leaned down and spoke softly. "It's so good to see you, Mrs. Sheffield. I'm sorry I haven't been to visit you since I've been home. I hope to call on you soon."

The older woman smiled and patted her hand, matched

her hushed tone. "I know you've been busy, Ellen. And to good effect. I've been sitting here admiring the decorations." Sophia Sheffield's lovely violet eyes, so like Callie's, warmed. "You come calling when you find the time, dear. I'll have the 'brown' cookies waiting."

Brown cookies. Memories of Sophia's large hotel kitchen rich with the mouthwatering smells of food cooking and desserts baking rushed upon her. She could almost taste the warm, spicy ginger cookies. She nodded, then pulled her lips into an appropriate, sophisticated smile and turned back to Harold Lodge. The happy memories and Sophia's praise of the decorations had acted as balm on the sore spot created by Harold Lodge's remark and her parents' absence of comment. She swept her gaze over the garland-draped windows and her sense of satisfaction returned. Not even her father's quick disapproving look as Mr. Lodge bowed her through the opened pew door erased it.

She gathered her skirts close and took her seat beside her mother. Gold twisted-silk fringe edged a purple velvet cushion that padded the bench. She ran the fringe through her fingers, smiled and leaned close. "The new cushion is lovely, Mother." Hope rose. Perhaps her mother would take advantage of the private moment to say something about her decorations.

Her mother tilted her head and whispered behind the hand she lifted to adjust her bonnet. "I finished it last night and had Asa bring it over. Hopefully, your Mr. Lodge will be suitably impressed."

The hope died—and took her sense of satisfaction with it. She nodded, unfastened her cloak and pushed her bonnet back to hang between her shoulders. At least her mother and father approved of her beau. She had pleased them in that.

Harold Lodge unbuttoned his coat, seated himself beside her and bowed his head to her level. "A small, pitifully plain church, isn't it? Despite someone's attempt to adorn it for the coming festivities."

His whispered comment sent a spurt of irritation through her. *Attempt to adorn it, indeed!* "There is no need here for a grandiose church such as you attend in Buffalo, Mr. Lodge." She ruffled the curls at her forehead and temples, reminded herself that every young woman in the church was envying her at that very moment. And their mothers and fathers, too. She sat a little straighter, held herself from glancing around to see who might be looking at them and made up her mind that she would not allow Mr. Lodge's ill-conceived comments to ruin her enjoyment of her triumphant day.

"It doesn't even have stained glass windows." Harold Lodge's voice dropped lower. "Of course, that could be changed easily enough, if one had an incentive to donate them. It would be an appropriate gift to commemorate a wedding, even if that socially significant event took place in another larger and more appropriate facility."

Her breath caught. She turned her head and looked up at him through her lashes, everything but her goal forgotten. "Why, Mr. Lodge…surely, I am misunderstanding you, sir."

His gaze fastened on hers. A smile touched his lips. "Not at all, Miss Hall. I shall mention making the church such a donation to your father when—"

˙ "Good morning, all!"

She started and gazed front as the congregation responded. David Dibble was standing at the end of the center aisle. *What poor timing!* She dipped her head and curved her lips into a smug smile at the thought of Harold Lodge's eagerness to have her for his bride. Of course, that could be because he wanted to best Earl Cuthbert. The thought dampened her elation.

"Please stand with me as we sing a song of praise to our God."

She rose with the others and took advantage of the moment when everyone was stirring to surreptitiously glance over at the Calverts' pew. If she could catch Willa's attention, she would— *Daniel.* Her intent flickered and died like a guttering candle. Her gaze faltered over Willa tucking a blanket more securely around baby Mary and settled on the tall figure standing in the Townsend pew across the aisle. Daniel was wearing a brown suit of coarse wool, his curls tamed down into those crisp waves, his strong jaw clean shaven and his green eyes focused on David Dibble.

Look at me. The hope sprang to life unbidden. And unwanted. She jerked her gaze away, assuring herself the only reason she wanted Daniel's attention was because of the work they'd done together on the decorations. She wanted nothing from Daniel. What she wanted was that feeling of…of satisfaction she'd known while working with him—which was foolish in this moment of triumph.

She looked up at Harold Lodge, admired the jeweled pin that held his snowy cravat in place. Daniel wore a plain stock. And he didn't even have a proper coat. Only that mended wool jacket on the pew seat. Odd that she could pick his voice out of all the others who were singing. But then again, perhaps not. She'd heard him sing often enough—silly songs he made up and taught them.

We'll march, march, march through
   the woods
Quiet as ever we can be.
No animal shall run
We'll see them every one
As we march through the woods
   happy and free.

The song flowed from her memory, tugged her lips into a grin in spite of the time and place. And situation. She stole another look across the aisle wanting to feel that sense of connection that was there whenever their gazes met—even when she was furious with him. She sobered, took a closer look. Daniel had stopped singing. He was facing front, and…yes, that little muscle along his jaw was twitching.

A clearing of throats and the rustle of clothing as people seated themselves alerted her that the singing was over. She sank gracefully to her seat between her mother and Mr. Lodge and folded her hands in her lap, wondering what had angered Daniel.

Popinjay! If the man's nose got any higher in the air, he'd drown in a summer rain! Daniel yanked his gaze from the stylish dark-haired man sitting beside Ellen looking as if he owned the place—as if he owned Ellen.

His stomach knotted. He clenched his hands into fists and stared at the pew ahead. Willa was there holding the baby and sitting beside her mother and her stepfather, David Dibble. He glanced toward the door to the back room, assailed by thoughts of working there alone with Ellen. He jerked his gaze back to stare at his boots.

I wish you were here, Ma. I need your wisdom. I'm not feeling very Christian at the moment.

Have faith, son. God will work it out.

He pulled in a breath, stopped the growl climbing his throat. How many times had his mother spoken those words to him in the past twelve years? Worse yet, how many times had she prayed that prayer? No matter how many times he'd told her there was nothing for God *to* work out, she persisted. It made him crazy! He knew full well he was not good enough for Ellen. That he had nothing to offer her—nothing to recommend him even as a suitor, let alone a husband. And he had accepted that. It was that…that…*cockalorum* across the aisle that bothered him. Within minutes of the man's arrival at the Sheffield House last night, word had spread about his arrogant, overbearing behavior and his demeaning attitude toward Mrs. Sheffield and the hotel—toward Pinewood itself.

He shot another look across the aisle. Harold Lodge loved himself too much to love Ellen the way she deserved. But there was nothing he could do about it. The knots in his stomach twisted tighter. He blew out breath to ease the tautness in his chest and closed his eyes. *Lord God Almighty, please don't let Ellen be blinded by Harold Lodge's wealth and its trappings. Please open her eyes and let her refuse his hand. I know I'm not supposed to judge another's heart, but his actions prove he's not good enough for her. Please let her refuse him and accept another who will love her and treat her with respect and tenderness. And help me, Lord. Help me to fully accept what is Your will. Amen.*

"Before I begin my message this morning, I'd like to acknowledge and thank the people who made these

lovely decorations for our Christmas service." Reverend
Matthew Calvert spread his arms, encompassing all of
the church in his gesture.

The congregation erupted in applause.

Ellen caught her breath and glanced at her parents.
They'd gone as stiff as statues. She looked up at Harold
Lodge, saw the slight curl of his lip and panicked. How
would she explain?

He smiled and leaned toward her. "The minister
would do better to dismiss those people and find others with more refined tastes to do any future decorating. Though it seems these people share their preacher's
opinion. Still, what else can one expect from *villagers,*
my dear Miss Hall."

How condescending! She stared at Harold Lodge's supercilious smile and all thought of explaining fled before
a rush of anger that turned her as stiff as her parents.
Those *villagers* were smiling and clapping for her. They
knew she'd helped to make the decorations. Warmth at
their kindness flooded through her, thawed her frozen
posture. This charade of deceit was over. She lifted her
chin, prepared to tell Harold Lodge that she was the one
who had made the *paltry* bows.

"Whoa! Hold on, everybody."

She held her words, turned her head to face the pul-
pit. Matthew Calvert was laughing.

"I said I'd *like* to acknowledge and thank our deco-
rators. But as Willa was the one who thought of making the decorations and enlisted the help of those who
stepped in and actually made them when she became
unable to do so, she wants to publicly thank them at our
Christmas program. Therefore, I will delay that pleasure
until our Christmas service."

Beside her, her mother gave a soft sigh and relaxed her stiff posture. From the corner of her eye she saw her father's hand release its white-knuckled grip on his knee and watched the scowl leave his face. She couldn't tell Mr. Lodge the truth now. If only there were someone who would understand. She glanced over at Daniel, but he was facing forward, and she could not draw his attention. Willa was engaged with the baby.

She looked down and toyed with the fur edging on the cloak's capelet that draped her shoulders, feeling abandoned, though she knew it was ridiculous. Daniel owed her no allegiance simply because they were once friends and had worked together on the decorations. And she should be feeling proud and happy to be sitting beside the wealthiest, most stylish man in the sanctuary. So what if Harold Lodge's disparaging comments had stolen the luster from her day? Why, she was soon to be betrothed to a man who could give her the best of everything, a life of ease, all that she desired. Why should she let such a small thing disturb her? Was she so foolish she would risk losing what was within her grasp? Indeed not! She curved her lips into a smile, lifted her head and set herself to listen to the sermon.

"'Be not high-minded, nor trust in uncertain riches, but in the living God, who giveth us richly all things to enjoy.' This time of year our thoughts turn to gifts for our loved ones, and perhaps for ourselves. And there's nothing wrong with that. I'm hoping for a new pair of gloves." Matthew Calvert laughed and swept his gaze over the congregation, then sobered and leaned forward. "But if I never receive them, or any other worldly gift, I count myself among the men most blessed, for the Lord has given me the gift of salvation. I will speak more of that on Christmas. Today I want to speak about other true gifts—gifts that bless us and last for all of eternity." He placed his hand on the open Bible in front of him. "In this book I have the assurance of God's love and care for me and mine. What more have I need of? The riches of this world? Gold? Silver? New gloves?"

Had Reverend Calvert read her thoughts? She stiffened and stared up at him, then dropped her gaze to Harold Lodge's expensive gray kid gloves and smiled. She would certainly have the riches of this world as his wife.

"I'd rather have the loving touch of my wife's hand on mine than a dozen pair of the finest gloves money can buy. And what amount of gold can equal the friendship of an honest man whose word you can trust, whose handshake is his bond?"

Murmurs of agreement hummed in the air. She glanced up at Harold Lodge, shifted her gaze to Daniel. She'd always trusted him. He'd never lied to her.

"Or what earthly riches can compare with the peace that comes when you have a home full of love? Can you put a price on the joy that fills you when you hold your baby or receive a hug from your child?"

Matthew Calvert's voice rang with conviction. It was obvious he was speaking from his heart. No wonder Willa was so happy. A twinge of uneasiness wriggled through her. She ran her hand over the fine wool of her cloak, touched the soft fur.

"Love…honesty…peace…joy…whatever has virtue, is pure or lovely, these are things the Bible says we are to think on and value. We are warned not to put our trust in the riches of this world that moth and rust can destroy, that thieves and the unscrupulous can steal from us."

"Fool."

The whispered word was filled with contempt. She looked up at Harold Lodge. His eyes were dark, his face tight with scorn. He leaned down and placed his mouth by her ear.

"Pay no attention to this *drivel,* my dear Miss Hall. It is merely the panacea used by the clergy to comfort all those without worldly possessions or the means or talent necessary to obtain them. He has a congregation full of such people." He drew back far enough to see her face and smiled. "But do not count yourself among them, Miss Hall. You will not have to concern yourself with such matters after tomorrow."

"There you are, Big Girl." Daniel fastened the blanket on the Belgian, patted her neck and left the stall. He'd taken both horses out to exercise them, then groomed and fed them. There was nothing left to do.

He strode to the door, the thud of his boots on the stable's plank floor accompanied by an occasional snort or the thump of a hoof. The hinges creaked. *No way to stop that in the cold.* He stepped outside and closed the door, checked to make sure the latch was secure and headed across the snow-trampled lot toward Main Street. On his left, lamplight poured out of the windows of the Dibble home, staining the snow beneath them with its golden hue. The house looked warm and inviting. A safe haven from the world. One full of love.

Stop it! He shoved his gloved hands in his jacket pockets and hunched his shoulders against the cold, tramped across the Stony Creek bridge and turned onto Brook Street. Across the frozen, rutted road, Nate Turner's wagon shop loomed black against the night. He continued down the snow-packed road, choosing a path along the edge where the footing was easier, passing cabin after Townsend Timber company log cabin, with flickering firelight or golden lamplight shining in the windows. The smell of burning wood from stoves and fireplaces hung on the cold, still air.

He turned toward his dark, unlit cabin and strode the path, between thigh-high banks of snow, that led around back. *Take in an armful of wood every time you go in the house, son, and you'll never have to go out in the cold and dark because the woodbox runs low.* His pa had drilled that truth into him when he was barely old enough to carry a piece of wood, and it had held him in good stead all these years. His pa had been a wise man—uneducated but wise.

He loaded his arms, shoved open the kitchen door, back-kicked it shut and walked through the dark room to the woodbox by memory, trying not to think about Ellen and Harold Lodge sitting in front of a roaring fire in her parents' comfortable, well-lit sitting room.

In this book I have the assurance of God's love and care for me and mine. What more have I need of? The riches of this world? Gold? Silver? New gloves?

It was certain Harold Lodge had all of those things and more besides. He could give Ellen whatever she deserved or desired. But he'd seen the way Lodge looked at her. And it wasn't the look of a man in love. It was the smug look of a man who had obtained a wanted prize. Her other beau had to be better than Lodge. "He's not good enough for her, Lord. Harold Lodge doesn't love her. Please don't let Ellen be lured into marrying him because of his money. Please let her refuse him and marry Cuthbert, or someone who will truly love her."

He dumped the wood into the box, squatted and raked

the ashes off the banked embers of his supper fire. He spread a handful of kindling over the massed embers and blew until they winked red, then added a few short pieces of small branches as the kindling caught fire.

I'd rather have the loving touch of my wife's hand on mine...

He'd never experience that. His chest tightened with the ache that had wormed its way into his heart during the past few days. He rose and gripped the log mantel, hung his head between his outstretched arms and stared at the flames licking at the wood. There was no point in continuing to lie to himself. Willa's scheming had worked. Working with Ellen, spending time with her the past two days, had stirred emotions he'd thought dead and buried. All of the old yearnings were back, worse than when he was young because he knew there was no hope. All he could do was to hold his tongue from speaking and endure.

Ellen stared up at the canopy overhead wishing she could fall asleep, but her turbulent thoughts made it impossible. One moment she decided yes, and the next moment she decided no. She had to make up her mind, but there was so much to consider. If only today had never happened.

She let out a long sigh, threw back the covers, pulled on her slippers and climbed from bed. Reflected firelight danced on the silk of her dressing gown as she slipped it on and walked to the fireplace. If only she could talk to Willa. But she simply couldn't. She hadn't the courage.

I'd rather have the loving touch of my wife's hand on mine than a dozen pair of the finest gloves money can buy.

Tears stung her eyes. How much Willa's husband loved her! Try as she might, she could not imagine Mr. Lodge or Mr. Cuthbert speaking those words. The men who courted her coveted the things of this world. They would never put love of her above possessions. She would *be* one of their coveted possessions! She blinked the tears away and stared at the flames, her thoughts churning, her temples throbbing. Mr. Lodge had confided that he was going to ask her father for her hand tomorrow when he took him for a ride in his enclosed sleigh. Of course, her father would agree. But he would also tell Harold Lodge the decision to accept or refuse his proposal of marriage was hers.

Oh, she wished she'd never come home! And that Mr. Lodge had never come to visit. He seemed different here. The way he had spoken about the people of Pinewood today was so insolent and patronizing. He acted as if they were beneath him. And he didn't even know them. *Villagers.* How derisively he'd spoken the word. Her stomach soured. She took a breath and pressed her hand against the silk fabric that covered it. *She* was one of those *villagers.* Should they wed, would he turn his scorn on her when her beauty faded?

The throbbing in her head increased. She rubbed her temples, but it didn't help. And she had no desire to ring for Isobel and have her report her agitated state to her mother. She crossed to the window, pulled back one panel of the woven coverlet drapes and leaned her forehead against a frost-coated pane. Shivers ran up and down her spine, prickled her flesh. She tugged the curtain in front of her to block the cold air and held it close beneath her chin.

Paltry bows.

She glanced through the night toward the gazebo sitting in the field at the corner of the road. Mr. Lodge might belittle the decorations, but the *villagers* liked them. And Daniel liked them. He'd said so. And Daniel never lied.

I'd rather have the loving touch of my wife's hand on mine than a dozen pair of the finest gloves money can buy.

Her throat tightened. She could imagine Daniel speaking those words. Daniel was the sort of man who would love a woman with all of his heart.

Chapter Eleven

Ellen laid the magazine on the settee, rose and walked to the window. Willa's meeting with the children's mothers about the Christmas pageant had put off decorating the parsonage until tomorrow. She crossed her arms, drummed her fingers against her upper arms and stared into the distance wishing for something to do. The idleness of her day was most annoying. It made her...restless.

And Mr. Lodge's call upon her that morning had made it worse. The man was so...so *pompous!* Why had she never noticed? All he did was talk about himself and how clever he was, twisting things to his advantage in numerous business deals and using his prestige to make those less fortunate yield to his demands. And the way he *looked* at her, as if he were assessing her value to him.

She pressed her lips together and touched the dark blue braid her mother had used on her new dress to emphasize her small waist. Obviously, he found her pleasing. He had deemed her worthy to become his wife. But then, the Buffalo elite had judged her the "prize" catch of the season because of her beauty, and Harold Lodge always obtained the best. His overweening pride would accept nothing less. But shouldn't there be something more? Shouldn't she be more to him than another acquisition that bested that of his peers?

Oh, what was wrong with her! She had been elated before she came home at the thought of marrying Mr. Lodge. So what if he was pompous? It was the way the socially prominent were. And why shouldn't they be? They had the best of everything. And soon she would, also.

She waited for the rush of excitement that thought should bring, but there was only that nagging uneasiness. She watched two boys running down the road trying to stay in the tracks of a passing sleigh, then gazed across the empty field to the parsonage. Willa had asked her to come to the meeting, but she couldn't go with Mr. Lodge here.

Coward! Spineless fribble! The name-calling did no good. Her feet stayed rooted to the spot. The boys left the road and waded through the deep snow of the field. She caught sight of the face of one as he looked up and pitched a snowball at the other. *Joshua.* Sally must be indoors. Would they decorate tomorrow evening after the children were abed, or—

She inhaled sharply, taken by a sudden thought. She stared at Joshua and smiled, lifted her gaze to the parsonage. She would go see Sadie. The weather was fine. It wasn't snowing or blowing. And the roads were passable. People had come to church from the outlying farms yesterday. She moved a curtain aside and glanced up; the sky held no threat.

"Pardon the intrusion, Miss Ellen, but I need to tend the fire."

She nodded, let the curtain fall back and turned from the window. "When you're finished with the fire, Asa, please hitch up the cutter and bring it around to the front for me. I'm going calling." She lifted her hems and ran into the entrance and up the stairs to change her gown.

"A few more nice days like this one, and I figure the snow will have melted down enough you men will be going back to work."

"You figure right, Mr. Roberts." *And it can't be too soon for me.* Daniel added coffee to the flour and molasses he had sitting on the counter, stiffened as the bell jingled. *Please don't let it be Ellen and that popinjay that's courting her.* He relaxed and smiled as Sophia Sheffield entered and walked toward the counter. "Good morning."

"Good morning, Daniel…everyone." Sophia laid a list on the counter, then swept her gaze over the people in the store. "I don't know about the rest of you, but I think someone should clear the ice for a skating party tonight. It's past time we had one."

"Oh, that's an excellent idea, Sophia! We've all been so hemmed in by the storm, it will be good to get out and socialize a bit." Judith Brody looked up from the basket of yarn she was sorting through and smiled. "I'll bring some cookies." Her gaze shifted to him. "I mean, if the ice gets cleared, of course."

"Will it, Daniel?"

He looked down at Sophia Sheffield and grinned. "I'm not busy today, so…sure—*if* I get at least a half dozen of your br—ginger cookies at the party tonight."

"I shall bake an extra dozen, all for you. You need some spoiling with Dora gone to Syracuse to help Ruth." She smiled and patted his arm, then fixed her gaze on the proprietor. "I trust we can count on you for chest-nuts to roast, Mr. Cargrave?"

Daniel looked at him over the top of Sophia's head and grinned. It wasn't a question.

"Of course."

"And chocolate so there is something warm for the children to drink?"

Allan Cargrave looked pained, but he nodded.

"Wonderful! You can include it when you bring my order, and I'll prepare it tonight." Sophia turned, her violet eyes twinkling. "I trust you will see to the wood for the bonfire, Daniel?"

"I'll have it there."

"That's everything, then." She waved her gloved hand through the air and headed for the door. "Spread the word, everyone! We're having a skating party tonight." The bell on the door jingled its approval.

"Well, I'd best go home and start baking. Thank you for volunteering to clear the ice, Daniel." Judith Brody hurried out the door after Sophia.

Did Harold Lodge skate? He thrust the sour thought from him and looked at Allan Cargrave. "Is it all right if I use the sidewalk plow to clear the ice? Or do you need approval from the other city elders? It would save me a lot of shoveling."

"Use it. It's stored at Dibble's stable."

"I know." Daniel gestured toward his burlap bag on the counter. "I'll come back for those things when I've finished."

"Hey, Mr. Braynard! Where you going with that plow?"

Daniel halted Big Boy, glanced across Main Street and grinned at the expectant look on Kurt Finster's and

Danny Brody's young faces. They already knew—and were hoping. "I'm going to clear the snow off the creek for the skating party tonight. Want to help?"

"Woo-hoo!" The boys jumped off the raised walkway and came running, their grins as wide as their lips would stretch. "Whatta we do?"

"Well, first, go and spread the word. Then you and your friends bring your shovels and meet me under the bridge. I need all the help I can get."

"Yes, sir!" The boys spun about and raced up Main Street shouting the news.

Daniel grinned, splayed his legs to balance himself on the floorboards of the inverted-V-shaped plow and clicked his tongue. "Let's go, Big Boy." The huge Belgian leaned into his harness and the plow skidded forward, skipping over the frozen ruts in the road and lurching onto the bridge. Ice crystals clattered along the high wood wings that formed the sides and flew off in a white cloud.

"Haw, Big Boy!" The Belgian turned left onto Brook Street and the plow slid sideways. Daniel shifted his weight to balance it and reined the chestnut off the road. The V nose of the plow bucked, then bit into the deep snow on the sloped bank, the sides making a yard-wide furrow at an angle down to the frozen creek.

"Whoa, boy." He removed the short reins, tied longer ropes to the plow, then hooked another rope to the Belgian's harness. A door slammed in the distance, then another. Children's shouts floated on the cold, still air. He tugged and slid the wood plow out to the center of the ice in the protected area beneath the bridge where there were only a few patches of blown-in snow. Young boys and girls of all ages and sizes came sliding and skidding down both banks to the frozen creek. Tommy Burke reached him first.

"We come to help, Mr. Braynard." The boy grinned and slapped snow from his jacket and pants. "What do you want us to do?"

"Stack your shovels out of the way on the bank, then take this rope—" he reached inside the plow and pulled out the attached rope and handed it to Tommy "—and all of you older boys go to the other bank."

"Wait!" He laughed and grabbed shoulders as several boys whipped around toward the other side of the creek. "I haven't told you what to do yet. Play out the rope, and when you get to the creek bank, take a good hold—the oldest of you in front, the youngest at the end. And then brace yourselves." He stifled the grin tugging at his lips. "When Big Boy moves ahead, the plow is going to skid sideways and that rope is going to pull hard. Your job is to keep the rope you're holding taut so the plow stays straight as we move forward. That's important. Think you can do that?"

"Sure we can!"

"All right, then." The boys raced for the opposite side of the wide creek, the rope stretching out behind them.

"What do we do?"

He looked down at Trudy Hoffman and the girls and younger boys clustered around her. "I need you all to stand in the plow to weight it down so it will dig into the snow. The oldest and biggest of you keep to the back so it doesn't flip over. And no leaning over the sides. I don't want anyone falling out where the plow can run over them." He gave them a stern look. "Trudy's in charge. Understand?"

Trudy beamed, then sobered. The others nodded.

"All right, climb in." There was a mad rush toward the plow. He left Trudy to manage the scramble and walked to Big Boy. Men stood by Dibble's house, watching with grins on their faces. He looked over at the boys across the creek. "Keep that rope tight, now! Brace yourselves, everybody—here we go!"

The boys gripped the rope and dug in their feet. The girls and boys stuffed into the plow grabbed hold of the sides and each other. He chuckled, fisted his hands around the reins and waded forward through the deep snow. "Hup, Big Boy, hup!"

Squeals and shouts and laughter filled the air as the Belgian trotted ahead. Daniel looked over his shoulder, grinned at the boys on the opposite bank slipping and sliding, losing their balance and falling, being tugged into the deep snow as they struggled to counter the pull of the horse while the plow zigzagged forward and jolted into the deeper snow. Children tumbled, laughing and squealing, from the back of the plow.

"Whoa, Big Boy!" He laughed and waved back the men who had started toward the creek bank to help, received nods and grins of understanding as they stopped and crouched down to wait. "Keep that rope tight, men!"

"Yes, sir!"

The boys scrambled to their feet, picked up the rope and pulled it straight. They splayed their legs and dug in their feet, determined looks on their young faces. The children that had tumbled out of the plow on impact scrambled back to their places.

The thud of hoofs on the bridge echoed in the hollow beneath. He glanced up, stiffened at the sight of a dark bay with black points pulling a green cutter with red striping. *Hall's rig.* He pretended not to see Ellen driving, turned to urge Big Boy forward. The ploy didn't work. Ellen stopped the cutter, looped the reins over the branch of a bush beside the road and started down the bank following the path he had made with the sidewalk plow. *What was she doing?*

He motioned to the men on the bank to take over, braced himself and strode across the creek. "Wait where you are, Musquash. I'll come help you."

"That's not necessary. I am perfectly able— Oh!" Her feet shot out from under her.

He leaped toward the bank, stretched out his arms and caught her as she came sliding toward him. "You little fool! Are you trying to maim yourself?" He growled the words, slid his arms around her and hauled her to her feet. The slope of the bank brought her face almost level with his. He looked into her blue eyes, and the shouting and laughter of the men and children faded away. The look, the smell, the touch of her filled his senses. He tightened his arms, pulled her close and lowered his head. Her tremble brought him back to reality.

He sucked in cold air, then loosened his hold and stepped back. "Are you all right?" He wasn't. Everything in him was yearning to kiss her, to confess the love he now knew had never truly gone away, to make her his own. And that could never be. She was too selfish and grasping, and he was too poor and proud. Anger boiled up, heated the blood racing through his veins.

Ellen nodded, grasped her long skirts and shook the snow from them. Her cheeks were overspread with red as bright as apples.

Cold or anger? Had he betrayed himself to her? Had she guessed he'd been about to kiss her? He couldn't tell without looking into her eyes, and her head was bowed so that he couldn't see them. "That was a fool thing to do, trying to come down that bank by yourself." *Let it work, Lord. Let her get angry and forget what almost happened.*

"I've done it before."

"Back when we were young!"

"Yes, back then. I forgot how much has changed!" She bit out the words, stopped brushing at her cloak and looked up.

The defiance and hurt in her eyes tore at his gut. "Did you want something?" He winced inwardly at his curt tone, but reinforcing her low opinion of him was his best defense.

She nodded, reached up and jerked her bonnet straight. "I thought Joshua and Sally might enjoy a Christmas tree. And when I saw you, I thought I would ask if you would cut one for them if Grandfather Townsend gives his permission. I'm on my way to see Sadie now to ask about the tree."

He stared. "*You* thought of a Christmas tree for Josh and Sally?"

Her face tightened. "I'm not entirely selfish, Daniel." She looked down, brushed at some snow still clinging to her cloak. "Will you cut the tree, or not?"

He nodded and pulled an image of Joshua and Sally into his head to calm his churning thoughts and emotions. "Of course. I'd do most anything for Josh and Sally." That should take away any thought that he was doing it for her. "What did Willa say about the tree— that we'll have to decorate it?" He was only half joking. He blew out a cloud of breath at the thought of spending more time with Ellen. There was no doubt Manning would let them have a tree.

She stopped fussing with her cloak and looked up at him. "Willa doesn't know. She is busy and I couldn't ask her." Her teeth caught at her lip, worried the corner. "I hadn't thought about decorating the tree. I guess I'm not very good at this sort of thing." She sighed, gave him a look that took his breath. "Would you help decorate the tree, Daniel?" Her face tightened. "For Joshua and Sally, I mean."

He lost his good sense somewhere in the blue of her eyes and nodded agreement, then hastened to put a good face on it. "As I said, I'd do most anything for Josh and Sally."

She took a little breath and nodded. "Then I shall ask Grandfather Townsend if we might have one." She turned and planted her booted foot firmly in the snow along the bank, wobbled and flailed her arms when it gave way beneath her.

"You trying to fall again?" He grabbed her arm, steadied her, then tromped up the bank tugging her with him, his heart thudding at the feel of her hand in his. He handed her in the cutter, freed the reins and gave them to her. "Tell Quick Stuff to get my cookies made. I'm busy with the skating party tonight, but I'll collect them when I go out to cut the tree tomorrow."

"But not by yourself at night."

Was she concerned for his safety? The thought gave him far too much pleasure. He slanted his lips into a teasing grin. "You worried about me, Musquash?"

Her cheeks flushed. "I wouldn't want your demise on my conscience. And, yes, I have one!" She snapped the reins and lifted her chin. "I shall give Sadie your message."

He stood and watched as the horse broke into a brisk

trot and the cutter glided down the road. Ellen had believed his performance, and it stuck like an icicle in his heart. He blew out another cloud of breath and loped down the bank to clear the ice.

"It's nice to see you again, Ellen." Cole Aylward shrugged into his jacket. "But I'm a bit pressed for time on an order, so if you ladies will excuse me, I've work to do in the shop."

"Of course." Ellen nodded and busied herself removing her cloak and bonnet but still caught a glimpse of the look Sadie and her husband exchanged, the way he touched her hand before he went outside. It almost seemed a…a promise of some sort. She glanced away but couldn't forget the look in Cole's eyes. It was the same way she'd seen Matthew look at Willa. And not at all the way Mr. Lodge looked at her. Her unease returned.

"I'm so glad you've come to visit, Ellen." Sadie took her cloak and bonnet from her and hung them on a peg. "You must be chilled after your ride from town. Shall we have a cup of hot cider or tea to warm you?"

"Tea sounds delightful." She looked down, shook out her skirts and smoothed her bodice. Thinking about Sadie and Cole only added to her confusion. She'd do best to concentrate on the reason she'd come.

"Why don't you come into the kitchen with me while I prepare it. This is Gertrude's day off, and Nanna is… having a bad day." Sadie sighed and turned toward the kitchen.

Ellen fluffed her curls and followed, latched on to the safe topic, determined to shake off her growing disquiet and return to her purpose. "I'm sorry about your grandmother, Sadie. How is your grandfather faring?"

"Poppa is doing well. The rolling chair Cole made for him has given him a large measure of his independence back. At least around the house. It's an amazing creation. And it's turned into a very lucrative livelihood, better than even the shingle mill provides. It seems there are a lot of infirm people in New York City." Sadie opened the drafts and pulled the teakettle forward. "It's astonishing how God took Cole's act of kindness toward grandfather and turned it into a blessing for Cole...for us. God truly does work in mysterious ways."

Be not high-minded, nor trust in uncertain riches, but in the living God, who giveth us richly all things to enjoy.

The topic wasn't as safe as she'd assumed. It had brought to her memory another bit of Scripture from Matthew Calvert's sermon. They kept coming to her. She shoved the verse to the back of her mind and tried again. "Have you tried the chair?"

"Not exactly."

A blush stole across Sadie's cheeks. Ellen stepped closer, intrigued by her friend's reaction to the harmless question. "What does that mean?"

"Nothing. It's—" Sadie turned and took a tin of tea from the cupboard. "Cole gave me a ride to show me how the chair worked."

"You mean on his *lap?*"

The pink in Sadie's cheeks turned a dark rose.

"Why, Sadie Aylward!" She choked back her laughter, raised her brows and tsk-tsked.

"He's my husband! Now stop teasing."

Sadie laughed, but her cheeks were flaming. Sadie, who had been terrified of men for so many years. She studied her friend's eyes. The fear that had shadowed them for so long was gone. Sadie looked like the happy person she'd been before the attack. And Cole Aylward had brought about that remarkable change.

"You truly love him, don't you?" The thought popped out of her mouth. *So much for staying on a safe subject.* She waved her hand through the air, trying to erase her words. "I'm sorry. That was rude. I didn't mean to—"

"Yes. I truly love him." Tears pooled in Sadie's eyes. "It's—it's *wondrous,* Ellen. After Payne's attack I was certain I would never trust another man, let alone love one. The very thought of marriage made me shudder. But Cole is *so* wonderful! He's so good and honest and kind and generous and loving and…and…"

"Thoughtful? Tender?"

"Yes." Sadie laughed and brushed tears from her cheeks. "Thank you. I'd run out of adjectives."

"It's an impressive list." Remarkably akin to the one she'd heard in church on Sunday. A list she could not apply to Mr. Lodge.

"I'm sorry, Ellen. I've been talking only about my-self." Sadie smiled, gave her an expectant look. "We heard your beau is in Pinewood. You must be very excited. Has he asked for your hand?"

"Not yet, though he confided he is going to." She rubbed her temples to hide her face lest Sadie see her lack of enthusiasm. "He has taken Father to Olville for a demonstration ride in his booby hut sleigh and intends to ask for my hand when they return." Where was the excitement she should be feeling? The satisfaction? She had reached her goal.

"That's wonderful! I'm so happy for you, Ellen!" Sadie gave her a hug, then stepped back, a frown on her face. "Is something wrong, Ellen? You're very quiet and contained for a soon-to-be-betrothed young woman."

She squared her shoulders, took a breath. "The truth is I don't know if I will accept Mr. Lodge's offer. There are many things I must consider—including Mr. Cuthbert."

"I see." Sadie picked up the tin of tea and tugged the cover off. "Forgive me for prying, Ellen, but…do you not love Mr. Lodge?"

No. Only the things he can give me. The truth hung in her thoughts, bald and ugly. She wrapped her arms about herself, feeling sick. Was she truly prepared to marry a man she had discovered she didn't even like— for *things?* Was that what her parents—

"Does Willa need more greens or firewood, Ellen?"

She lifted her head, grateful for Sadie's tactful change of subject and the interruption of her uncomfortable thoughts. "I don't know about the firewood, but we have more than enough greens. Daniel and I finished the church decorations Saturday."

"Yes. Matthew told us how lovely the church and gazebo look when he came to minister to us on Sunday afternoon. But I wasn't certain about the parsonage."

"We made a wreath for the door and a few sprays and garlands. They're not hung yet, however. They're waiting for when Willa is ready for them. The baby has been fussy and taking a good deal of her time, and Bertha has gone to visit her niece." She blew out a breath, rubbed the tense muscle at the side of her neck. "I did want to ask you if you thought Grandfather Townsend would allow us—I mean Daniel, of course—to cut a Christmas tree for the parsonage. I think Joshua and Sally would like one. And Daniel has agreed."

"A Christmas tree? What a wonderful idea. The children will love it." Sadie smiled and picked up a spoon.

"I know Poppa will agree. Though it would be dangerous for Daniel to go alone into the woods to cut one in this deep snow."

"Yes. He endangered himself cutting the greens." *You worried about me, Musquash?* She frowned. Was that so inconceivable? Did she seem that callous to her old friends?

"I heard. Perhaps Matthew will go with him to cut the tree." Sadie spooned tea into a red-and-white china teapot, placed matching cups and saucers and spoons on a pewter tray, then added a sugar bowl and creamer. "It must have been fun working on the decorations with Daniel. He hasn't changed a bit. He's still as kind and generous and—"

"Are you going to go through the list again?" She tried to make it sound amusing, but it came out a little too acerbic. She couldn't help it. She did not want to hear those attributes ascribed to Daniel—not even if he deserved them.

Sadie looked at her.

She sighed, raised her hands and rubbed her temples. "I'm sorry, Sadie. I didn't mean to sound waspish. I have a bit of a head."

"Perhaps the tea will help." Sadie poured the hot water into the teapot and covered it with a towel to steep. "Why don't you sit at the table and rest, Ellen? I'll be right back. I want to ask Poppa and Nanna if they would like tea."

"I'm not in pain, Sadie, only a bit uncomfortable." *And growing more so.* "I don't need to rest. I'll go in with you and pay my respects. And ask about the tree."

"Nanna may not recognize you, Ellen."

The sadness in Sadie's voice brought her self-centered

thoughts to a halt. "I know." She stepped to Sadie's side, smiled and gave her a quick hug. "But it doesn't matter, because *I* will know that inside, Grandmother Townsend is as sweet and gracious as she's always been."

Sadie caught her breath and nodded. "Thank you, Ellen. I…cling to the thought that somewhere inside, Nanna is still the same."

"I'm certain it's so." She stepped back, unaccustomed to the role of comforter. "I meant to tell you how much I like the wreath on your door. That carved wood bird attached to it is lovely. And I've recently become an expert on decorations, you know." She gave a self-deprecating wrinkle of her nose.

Sadie laughed and headed for the hallway. "Daniel carved the chickadee and gave it to us for a wedding present. I've always enjoyed feeding the birds, of course."

"I didn't know Daniel did carvings."

"Oh, yes. He gave us all one as a gift when we married. He carved Willa a horse, because she'd always wanted one. And Callie a deer, because she loved going to the deer path and watching for them."

"I remember." *She'd been forbidden to go into the woods, so she'd pretended she no longer wanted to.*

"I'm sure he will make you a carving for a gift, as well. Why, he's probably already working on it as you will be announcing your betrothal to one of your beaux soon."

Sadie was wrong. She was certain of that. Sadie was thinking of the way it was when they were all friends. But that time had passed. Daniel would not spend his time making a carving as a wedding present for her— not the way he felt about her and her beaux. And if he did, it would probably be a *muskrat.* She thrust away the hurtful thoughts and followed Sadie through the arched doorway into the sitting room, where Manning Townsend was reading aloud to his wife.

"Nanna, Poppa, we have a visitor, and I thought you might like to join us for tea."

Ellen crossed the room and smiled at the elderly couple. "Good afternoon, Grandmother Townsend, Grandfather Townsend. It's so good to see you again."

"And you, Ellen." Manning Townsend tucked his fingertip in his book and looked up at her. "It's kind of you to call."

Rachel Townsend stared at her. "Do I know you, young woman?"

She nodded and smiled. "I'm Ellen Hall, Sadie's friend."

"Sadie went away."

"Yes. But she's come home, and now Ellen has come to call." Manning Townsend's voice seemed to penetrate his wife's confusion. Rachel Townsend turned toward him. He took her hand in his and smiled.

Her throat squeezed at the look in his eyes. She cleared away the tightness, drew a breath. "I wanted to tell you, Grandfather Townsend, how lovely the greens you donated make the church look." She smiled as they both looked up at her, noted the spark of interest in Rachel Townsend's eyes and hurried to describe the decorations. "There is a large wreath on the front door, garlands at the top of the windows and sprays on the pew doors. We haven't yet decorated the parsonage. We were hoping that perhaps you would donate a Christmas tree for the children to enjoy? Daniel would cut it for us."

"A Christmas tree? That's a wonderful idea. I should

have thought of that. Those children will love a tree." Manning Townsend smiled and nodded his consent.

Rachel Townsend looked perplexed. "What is a Christmas tree?"

"It's a decoration, Nanna." Sadie smiled, glanced her way. "Ellen has decorated the church and also the gazebo. It looks very festive with the greens swooping in graceful loops from pillar to pillar and pretty red bows with long ties that flutter in the wind."

"My, that must be lovely. I like bows...." Rachel Townsend sighed.

Manning Townsend straightened, took the book off his lap and placed it on the lamp stand beside him. "Sadie, I want you to ring the bell for Cole and ask him to please hitch up the sleigh. You young ladies may have your tea. I'm going to take your grandmother into town to see the gazebo."

"I'm sorry, Poppa, but Cole is too busy to drive you to town today. Perhaps—"

"We're going alone."

Alone! She glanced at Sadie, saw the concern leap into her friend's eyes.

"That's not necessary, Poppa. I can—"

"No, Sadie. We're going alone." Her grandfather's tone was firm, his expression resolute. "I still have one good hand, and it won't be the first time I've driven a horse one handed while your grandmother was with me—though then it was for a very different reason."

"Poppa!"

Ellen gasped, tried to hide her shock behind a cough.

Manning Townsend chuckled. "My apologies for the indelicacy of mentioning our spooning in front of you, Ellen." He sobered and waved his good hand toward

Sadie. "Go on now and ring for Cole, while my best girl and I get ready to go for a sleigh ride."

Spooning...his best girl... The words repeated themselves in time with the swish of their long skirts as she hurried with Sadie to the kitchen. Did her father feel that way about her mother? Had he ever?

"I'll be back in a minute, Ellen. I have to ring the bell for Cole." Sadie took a cape off a peg by the door, pulled it on and stepped out onto the porch.

Spooning. She uncovered the teapot and set it on the tray, tried to remember if she had ever seen or heard any signs of affection between her parents. It was certain she had never seen them look at one another the way Willa and Matthew and Sadie and Cole and even Rachel and Manning looked at one another. Still, they had a beautiful home—one of the best in town. There was no discord between them. And they were unfailingly courteous to one another. Was that what she wanted? Courtesy and comfort? Was that enough?

The door squeaked open. Sadie slipped back inside, hung the cloak on the peg and turned toward her, rubbing her hands together. "Now, I'm ready for that tea."

She stared at Sadie's shining eyes, the mussed hair on the right side of her head, as if fingers had burrowed through it, and the disquieting question returned. Were things enough?

Chapter Twelve

"I understand you took the cutter out while Mr. Lodge and I were in Olville, Ellen."

Isobel or Asa? Ellen laid her fork on her cake plate and glanced toward her father sitting at the head of the table. "Yes, I did. I went to call on Sadie and Cole, and Mr. and Mrs. Townsend. But you've no need for concern, Father. I haven't forgotten how to handle a horse during my time in Buffalo."

"Had it not been in use, the booby hut and my driver would have been at your disposal, Miss Hall. It would have kept you warm."

She glanced across the table, met another of Harold Lodge's smug smiles. The message he'd been sending her during the meal was clear. He had gained her father's blessing to ask for her hand—not that there had ever been any question as to her father's response. The only doubt involved was hers. She still hadn't decided how to answer when he posed the question to her, and she was feeling surrounded and pressured and…miffed. She pulled up one of her practiced smiles and reached for her glass. "The weather was agreeable. I was quite comfortable in the cutter. And I found driving myself quite enjoyable. I'd forgotten how invigorating it could be."

"I trust you had a nice visit, dear?" Her mother gave her a warning look over the top of the napkin she was using to dab her lips.

Evidently, she hadn't been fawning enough in her response to Mr. Lodge. "Yes, very nice, Mother. Sadie sends her regards. And I'm sure Grandmother Townsend would, too, were she able." The mention of Rachel Townsend's infirmity earned her another look.

Her mother dipped her head and smiled, then swept her gaze across the table. "Would you care for more dessert, Mr. Lodge?"

"No, thank you. It is excellent cake, Mrs. Hall, but I've had my fill."

"Very well, then. Ellen and I will leave you gentlemen to enjoy an after-dinner cigar and await you in the sitting room."

Her father and Mr. Lodge stood as she rose and followed her mother from the dining room. It wouldn't be long now. She pressed her hand against her stomach, regretting the little supper she had eaten.

"What is wrong with you tonight, Ellen!" Her mother spun about and all but hissed the words at her as they entered the sitting room. "You know perfectly well Mr. Lodge has spoken with your father and intends to ask you for your hand this evening, and you—"

"Don't know what I will answer."

Her mother stared, took in a breath. "You are playing a dangerous game, Ellen. Mr. Lodge does not seem a patient man. He may not be willing to wait for your decision until after Mr. Cuthbert's visit."

"Then the decision will be made for me." She stepped

past her mother, crossed the room and stood by the hearth, soaking up the warmth of the fire, wishing it could reach her heart. Wishing her growing disquiet would go away.

"Ellen, consider what you are—"

"Are you happy, Mother?"

"I beg your pardon?"

She lifted her gaze from the dancing flames to her mother. "I asked if you are happy."

"Don't be ridiculous! What has that to do with—?"

"Does Father have an endearment for you? Has he ever called you his best girl?"

"Certainly not! Your father would never use such a vulgar expression." Her mother's eyes narrowed, and her long skirts swished as she rushed over to her. "Sadie has put this nonsense into your head, hasn't she? 'Best girl' is the exact sort of thing Cole Aylward would—"

"Not Cole, Mother—Grandfather Townsend."

"One and the same." Her mother sniffed, waved her hand. "Manning Townsend was lowborn, too. Rachel married beneath her, against her parents' wishes. Who knows to what heights in society Rachel would have risen had she listened to them. She was a beautiful, wellborn young woman with wealthy beaux, but she and Manning were besotted with one another and she'd have no other."

The look she'd witnessed between the Townsends that morning swept into her mind. A smile curved her lips. "They still are."

"How inappropriate at their age. But Manning and Rachel have nothing to do with the decision you must make." Her mother lifted her hands and gripped her shoulders. "Listen to me, Ellen. You are young and beautiful. But beauty fades, and other, younger women take a man's eye. Unless you are very certain Mr. Cuthbert intends to call upon your father to request his blessing to ask for your hand, you must thrust all comparisons and indecisions aside and accept Mr. Lodge's offer. You do not want to miss your opportunity to gain all your father and I have raised you to achieve, all you have dreamed of."

All she had dreamed of... Something stirred deep inside her. That nagging sense of dissatisfaction strengthened, no doubt because of her indecision. She had to do something that would help her choose.

"Why did you insist on our taking a walk, Miss Hall?" Harold Lodge tucked his gray wool scarf more closely beneath his long chin with his free hand. "It's turning colder since the sun has gone down. I should think you would prefer to stay indoors in front of the fire."

Not tonight. "My cloak and bonnet are warm. And there is something I want to show you." Moonlight glimmered on a patch of ice on the walkway. She took a firmer hold on his arm.

"The footing is treacherous. Ease your grip, Miss Hall, or you'll make us both fall." He stepped ahead, led the way around the ice and stopped at the corner.

The memory of Daniel moving to block the force of the blizzard from her flashed into her head. She'd walked blind, with her face hidden behind his shoulder, trusting him to lead her. *Trusting him.* She'd always trusted Daniel. He'd always protected her. Like this afternoon.

"Which way do we go?"

She looked up at Harold Lodge, his tall, slender form a shadow against the lamp-lit windows of the Sheffield House Inn and Restaurant standing across the snow-trampled expanse of Main Street. "To the left, past the church." She kept her gaze from the gazebo and focused instead on the parsonage, thought about the Christmas tree and had a sudden wish that she might go to the woods with Daniel to cut it down. They'd all spent so much time in the woods as children. She'd always loved going on their adventures.

"It's so silent and lifeless here." Harold Lodge gestured across the road to the block of stores with their closed doors and dark windows. "The only place that shows any activity at all is the Sheffield House, and, staying there, I know that is trifling. Whatever does one do for entertainment in this…village?"

Trifling? She fought back the urge to spring to Sophia's defense. "It is true that compared to the city, Pinewood has little in the way of formal entertainment, Mr. Lodge. But there are sleigh rides, and sledding, of course. And hymn sings and skating parties."

"How very amusing."

His tone said different. They passed the church and the Cargrave home, then picked their way over the snow- and ice-covered planks that formed Church Street. She could hear shouts and laughter faintly now, could smell the bonfire. She glanced up at him. "Do you skate, Mr. Lodge?"

He laughed and looked down at her, his top hat a small dark tower against the night. "That is an odd question for you to ask, my dear Miss Hall. You know people such as you and I find our entertainment in the theater and opera, in fine dining and soirees." He placed his gloved hand over hers. "All places where beauty such as yours is admired and, I dare say, envied."

Which is why you covet to possess it. The truth was

too blatant to ignore. She quelled the urge to pull her hand from beneath his, took a breath and forced another smile. "You're too kind, sir."

"Not at all. You are an extremely beautiful young woman, Miss Hall." He lifted his head, looked around. "I see nothing but a livery beside us and closed stores across the way. Where is this thing you want me to see?"

Faint light glowed against the darkness ahead. Her stomach tightened—the way it had when she was young. "We're almost there."

"Is that shouting I hear?" He started forward into the night. "It seems to be coming from around that bridge." He stopped, glanced over his shoulder. "I think it would be wise if we turned back, Miss Hall. There could be danger from ruffians lurking ahead."

"There is no danger, Mr. Lodge. It's a skating party." She looked up at him, watched his face to catch any change of expression. "I saw them clearing the snow from the ice today when I was on my way to my friend's home—" *Daniel, holding the horse's reins and laughing with the children and other men, until he'd looked up, seen her and then…* "—and I thought perhaps we might come and watch the festivities."

"Skating?"

His lip didn't quite curl. "Yes." She released her grip on his arm, gathered her skirts close and stepped off the walkway onto a trodden path through the deep snow that led past the Dibble house. The path curved to the top of the creek bank, then descended in a series of steps cut into the snow. Swaths and ruts on either side testified of the children who preferred to slide down to the creek. Her pulse quickened at the memory of her afternoon slide into Daniel's arms. She hurried her steps.

Torches atop posts thrust into the deep snow piled on the edges of the far bank shone on laughing boys trying to outskate one another on a long cleared path of creek ice while others awaiting their turn to race cheered them on. Lanterns that would be used to light trips home hung from pegs driven into the bridge supports, and people of all ages skated in and out of the golden pools of light mirrored by the ice. On the creek bank below them, people stood eating roasted chestnuts while they visited and warmed themselves around a large bonfire.

She caught her breath. It was exactly as she remembered, though it had been years. She turned to look up at Harold Lodge. "Your hand, sir. They've cut steps in the snow, but—"

"Surely you are not thinking of going down there, Miss Hall."

"Why, yes." She looked at his stiff posture, his taut face. "Is it that you do not wish to go down and stand among the villagers, Mr. Lodge? Or that you do not wish to watch the skating?"

"Both, my dear Miss Hall. Such activities are for children and…others. Not for us." He smiled, reached out and took her gloved hand in his. "I have seen your quaint little village party. Now let us return to the quiet and warmth of your parents' home. I must leave for Buffalo tomorrow, and I have a question to ask you."

Her stomach churned. This was not working out as she had hoped. She nodded and turned. A victorious shout turned her back around again. The race was over. She looked at the boys happily thumping one another and moving out of the way as others skated to the starting line. *Daniel had always won. And he'd taught her how to skate backward….*

"Are you coming, Miss Hall?"

"A moment, Mr. Lodge." She stepped closer to the top of the bank, scanning the skaters. He wasn't there. But Sadie was. She watched her friend glide into view from the protected area beneath the bridge, skating with her arm linked with Cole's as he pushed her grandfather across the ice in a chair that had a footboard and runners attached to the bottom. Sadie's grandmother skated beside the chair, holding to her husband's good hand and laughing. They were all laughing. Her throat swelled at the happiness on their faces.

"Miss Hall?" Harold Lodge stepped close, again took hold of her hand.

She nodded and started to turn, looked down for one last glimpse and froze. Daniel was standing by the bonfire looking up at them, the leaping flames throwing flickering light across his face. Their gazes met. He gave a curt nod, then turned and added a log to the bonfire. Clearly their meeting earlier had meant nothing to him. He'd only been helping her. He helped everyone.

"The moonlight is fading, Miss Hall, and it's beginning to snow. We'd best hurry before it becomes too dark to find our way."

She tucked away the hurt of Daniel's snub and led the way back to Main Street.

Snow crunched beneath their feet as they traced their steps back to Oak Street and turned the corner. *Paltry bows.* She should have known then what her answer to Harold Lodge's proposal should be. She yanked her gaze from the dark form of the gazebo and fixed her sight on the shadowed shape of her home. A flame burned in the post lamp at the end of the shoveled walk.

Harold Lodge took her elbow and climbed the porch

steps beside her, reached for the door. She took a breath and turned to face him, pasted on her phony smile. "I'll say good evening here, Mr. Lodge."

His face tightened. "I'm afraid that will not do, Miss Hall. As I mentioned earlier, I must leave for Buffalo tomorrow, and, though I realize I have not yet asked my question, I must state that there are matters of importance concerning our wedding that need to be discussed before I go."

"There is no such need, for there will be no wedding, Mr. Lodge."

Shock spread across his face. "You are refusing my hand?"

She dipped her head. "I am most flattered by your offer of marriage, of course, but I must decline." She would have been sorry had there been any sign of hurt, but anger had already taken the place of his shock. His dark eyes glittered in the light from the lamp by the door.

"You are young, so I will give you a chance to reconsider your answer, Miss Hall. You will be making a serious error in choosing Mr. Cuthbert over me. His fortune does not compare to mine. And I am already taking steps to ensure his political future will be a short one."

How had she ever considered spending the rest of her life with this man? "I appreciate your concern for my well-being, Mr. Lodge. Nonetheless, my answer stands."

"Very well, but you and Cuthbert will both live to rue your decision! Good evening, Miss Hall."

She watched him pivot and stride down the steps and sidewalk, then lifted her chin and went inside to tell her parents she'd made her decision. Mr. Cuthbert's fortune might be less than Harold Lodge's, but combined with his political prominence it was more than enough to please her mother and father. And he was not as unbearably arrogant as Harold Lodge had turned out to be.

Ellen hung her bonnet and cloak on a peg, took a deep breath and walked to the sitting room. Her parents looked up, expectant expressions on their faces. "I refused Mr. Lodge's proposal." She smoothed her hands down over the front of her dress, shook out the long skirt and crossed to the hearth to warm herself.

Her mother drew an audible breath. "We discussed this before you went for your walk, Ellen." She rose from the settee and came to face her. "Why would you refuse Mr. Lodge? He—"

"Is prideful and—"

"And has every right to be so! You told us yourself he is one of the richest men in Buffalo. That he has one of the finest homes and the best of everything. And his appearance is impeccable. Why, his clothes are rich and… and…" Her mother stuttered to a halt, spun around. "Perhaps it's not too late, Conrad. You can go to the Sheffield House to see Mr. Lodge and explain that Ellen was… was overly excited at his proposal and refused his hand because she did not consider herself worthy to be his bride. Yes, that—"

"Is untrue, Mother."

"What reason did you give Mr. Lodge for your refusal, Ellen?"

She looked over at her father, lifted her chin at his disapproving expression. "None, Father. I merely said I would not marry him."

"That's not what we discussed." Her father removed his pipe from his mouth and pointed the stem toward her. "You were to tell Mr. Lodge you would give him your answer after Mr. Cuthbert's visit." His brows lowered. "I would have met both men, and you and I would have had time to discuss their prospects and come to a decision then."

"I made my decision, Father." She lifted her chin higher, met his gaze. "You told me the choice was mine."

"*After* we had discussed the men's merits."

"I believe you mean finances, Father." She held her voice steady, denying the tremor traveling through her at the chill in her father's gaze. "As for merits, I found Mr. Lodge quite lacking in them. And I was right. He threatened me."

"Threatened you?" Her father's eyes narrowed. "In what way?"

"He said that Mr. Cuthbert and I would both rue my decision. That he was already taking steps to ensure that Mr. Cuthbert's political future was a short one."

"I see. Well, that puts a different face on things." Her father rose, stepped to the hearth, tapped his pipe against a log and set it in its holder.

She relaxed and glanced toward her mother, wished she were as reasonable as her father.

"If Mr. Lodge is that powerful, he could disrupt Mr. Cuthbert's career—and after talking with him, I am convinced he is. You have made a serious mistake, Ellen."

She shot her gaze back to her father. "But—" His raised hand stopped her from speaking.

"However, I believe your mother is right. As are you." He looked down at the fire, stroked his beard, nodded. "Yes, you are both right. Harold Lodge's pride is such that he may be willing to accept the excuse your mother concocted for your refusal, if it comes from me." He brushed his hands together over the fire, looked at her and smiled. "Don't be concerned. It's not too late. I'll go to the Sheffield House and speak with him. I'm not without persuasive powers."

She stared at her father and shook her head. "I'm not concerned, Father. And I am not going to marry Mr. Lodge. I find I cannot abide the man." She lifted her hand and tucked a curl tickling her cheek behind her ear. "And as for his threat—you need have no fear. The governor is Mr. Cuthbert's close friend, and Mr. Lodge has no power to equal that connection. Now, if you will excuse me, I'm weary and am going to retire."

She dipped her head toward her mother and swept from the room, leaving them staring after her. She had been well trained in making entrances and exits.

Daniel checked to be sure the fire was out, picked up the lantern and left the cabin. The clothes he'd stuffed in the burlap bag slung over his shoulder bumped against his back with every stride as he walked up Brook Street, turned onto Main Street and tramped across the Stony Creek Bridge. Smoke rising from the embers of the bonfire stung his nose, sharpened the memory of Ellen standing on the creek bank holding to Harold Lodge's hand while he sneered down at them all. His fingers clenched the neck of the bag. It would take some time, but the feel of Ellen's hand in his as he helped her up the creek bank this afternoon was a memory he intended to forget. He'd forget them all if he had a lick of sense!

The squeak of the stable door brought forth a series of snorts and whickers. He set the lantern and his bag on the floor and crossed to the stalls in the shadowy light. "Hey, Big Boy." He stroked the velvety nose, opened the stall door and led the Belgian into the open area in the center of the barn. "Stand, boy. I've got to get Big Girl."

The mare lifted her head and whinnied at her name. He hurried to her stall, pulled a note for David Dibble from his coat pocket and stuck it on a nail, then led her out to stand beside her mate. "Quiet, now. Don't be stirring up the rest of the horses."

He slipped off their blankets, buckled on the harness, replaced the blankets and took hold of the reins. "All right, let's go."

Their hoofs thudded against the planks. The door hinges squeaked. He led the team outside, went back for his things and closed and latched the stable door. The snow that had started earlier that evening was coming harder. He gripped the reins and his bag in one hand, the lantern in the other and turned the horses toward the street. A door opened and closed.

"Everything all right, Daniel?"

He looked over at David Dibble standing on his porch and nodded. "I left a note telling you I was taking the horses back to camp. It's in Big Girl's stall."

"You need anything?"

"Only to get back to work, limited as it will be without the loggers cutting timber." He pulled up a grin. "That cabin's fearsome quiet with Ma gone." And neither one of those reasons were the whole truth. Nor was the Christmas tree he'd promised to cut. That was only a convenient excuse.

He lifted the lantern in farewell and walked the horses out to Main Street, the thud of their hoofs muted by the packed snow. Circles of gold bobbed at his feet, cast by the lantern dangling from his hand. He led the Belgians onto Church Street, walked them by the Cargrave house, dark and quiet against the night, and turned into the parsonage carriageway.

A lamp glowed in an upstairs window, a shadowy figure moving behind it. *Willa, holding the baby.* He set his mind against the ache that spread through him, tossed his bag in the pung and put his lantern on the seat.

"Back, back, now." He positioned the team and set about hitching them to the pung, working quickly, wincing at every unavoidable sound.

The kitchen door opened and closed. "No. Stay, Happy, stay!"

Willa. There was no avoiding her now. He turned, strode to the bottom of the porch steps. "Go back inside, Pest. It's snowing. There's no reason for you to come out and get chilled."

She grabbed her cloak close and came to the top of the steps. "What are you doing, Daniel? No one has been called back to camp."

"Ma's gone. There's no reason for me to stay in that empty cabin." *It's no lie, Lord. Please let her accept it and go inside. I can't tell her about the Christmas tree, and she wouldn't believe me anyway.*

"So you're leaving in the middle of the night?" She moved down the steps until she was looking him straight in the eye. "This is about Ellen, isn't it? Matthew said her beau—"

"*Hound's teeth*, but you're a persistent woman, Pest! I'm not going to discuss this." He turned away, took a couple of steps, then went back. "I'll be back to finish the decorations tomorrow afternoon."

She reached out and touched his sleeve. "Daniel, I'm sorry things—"

The muscle along his jaw twitched. He stepped back, nodded. "I know, Pest. Now go inside."

"There's still time. Ellen may—"

He scooped her up with one arm and started up the steps.

"Put me down!" She pushed at his shoulder.

"You're a good friend, Pest, but you don't know when to stop trying." He set her down by the door and yanked it open. "Now go inside. I'll see you tomorrow." He moved to the steps, leaped down and strode to the pung, wishing his conscience would let him break his word—wishing that he'd never given it.

"Let's go, Big Boy." He hopped to the seat, set the lantern between his feet to keep it safe, picked up the reins and clicked his tongue. The horses leaned into their harness, the runners broke free from the ice holding them and the pung lurched forward. He reined the team out to the road, then looked back over his shoulder across the field to the Hall house. Lamplight glowed in Ellen's window.

Probably planning her big society wedding. It was for sure she wasn't losing sleep because he'd held her in his arms this afternoon. It had meant nothing to her. And that was good. His stomach knotted. He urged the horses forward, then had them pick up their pace when they reached Main Street. He couldn't get back to camp fast enough to suit him.

Chapter Thirteen

Water slipped down the icicles gripping the edge of the roof, gathered into drops at the tips and fell. More drops formed. Fell. Ellen stared at the shimmering, quivering drops and worried the corner of her bottom lip with her teeth. The icicles had been melting all morning. And if the warmth continued...

"Not now, Lord. Please don't let the weather warm now. I need time to think of what to do." She stepped out of the sunshine pouring in her bedroom window, walked to the fireplace, then to her bed and on to her dressing room. She was pacing again.

She made herself stop, snatched the cold, damp cloth out of the washbowl and held it to her tired eyes. Again. She was fooling herself. Even if the deep snow kept Daniel in town longer, there was nothing she could do to change things. How did one revive a friendship that had died? Especially with someone who now found you repugnant.

The way he had looked at her before he turned away... A vision of Daniel standing beside the bonfire with the light flickering across his face floated against her eyelids. She blew out a breath, removed the cloth and opened her eyes. *The distaste on his face...*

She wrapped her arms about the tightness in her chest and went back to the window, looked at the gazebo. The deep snow that had fallen during the blizzard covered the conical roof that overhung the dark green garlands and the red bows whose long ties hung straight down the pillars. There was no wind fluttering them today. Her throat constricted. It had seemed when she and Daniel were working together on the decorations that things were improving between them. And then Harold Lodge had come to town. And now...now Daniel thought less of her than ever. The look on his face had made that clear. And she couldn't blame him. She winced, rubbed her temples with her fingertips.

Thankfully, Mr. Lodge was gone back to Buffalo. He and his threats with him! The man was insufferable! She frowned and let out a long sigh. It was odd that she had not found him so until he'd come to Pinewood. But then again, perhaps not. He didn't *strut* among the elite in Buffalo. Of course, he couldn't. It wouldn't be tolerated. They *all* thought their wealth made them superior to others. As did her parents. As had she.

Had? What did that mean? Was it she who had changed? Her breath snagged. Perhaps that was the answer to her change of heart about Mr. Lodge and the disagreement with her parents. Perhaps she was looking at people and things through a different prism since coming back to Pinewood and being with her old friends. Were her parents right last night? Had she made the wrong choice?

Be not high-minded, nor trust in uncertain riches, but in the living God... The Scripture Matthew Calvert had

quoted in church floated into her head. *Love...honesty...
peace...joy...whatever has virtue, is pure or lovely, these
are things the Bible says we are to think on and value.*

No. She had made the right choice. Hadn't she?

Movement caught her attention. She looked across
the field to the parsonage. Matthew Calvert was leaving
in his sleigh, no doubt paying another comfort call on a
sick parishioner. A preacher was almost as busy with the
sick as a doctor. She'd learned that when she'd tried to
win Matthew Calvert's affection. That had ended with
her fleeing to Buffalo when his wards took sick. It still
made her shudder to think of the illness he could bring
home. *Please keep Willa and her family healthy, Lord.*
She watched until Matthew was out of sight, then shifted
her gaze back to the parsonage. If Matthew was gone,
who would help Daniel cut the tree today? The tree! She
had to get decorations!

She shrugged out of her morning gown, opened the
wardrobe and scanned her day dresses. A rose barège
gown caught her eye, its only adornment faux-pearl buttons that secured the bodice from the neck to the point
at the waist. It was her plainest dress. And exactly what
she wanted. She slipped it on, grabbed her brown leather
boots off of the wardrobe floor and closed the doors.
What should she buy to adorn the tree? She couldn't ask
for help. The way news flew around the village, Joshua
and Sally's surprise would be ruined.

She peered into the mirror on her dressing table and
brushed her hair toward the back of her head, allowing
a few curls to dangle on her forehead and in front of her
ears. A few quick twists of the rest turned her long, way-
ward curls into a loose cluster at the crown of her head.
She pinned them in place, laced on her boots and went

back to the wardrobe for her velvet coat with its matching hood. It was too warm for her new cloak and bonnet.

She went back to the mirror and adjusted the hood and fluffed her curls. Should she see Daniel, she wanted to look her best. Not that it would matter.

"Give over now!" Daniel shoved aside the pigs that snorted and snuffled around his feet investigating every thrust of his shovel. "Go on, get out of here!" He swatted their round hams with the flat side of the shovel blade to no avail. The pigs merely grunted and crowded closer. Gluttonous beasts. Smiley's dinner leavings had been scant with most of the men gone. That would change now. If this thaw kept up, the men would soon be drifting back.

He leaned on the shovel handle, pulled off a glove and ran his finger under the high rolled collar of his gray sweater. The heavy shoveling in the sunshine was making him too warm. The wool was beginning to itch. His face tightened. It was certain the fine wool of Harold Lodge's coat and scarf wouldn't dare prickle his skin. *Pompous dandy!*

His snort rivaled those of the pigs. He clenched his jaw at the memory of Harold Lodge standing beside Ellen in church in all his finery while looking down his long thin nose at them all. And at the skating party, too. It had taken all of his self-control not to run up that creek bank and wipe the supercilious sneer off of his face! If it hadn't been for Ellen standing there holding Lodge's hand—

He tugged his glove back on, scooped up a shovelful of snow and tossed it atop the pile beside the path. The sun was climbing overhead and Smiley would be calling him in to dinner soon. Hopefully, Ellen and Lodge would linger over their meal, and he and Willa could get most of the decorations hung before Ellen even came to help. If it weren't for the tree...

He scowled at the small pine in the pung, pushed through the rutting pigs and attacked the snow with renewed vigor, trying to drive the thoughts of Ellen and her wealthy beau out of his head. If only he'd never held her in his arms... The clang of a poker striking the metal stove chimney drew him up short. Time to eat—if he could swallow.

He jammed his shovel in the pile at the edge of the path, tromped to the kitchen and kicked his boots against the door to rid them of snow. An icy drop off of an icicle hit his cheek and slid down to his neck. He wiped it off and ducked inside before another drop caught him.

Smiley glanced his way. "Looks like you could use some dryin' out."

"A little." He tugged his gloves off and shoved them behind the waistband on his pants. "Food smells good."

"Beans an' biscuits, is all. Grab a plate an' set yourself down. We're eatin' here." Smiley limped his way to the table by the stove, set the plate of biscuits he carried down beside a crock of butter and another of molasses. "Ain't no sense stokin' up the dinin' room stoves when there's only the four of us."

He stepped to the table, chose a chair close to the stove and stretched his legs out to dry his pants. "Four? Who's here?"

"Us an' Irish and Hans. Those two never left. But I figure the rest of the men will be trailin' in this afternoon an' tomorrow, does the warm weather hold."

The door to the dining room opened. A blast of cold,

stale air hit him. He looked up and nodded. "Hey, Irish... Hans."

"'Bout time you two got here." Smiley scowled and growled. "I was figurin' on throwin' your share out to the hogs."

The loggers grinned, grabbed plates and sat down. "Heard you come in late last night, Danny-boy-o."

"He misses us too much to stay avay, *ja?*"

"Irish mayhap, but not your ugly mug, Hans." Smiley punctuated his snarl by slamming a spoonful of beans onto the laughing German's plate, then served Irish and came to him. "You plannin' on eatin' beans out of your hand, Teamster?"

He grabbed a plate off the pile and held it up. The large metal spoon clanged against the tin, sent reverberations up his arm. A goodly portion of beans spilled onto the plate.

"I'm runnin' short on flour and sugar and some other things I'll need for when the men return." Smiley plunked the iron pot back on the stove. "I'll make a list, and you can go to town for supplies tomorrow. I don't wanna be caught short."

And I don't trust myself if I see that popinjay with Ellen again. His stomach knotted. He stared at the beans, wanted to throw them at something instead of eating them. He would not see Lodge at Willa's, but if he went shopping for the supplies—

"Bless *die* beans *und* biscuits, *Gott.*" Hans put four biscuits on his plate, smeared them with butter and ladled molasses over them.

Irish dug into his beans, his spoon scraping against the tin plate.

"Somethin' wrong with the food, now you been home eatin' your ma's cookin'?"

He looked up at Smiley's scowling face and shook his head. "The food's fine, Smiley. And Ma's in Syracuse. I've been eating my own cooking." He pulled up a grin. "It's what drove me back here early." He grabbed a biscuit, split it and buttered it. "The thing is, I came back from town last night and I have to deliver the tree I cut this morning to the parsonage today. I'll leave as soon as I'm through eating, but I won't have time to go to the mercantile, and I'd rather not go back tomorrow." He put the biscuit on his plate and drizzled molasses on it. "What about you, Irish? You and Hans have been here the whole time the rest of us were gone. What if I hitch up the pung in the morning and you go to town for the supplies? Does that suit you?"

"*Und* vat about me? Ve vere going to vork, *ja?*"

He looked over at Hans. "I'll work with you. If it's all right?"

The German nodded. "*Ja.* I've seen you vork." His broad face broke into a wide grin. "You almost as goot as me, *ja?*"

Irish let out a snort. "'Tis circles Danny-boy-o can work around you, you braggin' Deutschman."

Hans chuckled and pointed his fork at Irish. Molasses dripped off the piece of biscuit impaled on the tines. "*Und* he vould have tree chopped down before you make first cut, *ja?*"

The sound of boots thudding against the plank floor in the dining room broke through the laughter. He glanced up, braced himself for the blast of cold, stale air. The connecting door opened and two loggers strode into the kitchen. The stockier one grinned and elbowed his partner. "Told you we'd be in time for victuals, Joe."

"Not if I had me a shotgun, you wouldn't!" Smiley grumbled the threat and grabbed up the pot of beans. "How many more of the likes of you are out there?"

"None that we saw." The loggers shoved their hats and gloves in their pockets, grabbed plates, sat down and reached for the biscuits.

"There better not be." Smiley dumped a spoonful of beans on Scudder's plate, spilled another spoonful onto Joe's and slammed the pot back onto the stove. "This here kitchen is closed!"

So is my heart. No more encounters with Ellen, chance or otherwise. After I deliver and help decorate the tree, I'm coming back to camp to stay. It's time to shut off the memories and truly let her go.

"Good morning, Mrs. Roberts." Ellen smiled at the older woman standing outside her husband's apothecary shop. "It's a lovely day."

"Indeed it is, Ellen. The sun is so cheering I'm loath to stay inside." The woman gave a soft laugh and pulled her shawl more closely about her shoulders. "The truth is, I keep coming out here instead of helping Mr. Roberts."

Ellen glanced at the sleighs nestled up beside hitching posts and the people hurrying in and out of the stores. "The sunshine has the entire village out and about today."

"Indeed. I only hope the break in the weather holds on long enough to stop the spread of the influenza. Some of those stricken have been taken hard and are quite ill. Which reminds me, I'd best go in and help Mr. Roberts mix his elixir. It's much in demand."

A chill chased up her spine. Her chest tightened, pushed the air from her lungs. *Some of those stricken have been taken hard.* She pressed her hand against the squeezing pressure and watched Mrs. Roberts go into the apothecary shop. *Keep me well, Almighty God. Please keep me safe from illness.* She finally managed a breath, lifted her hems above the melting slush and hurried to Cargrave's.

The buzz of conversation in the mercantile covered the jangling of the bell. She stepped inside and turned to the wall of small glass mailboxes on her right.

"Good morning, Ellen."

She glanced up, smiled. "How are you, Mrs. Grant?"

"Quite well, thank you. Unlike many others. Susan Carver is the latest that has been taken with this grippe that's going around. She's not doing well." The woman shook her head. "And you, Ellen. How are you? I heard your beau has gone back to Buffalo."

Was it her imagination, or had the store quieted? "Yes. Mr. Lodge has several businesses he must oversee." She swept her gaze over the customers in the store, looking for signs of illness. "Please give your family my regards, Mrs. Grant. Now, if you'll excuse me, I must see about my mail."

The postmaster had a smile on his face when she reached the shelf in the middle of the mailboxes. She glanced at the missive he held out toward her. It was sealed with red wax and had her name and the village name written on it in precise script.

"Looks like another letter from another beau, Miss Ellen."

It was so quiet now, she heard a clinker fall through the fire grate in the heating stove. She ignored the postmaster's quest for information and took the letter. "Thank you, Mr. Hubble. I've been waiting for this to arrive." She turned and headed for the dry-goods shelves to see what she could find for decorations.

"—operations will be starting again soon. The loggers are headed back to camp. I saw a couple of them walking up the road on my way in." Helmut Hoffman pointed behind the counter. "The missus wants some of that rose water."

Allan Cargrave nodded, took a bottle off the shelf and set it on the counter with the other items. "Daniel went back late last night."

"That so?"

Daniel went back to camp last night? She frowned, strained to hear Allan Cargrave's answer above the general hum of people shopping.

"I heard horses passing the house last night, shortly after I'd retired. I looked out—"

"Your move, Albert."

Hush! She glared at the men playing checkers and moved to the notions table, where she could hear better.

"—that team of Belgians to the parsonage. Wasn't long before I heard the horses going by again, headed back for Main Street. When I left the house to come open the store this morning, the pung was gone."

Daniel was gone. And her chance to earn back his friendship, however small that chance might have been, was gone with him. A horrible feeling of hopelessness swept through her, leaving a hollowness in its wake. She stared at the yarns, thought of the tree. Daniel would never break his word. Whatever his reason for leaving town last night, he would come back with the Christmas tree for Joshua and Sally.

She picked up two skeins of red yarn, four yarn needles and several lengths of white and green ribbon and made her way to the counter.

"That all for today, Miss Ellen?" Allan Cargrave glanced at the items on the counter and opened his account book to her mother's name.

"No. I want two of those bags of dried apples. Have you any other dried fruits?"

"I've got some cranberries, but they're not dried."

"All right, I'll take a large sack of those, also. And don't charge them to my mother or father. I will pay."

Someone behind her coughed. She stiffened, reached into her purse and handed Mr. Cargrave a half eagle, then looked longingly at the door while he wrapped her purchases. The sooner she got home where it was safe, the better.

Chapter Fourteen

Ellen donned her old cloak, tugged on the kid gloves spotted with pine sap and picked up the package she'd left on the chair while she ate her dinner. The brown paper crackled. A grin curved her mouth. Isobel must be beside herself wondering what was in the package and why she was taking it with her. She clutched it close and stepped outside.

The sun had disappeared. Thick clouds blanketed the sky, dropped their burden of snow in a heavy fall of large fluffy flakes. She glanced toward the stable behind the parsonage. There was no pung in sight. She would be there when Daniel brought the tree.

The thought lent urgency to her steps. She hurried down the shoveled walk to the road, lifted her hems and crossed, the freezing slush crunching beneath her booted feet. The shortcut through the field with its deep snow partially melted from the morning's sun now sparkled with ice crystals. She turned and headed for the corner, hurried down Main Street to the church.

The still air in the small back room felt colder than outside. She laid her package beside the decorations stacked on the table, shivered and cast a longing look at the cold stove. She should have paid attention when Daniel built a fire. The next time she would. The truth struck and brought back that horrid hollow feeling. There would be no next time. Willa would not need their help after today. How could she hope to restore even a semblance of her old friendship with Daniel in one afternoon?

Another shiver took her. She jerked her thoughts back to her task, frowned down at the decorations. They couldn't hang them without Daniel's help, but it was too cold for her to wait for him here. Her gaze shifted to the corner. She snatched up the empty water bucket, filled it with leftover pine sprigs, tossed a few pinecones on the top and grabbed her package. A gust of wind hit when she opened the back door. Snow blew into the room.

She tugged the door closed behind her, ducked her head against the blowing snow and ran to the parsonage. She stomped the snow from her boots on her way up the steps and shoved open the kitchen door.

Willa turned from the stove, the baby in one arm, a large metal spoon in her other hand.

"S-sorry for not knocking, Willa." She shivered at the prickle of warmth on her face. "It's t-too cold out there for manners."

"I heard the wind come up. I hope we're not in for another blizzard. Mama came for a visit this morning and took Joshua and Sally home with her so I could decorate without interruption this afternoon—except for Mary, of course." Willa pointed the spoon at the package and bucket. "What are they for?"

"We can't h-hang any of the decorations until Daniel comes, so I thought perhaps we could decorate your fireplace mantel with these while we wait." She removed her cloak and hung it on a peg, shoved her gloves in the fold of the hood and rubbed her cold hands together.

"That's a wonderful idea, Ellen." Willa smiled and put down the spoon, lifted the baby up and cuddled her against her shoulder. "You go in the sitting room and start. I'll join you as soon as I go upstairs and change Mary."

She nodded and hurried to the sitting room fireplace. Warmth from the fire wrapped her in a cozy caress. She set the package aside, placed the bucket on the hearth and let her cold feet soak up the welcome heat.

On the mantel to her left, a large pewter candlestick sat beside a small wood box with crooked words carved into the lid. She frowned and shook her head. Such a crude box would never be displayed in her parents' home. Perhaps she could arrange the greens around it so it would not be noticed. She snatched a handful of sprigs from the bucket and turned toward the box.

For my new mama.

The words evoked a picture of Joshua's curly blond head bent over the box as he carved the rough letters with his pocketknife. She stared at the sentiment on the lid, suddenly aware of the love revealed by those uneven words. Her throat tightened. No wonder Willa displayed the box. She placed a few of the greens around the candle's base, tucked more between it and the box, careful not to hide it, then snatched a few pinecones from the bucket, nestled them into the greens and stepped back.

It looked even better than she had pictured. She smiled at the thought of Willa's pleasure, grabbed another handful of sprigs and turned to the right. A matching candlestick stood beside a small framed piece of muslin bearing the message, *I love my new mama* in a child's uneven stitches worked in blue needlepoint wool. A disreputable looking cat worked in yellow wool stood guard over the name Sally at the bottom. She smiled and ran her fingertip over the cat's big, lopsided ears.

Can you put a price on the joy that fills you when you hold your baby or receive a hug from your child?

Or gifts like these? Perhaps she hadn't given motherhood enough consideration. She glanced down at the empty cradle on the hearth, pictured Mary's sweet baby face surrounded by her soft auburn curls. What would it be like to bear a child who was part you and part your husband? Mr. Cuthbert's image intruded into her musings. She stiffened, frowned. What was she thinking! She had no inclination to bear Earl Cuthbert's child. Besides, motherhood was different among society women. They had nannies who cared for their children until they sent them away to school.

She turned her attention back to the mantel and arranged the pine sprigs and cones she held around the needlepoint and candle, then shifted her gaze toward the carved horse at the mantel's center. The horse stood with its head high, its ears pricked forward, an alert wariness in every line of its beautifully carved body. Daniel's wedding gift. Her face tightened. Willa's mantel display was a testimony of people who loved her. What would she display on her sitting room mantel—the most expensive ornaments she could find to best those of the other members of the elite, and a carved muskrat that would be a constant reminder of Daniel's disdain?

That terrible feeling of emptiness returned. She took a breath and closed her eyes. *Please, Lord—*

"Where do you want me to put these things, Pest? There's more for me to bring in."

Her heart leaped into her throat. She whirled, her long skirts billowing out around her. Daniel was standing in the doorway with his arms full of decorations, staring at her, his green eyes dark and smoky. He looked…different. Her breath caught. She lifted her hand to press against a sudden throbbing at the base of her throat and tried to speak but was held mute by an odd shyness she'd never before experienced.

He took an audible breath, jerked his gaze away and nodded toward the hearth. "Your skirt is too close to that fire. You'd best step away, unless you want your gown to burst into flames."

No. He was the same. Still judging her to be a spoiled, incompetent bit of fluff despite the help she'd given Willa. Her eyes stung with a rush of tears. She blinked and looked down. Her hem had landed mere inches from the hot coals when she turned. She yanked it out of danger and shook off the ashes clinging to it. "Willa's upstairs tending the baby."

He gave a curt nod, cleared his throat. "Where should I put—"

"Daniel! I thought I heard your voice." Willa swept into the room, crossed to the hearth and laid Mary in the cradle. "You can put those decorations on the floor and then I'll show you where I want to hang them." Willa gave the cradle a gentle push to start it rocking and straightened. "Oh, my! The mantel looks beautiful, Ellen!"

"Thank you, but—"

"Willa, I'm home!" Boots thumped against the floor in the hall.

"We're in the sitting room, Matthew." Willa spun about and hurried toward the doorway.

Envy stabbed her at the happy look on Willa's face, the eagerness in her friend's steps. Movement drew her attention. Daniel was putting the decorations down on the floor, his jaw taut, the muscle jumping. So much for any thought of trying to regain his friendship. She blinked her eyes, pasted a smile on her face and added greens around the horse's legs.

"That looks very festive, Ellen." Matthew aimed a warm smile her way, then shifted his gaze across the room. "Hey, Daniel. Do you want some help hacking the limbs off of that tree in the pung?"

"A tree?" Willa frowned, looked at Daniel. "Why did you bring a tree? We don't need any more greens."

"Ask Musquash. It was her idea."

He needn't growl! She lifted her chin. "It's for a Christmas tree. I thought Joshua and Sally might like one. I should have asked, but—"

"Ellen!" Willa rushed over and gave her a fierce hug. "I've heard about Christmas trees, but I never thought to have one. Joshua and Sally will love it!" Willa stepped back, her eyes clouded. "But how will we decorate it? I've nothing—"

She sighed out her relief. "I've brought some things to make decorations."

"Then that's settled." Matthew stepped over and clapped Daniel on the shoulder. "Let's go get that tree."

Daniel butted the second crosspiece against the full-length board, hefted his ax and drove the nails into the tree trunk. "That's it. I think these boards are long enough the tree should stand without toppling over."

Matthew grinned down at him. "You think?"

"We'll know soon enough." He returned Matthew's grin, laid down his ax and motioned to the top of the tree. "You get that end—it prickles."

"Thank you."

"My pleasure." He chuckled, grabbed hold of the tree trunk behind the base he'd nailed to it and backed to the corner, careful to keep his gaze from where Ellen sat working with white paper and scissors. The earlier glimpse of her by the fire, her blue eyes soft and warm, her cheeks as pink as the dress she wore, still lingered. He knelt and set the base on the floor, settled back on his heels. "Is it straight?"

"Yes. Oh, it's wonderful! Look at the cluster of pinecones at the top. I can't wait to see it decorated!" Willa set the dried apples she was stringing on red yarn aside, rose from her chair and gave Ellen a quick hug. "And, as it was your idea, you must place the first ornament."

"No, Willa. Truly. The tree is for—"

"You've no choice, Ellen." Matthew's deep voice hushed the argument. "I agree with Willa. You must have the honor of placing the first ornament."

"But all I have ready is this star for the top, and I can't reach that high, Matthew. You or Daniel—" Ellen looked his way. His pulse kicked.

"Daniel will fetch you a chair to stand on and make certain you don't fall. Won't you, Daniel?"

He shot Willa a look. She smiled. Matthew grinned. Obviously, Willa had been confiding her matchmaking scheme to her husband. He stifled a refusal, grabbed the chair from the writing desk and swung it into place in front of the tree. "Let's get this done, Musquash."

She stiffened, picked up a large white paper star with

a white ribbon threaded through the middle and marched to the chair. She looked askance at the height of the seat. "How am I—"

"Like this." He stepped behind her, grabbed her waist and lifted her to the chair. She leaned forward, and he tightened his grip, his arms aching with his effort not to draw her close. He fixed his gaze on the star she stretched out toward the top of the tree, watched as she slid the loop of ribbon at the back of the star down over the topmost branch, then pulled the ends that dangled from slots in the front snug and tied them in a bow. "There. That should hold it in place." She adjusted the dangling ribbon ties down over the top branches. "Does that look all right?"

"It's perfect."

He wasn't at all sure Willa was talking about the star. Ellen straightened, turned and looked down at him.

"Ready?" His voice sounded like he had a mouth full of gravel. He frowned, tightened his grip. Ellen leaned into his hold and placed her hands on his shoulders. His heart thudded. He lifted her down, then made himself let go of her. The soft sound of her footsteps walking away tore at him as he carried the chair back to the desk. "What's next?"

"This. I need to help Ellen."

He looked at the dried apple slices and cranberries on the red yarn threaded through the needle Willa held out to him. There was a *long* string of bare yarn left. He scowled. "Look, Pest, I've done everything you've asked but—"

"It's for Joshua and Sally."

Matthew chuckled and held up the string of apples

he was working on. "You might as well give in gracefully, Daniel."

He glanced at the only empty chair—the one beside Ellen—and glared at Matthew. He didn't feel like giving in, gracefully or otherwise. He felt like punching something. "You condone blackmail, do you?"

"Only when it profits those I care about."

Matthew's smile was as irritating as Willa's. Daniel strode across the room, took the needle and plunked down in the chair, acutely aware of Ellen sitting beside him tying loops of red and green ribbons to the stars and angels Willa was cutting from white paper.

He shoved the needle into a dried apple slice, added three cranberries the way Matthew was doing, impaled another slice and glanced at the window. Snow was falling so fast it looked like a white curtain. He'd have to be leaving for camp soon. Ellen moved, and he caught a hint of the flower scent she wore. He'd probably smell it all night!

He shifted as far away from her as possible, grabbed apple slices and cranberries and threaded them as if his life depended on it. His sanity surely did.

Ellen tossed the *Godey's Lady's Book* magazine aside, rose and walked to the hearth. The evening was endless. There was nothing to do. No more decorations to plan.

"The magazine does not interest you?"

She looked at her mother, gave a dismissive wave of her hand. "I find the articles…bland."

"You are restless, Ellen." Her father turned a page, then looked up from the book he was reading. "I think you are missing your entertainments."

"Perhaps you're right, Father. If I were in Buffalo,

I would be at the theater or opera, or at a dinner party, or—" She stopped, surprised to find the list held no allure.

"Or attending a political function on Mr. Cuthbert's arm?" Her mother laughed, picked up the magazine and thumbed through the pages. "I saw a lovely dress in the latest Parisian fashion that would be perfect for such an occasion...."

Ellen nodded and looked down at the fire. Her parents had gotten over their irritation with her as soon as she'd received Mr. Cuthbert's letter today assuring her of his coming visit. Their agenda was again moving forward, and they were pleased. Did her feelings count for nothing? She glanced toward the window, sighed and fiddled with the satin roses clustered at her waist. *Will Daniel be back in Pinewood for Christmas? Will I see him before—*

"—I hope he is not too ill to come before Christmas."

"He's not ill."

Her father put down his book and looked up at her. "I thought that's what he wrote you in his letter?"

He'd been speaking of Mr. Cuthbert! She nodded and smiled to cover her error. "And you are right, Father. I meant Mr. Cuthbert is not ill *now.* He is already on the mend. His visit will only be delayed a few days."

"Here it is."

Her mother came to stand beside her and pointed at a picture in the magazine. Ellen looked at the dress, skimmed her gaze over the tiered lace of the off-the-shoulders bodice trimmed with a large silk rose where it met between the model's breast, the filmy puffs of fabric that formed the sleeves and the exaggerated fullness of the skirt that fell to the floor in two ribbon- and flower-trimmed ruffles from the deep V point at the narrow waist. "It's lovely, Mother. But please don't trouble yourself to make it for me. I'm tired of silks and satins and laces and flounces and frills."

"Why, Ellen!"

Her mother's shock was no greater than her own. "It's true, Mother. I find I much prefer the simpler designs of the two new dresses you've made me. They're…elegant. And very comfortable."

Her mother studied her for a moment, then nodded. "I suppose it's not surprising you would prefer the high collar and heavier fabric during the cold weather. Still, if you attend a society event or political gathering as Mr. Cuthbert's betrothed this winter, you must be stylish, Ellen." Her mother took a step back and narrowed her gaze on her. "With the lovely way you hold your head, elegance does suit you. And it could set you apart…draw every eye. Hmm…" Her mother looked down at the magazine and thumbed through the pages as she resumed her seat on the settee. "I could make an evening dress of pearl-blue velvet, with a cascade of lavender silk flowers…."

And I will again become an ornament with no purpose but to draw the envy of others to my escort. She pressed her lips together lest she speak the thought aloud and rekindle her parents' displeasure.

The window drew her like a magnet. She left the fire and went to stand looking through the snow toward the parsonage and the gazebo. For a few days she had felt useful, needed…appreciated for something more than her appearance. Even by Daniel. There had been a grudging respect for her work underlying his disdain. Perhaps there was a chance after all…. The hope refused to die.

She wrapped her arms about herself and lifted her

gaze above the parsonage to the hill that sheltered the camp where Daniel worked and lived. *I want so much to be friends with Daniel again, Lord. I miss his friendship. Please help me find a way.*

Sleep wouldn't come. Daniel swung his legs over the edge of the cot, tugged the blanket around his shoulders and rose. Every time he closed his eyes, he remembered the feel of Ellen in his arms, the way she had looked standing by the fire or decorating the tree. On the heels of those images came ones of her and Harold Lodge walking down the aisle in church, singing side by side or standing on the creek bank. His mind refused to stop dredging up the painful images.

He grabbed a chunk of wood out of the wood box, opened the door on the stove and tossed it inside. Smoke puffed out, stung his nose and eyes. He closed the door, waved the smoke away and looked around the small sloped-roof shed.

A cot with a straw tick and blankets…a chipped pitcher and washbowl…a heating stove with an iron kettle and pot…and a trunk that held his clothes. None of it his, save the trunk and clothes. His face tightened. Add in a small log cabin for his ma's use and a wage that provided food and a bit extra for her, and it was not much to show for twelve years of hard work. Well, that was over.

Twelve years ago he had resigned his counting-house apprenticeship and buried his dream of making himself into a man worthy of Ellen's love in a grave along with his father. He had turned from that grave, marched to the Townsend lumber camp and announced that he was there to take his pa's place. He'd had no choice. There had been no other way he could provide a home for his mother.

But he had a choice now. His mother was in Syracuse caring for Aunt Ruth, and she'd never come home and leave her sister in need. The log cabin was empty. And so was his heart. The remnant of the dream, the hope he had so stubbornly, *foolishly* clung to, had died with Harold Lodge's arrival and Ellen's imminent betrothal.

He stepped to the trunk, careful not to catch a sliver off of the plank floor with his stocking-clad feet, squatted and shoved his hand beneath the clothes. His fingers touched the rough wool yarn, felt the stitches knitted by his mother. He closed his hand and withdrew it, then went back to stand by the stove.

The hat was worn, frayed. And all he had left of his father. He stared at the small loop of gray yarn near the crown where a stitch had been pulled loose by a tree branch, most likely on the day of the accident when his father had been killed by a rotted tree that turned into a spinner. It had to have been that day, else his mother would have mended it. She was always careful to keep their clothes in good repair.

He touched the loop, worked at pulling in a breath. "I promised you I'd take care of Ma, and I've kept my word, Pa. You don't need to be concerned. I'll see to it that Ma's all right. But I've got to leave Pinewood."

He opened the hat's brim he held clutched tight and stared at the coins he'd set aside against any unexpected need. It wasn't enough. What he had left in the bank he would need to give his mother to keep her until he could find other work—maybe on one of those big ships that plied the Great Lakes. But he would be staying in camp now, and with his mother gone, he wouldn't have to buy any food or other provisions. He should be able to save enough to leave in a few weeks.

Leave Pinewood and all he loved. The thought took him like a kick in the gut. But it was the only answer. His love for Ellen would never die as long as he stayed where he would occasionally see her, where every place he went or looked, memories lurked and tore at him. He closed the hat over the coins, moved back to the trunk and tucked it away. *A few weeks...*

He stepped to the small window and stared out at the night, lifted his gaze to the pines standing like dark shadows against the falling snow and blew out a breath to ease the tautness in his chest. "Thy will be done, O Lord. Thy will be done."

Chapter Fifteen

"There, all hitched and ready to go, Big Girl." Daniel smoothed down the mare's mane. "Irish will be taking you to town today, so you go easy, you hear?" The Belgian huffed out a breath, shook her head.

"Don't play ignorant with me." Daniel laughed and stroked her nose, cast another look at the sky. The heavy cloud cover did not look promising.

He tromped to the kitchen, kicked his caulked boots free of snow and went inside.

"'Bout time you come in. I was thinkin' you supposed I'd keep this food hot all day." Smiley threw a scowl his way, grabbed the pot off the stove and slapped a heaping mound of oatmeal onto his plate.

He nodded his thanks, then looked at Irish. "The pung's hitched. I threw Big Girl's blanket into the back in case the temperature takes a dip. The sky's heavy." He yanked off his hat and gloves, shoved them in his jacket pockets and took a seat. Steam rose from the oatmeal. He spooned on butter, made a small hollow in the top of the pile and filled it with molasses. Hot coffee splashed into his cup, its fragrant steam tantalizing his nose.

Scudder held his cup up to Smiley for a refill. "If it comes on to snow again, the hicks will stay in town. Looks like we'll be the only ones cutting today."

"*Ja.* It be best if ve vork close by to each other."

"Me an' Scudder were planning to start cutting over by the creek where we were when the snow caught us." Joe scooped up the last of his oatmeal, took a swallow of coffee and looked his way. "Can you get the sledge in there, Daniel?"

"No, the snow will be too deep in that cut. But I won't be hauling logs without my team. And Big Boy can haul the tool cart in without a problem." He ate another spoonful of oatmeal and buttered a biscuit. "I meant to tell you, Irish, it's good to handle Big Girl gently. She's got a soft mouth and tends to fight the rein when you keep too tight a hold on her."

"I'll remember that, Danny-boy-o." The lanky Irishman looked around the table and grinned. "An' I'll be rememberin' the lot of you workin' downin' timber while I'm ridin' to town an' back at my ease."

Joe drained his cup, stood and clapped Irish on the shoulder. "Well, enjoy your 'ease' while you can, *boy-o,* 'cause you'll be back swinging an ax tomorrow."

Daniel cast a glance toward the window and slanted his lips in a grin. "Those of us who are actually going to *work* today had best get going. It's getting light out there."

Irish tipped his chair onto its back legs, crossed his hands over his belly and grinned. "May the good Lord rest His hand o' blessin' on you all."

"*Ja. Und* on you."

Chairs scraped against the floor as Hans, Scudder and Joe shoved away from the table. Daniel tugged on his hat and gloves, grabbed a couple of biscuits, wiped them in the molasses left on his plate and followed them out the door.

"Here you are, Big Girl." He gave the mare a biscuit, patted her mane and moved on. "Here you go, Big Boy." He fed the second biscuit to the Belgian, stepped up to his seat and took up the reins. Joe and Scudder and Hans climbed onto the cart and found seats among the tools, chains and coiled ropes.

"Let's go, Big Boy!" He clicked his tongue and the horse leaned into the harness. The runners on the cart skittered onto the logging road that wound through the forest. He splayed his legs and braced his feet against the front board to maintain his balance as they rocked over hummocks of frozen snow, released his breath in small gray clouds that disappeared behind him.

The growing daylight filtering through the trees revealed the deep cut ahead. "Haw, Big Boy!" The horse turned left, plodded along the trampled path at the edge of the iced-over creek. Light poured into the cleared area where they'd already downed timber. "Whoa."

The men climbed down from the cart, their caulks clattering against the wood, reached into the box and pulled out the tools they needed. "Joe and I will be cutting over by the creek."

He nodded to Scudder, hauled out his ax, some wedges and two shovels. Hans hefted the crosscut saw so the flat of the blade lay against his shoulder, grabbed his ax in his other hand and trudged to a huge pine at the edge of the clearing.

They worked in silence, the only sounds the soughing of the rising wind through the branches of the pines and the swish of the shovel blades against the snow as they each cleared an area to stand in on opposite sides of the tree.

"Ve fell him there, *ja?*"

He glanced in the direction Hans pointed, nodded and picked up his ax. He sank the blade deep in the tree trunk and pulled it free. Hans's ax blade flashed, hit exactly where his left off. They swung again and again, wood chips flying out to litter the ground as each picked up the rhythm of the other's strokes. The notch that would dictate the direction of the tree's fall deepened.

Craaack!

"Timber!"

Daniel pivoted, his heart leaping into his throat. The warning yell was supposed to come before a tree started falling.

Swish, thud!

The ground trembled beneath his feet.

"Help! Help!"

He gripped his ax and started running toward the creek, Hans's boots thudding against the snow behind him. Scudder lay on the ground beside the trunk of the fallen pine.

"Joe's in the creek!"

He veered left at the wave of Scudder's arm, his heart lurching at the sight of the dark pool of flowing water in the broken ice beneath the fallen tree. "Joe! Where—"

He caught a glimpse of the logger's arm flailing around, dropped his ax on the ice, jumped into the thigh-deep frigid water and dropped to his knees. Icy coldness soaked into his clothes and covered his chest, stealing his breath. He grabbed Joe's arm, followed it under the trunk with his hands, found a broken branch that had snagged the back of the logger's sweater and yanked it free. Cold air seared his lungs. He pulled Joe's torso toward him as far as he was able, lifted the logger's head out of the water and held him as he coughed and sputtered.

"I can't p-pull you any farther, Joe. Where are you c-caught?" He tried to stop them, but his teeth chattered like an angry squirrel. Shivers shook his body.

"F-foot."

He looked toward Hans on the bank, standing ready to help. "His f-foot's caught under the trunk. Can Scudder h-help you saw?"

"*Ja,* he's pinned by a branch. I get him free!"

He nodded, then knelt in the water holding Joe's head and listening to the thunk of Hans's ax while he studied the situation. Thankfully, the fallen tree spanned the creek, the top resting on the higher far bank. That, and the large limb that had broken the ice, held the tree up at an angle, else Joe would have been crushed.

His feet and legs went numb. He tried to wiggle his toes but couldn't tell if they moved. How much longer would Joe be able to keep breathing?

The chopping stopped. Hans and Scudder came running, the crosscut saw whipping wildly in the air between them. "You'll n-need chocks!"

Scudder spun at his call, ran to the base of the tree, snatched up the chocks and raced back.

"P-put them under this side of the l-log so it can't drop on Joe or r-roll back when it's cut. The bank will hold up th-that end."

Scudder dropped to his knees on the ice and shoved the chocks in place.

He looked at Hans. "Put skids on th-that side, then get Big Boy and wrap the chain around the tr-trunk. He'll pull it off when it's c-cut. Pivot it on that b-bank." He nodded toward the far side.

"Ja!" Hans and Scudder raced toward their cutting site.

His body felt like a block of ice, his hands stiff and numb. He fixed his gaze on them to be sure he still held Joe's head and prayed. He'd never heard anything as beautiful as the thud of Big Boy's hoofs trotting toward them.

Hans stopped the horse on the bank, dragged the chain out onto the ice and shoved it beneath the log to Scudder, who pulled it through, then tossed it over the top so Hans could hook it. Two quick thrusts and the skid logs were in place.

The numbness crept up his chest and arms. He kept his eyes on Joe while Hans and Scudder sawed the log from its heavy base on the bank. The ice creaked, started to crack when the log was cut through and the chocks took its weight. *It was now or too late.* "Hup! Hup!" The Belgian leaned into his harness at his call. The log slid onto the skids. "Whoa!"

Hans dug Joe's foot free of the impacted snow that imprisoned it, and Scudder pulled his partner onto the bank.

Daniel forced his lungs to suck in air. He tried to pull himself onto the ice but his body wouldn't obey. Hans grabbed him under the armpits and hauled him from the water, yanked off his sodden sweater, then tugged off his own dry one and slipped it onto his cold, wet torso. Scudder was doing the same for Joe.

He lay on the snow shivering and shaking, fighting to stay awake while Hans ran and unhitched Big Boy. The cold overwhelmed him. His eyes closed. Hoofs thudded and the ground beneath him trembled. His body jerked. He forced his eyes open, watched the German pull his soaked boots and socks off but felt nothing but the tugs. And then Hans lifted him, and tossed him across Big Boy's broad back like a bag of grain. Joe was plopped into place beside him, and the horse's thick blanket was thrown over them.

"Hup...hup..."

The Belgian's muscles rippled beneath him. The warmth of the horse's huge body seeped into him. And then the darkness came and all awareness ceased.

Chapter Sixteen

Daniel tugged the blanket closer around him and bent forward, convulsed by the force of his cough. He'd tried to hide how poor he felt, but with the coughing and the shivers that shook him it was a losing battle. And the pain in his head that stabbed deeper every time he coughed wasn't helping matters.

"You're getting worse, Daniel. You need some proper care." Doc Palmer frowned and closed his black bag. "Get your jacket on. I'm taking you back to town with me."

"No p-point, Doc." He coughed again, winced. "Ma's g-gone."

"I know that! I'm taking you to Willa."

"No." He would have shook his head for emphasis, but it hurt too much.

The doctor scowled, snatched his jacket from where it lay on the chest and tossed it on the bed. "Do you want to make Willa come all the way out here to the camp to get you? You know she will once she learns you're sick." The doctor fixed him with a look and tossed his gloves, hat and scarf on top of his jacket. "And I intend to tell her as soon as I get back to town, should you force my hand."

"Th-that's blackm-mail."

"You're right. But I've no wish to face Willa if she learns of your illness from someone else." The doctor gave him another look. "Well? The choice is yours, Daniel. But you know I'm right. You'll be going to Willa's one way or the other."

He tried to scowl, but it took too much effort. Doc Palmer was right. He might as well yield and save Willa the trouble of a trip. Because she *would* come after him. He released his death grip on the blanket and reached for his jacket while goose pimples raised on his flesh. "Get my b-boots. They're by the s-stove."

Winter had returned with a vengeance. It was cold and snowy and blustery. Ellen donned her cloak and bonnet, grabbed her muff and stepped outside. A gust of wind almost took her off her feet. She tugged the door shut, shoved one gloved hand in her muff, grabbed hold of her bonnet brim with the other and hurried down the shoveled walk to the road.

The garlands on the gazebo were swinging wildly, the red bows fluttering and their tails snapping in the wind. Snow blew off the conical roof in a white, swirling cloud, the icy particles stinging the side of her face. She turned the corner, glanced across Main Street at the Sheffield House with its windows aglow with warm, inviting lantern light and quickened her steps. She would call on Sophia as she'd promised. But first she'd go to Cargrave's and check the mail. Mr. Cuthbert might have sent her notice of the day of his arrival.

The footing was treacherous. The wind punishing.

She crossed the road, climbed the steps and hurried across the walkway, ducked into Cargrave's recessed entrance and bumped into someone coming out of the store. "Oh, I'm sorry!" She looked up.

"Ellen! How nice to bump into you, dear." Sophia Sheffield laughed, reached up and pulled the scarf wound about her neck closer. "I've been expecting you to call, but I know you've been helping Willa. And you are probably busy now making plans for your wedding to Mr. Lodge. Has a date been set?"

She shook her head, sending the snow clinging to the fur on her bonnet flying. "I refused Mr. Lodge." She brushed back the curls on her forehead and met the older woman's gaze.

"Should I offer my condolences, dear?"

"Only to my parents." The truth blurted out. Sophia always had that effect on her. She gave a little shrug. "Mother and Father were not pleased."

"I'm sure they were disappointed for you, dear."

"Perhaps, but there was no reason for them to be. The choice was mine. Anyway, it's of no importance. They are now looking forward to the arrival of Mr. Cuthbert—my other beau."

"Well, gracious, the people of this village are behind in the news. This storm is interfering with our...visiting."

"Visiting?" She laughed at Sophia's word choice. "There was nothing to *visit* about. You are the first person I've told."

"Hmm, then I must get this straight." Sophia's eyes twinkled at her. "You refused Mr. Lodge because Mr. Cuthbert is the man you have chosen to wed? You must be excited, waiting for his arrival."

She stared at Sophia, shocked to silence by the truth

that hit her at the comment. She wasn't at all excited about Mr. Cuthbert's coming visit. In truth, she had been relieved at the delay.

"Is something wrong, Ellen? You look— Oh, dear." Sophia's gaze shifted, her eyes clouded. "I hadn't heard any of Willa's family was ill."

"They're not." She turned, stared at the black buggy fastened onto runners standing by the parsonage's side porch and felt a chill that had nothing to do with the cold or the wind.

Ellen forced her feet to move down the steps to the road. She lifted her hems and picked her way over the ruts, stopped and stared at the black buggy. The old terror washed over her. Her heart thudded. Her breath shortened. She stepped over the piled snow at the edge of the road onto the walkway and forced her feet to carry her to the porch.

The wreath they'd made hung on the door, the festive red bow mocking the fear that filled her. She swallowed hard and closed her eyes. *Help me, Lord. Please help me.* She forced a breath into her constricted chest, opened her eyes and knocked. *Please, Lord. Please—*

The door opened and Joshua stood staring up at her, Sally standing beside him. *It was Willa.* Panic surged. She closed her eyes, tried to breathe.

"*Ellen!* What are you doing here? I mean—come in."

She opened her eyes and stared at Willa standing at the base of the stairs with a bowl in her hand. Tears filmed her eyes. "I saw the doctor's buggy and I thought— I thought you—" Her voice broke.

"Oh, Ellen…" Willa set the bowl on a table and hurried to her, pulled her inside and into a fierce hug. "I'm sorry you were so frightened. I'm fine. We're all fine. Truly. See?"

She blinked her eyes, glanced from Willa to Joshua and Sally, who were headed down the hallway toward the kitchen. "But Dr. Palmer—"

Willa's face sobered. "It's Daniel, Ellen. He's ill, and his mother is in Syracuse, so Dr. Palmer brought him here to me. He and Matthew are upstairs with him now, getting him settled in."

"Daniel?" His name came out a disbelieving breath. She shook her head. "Daniel is never sick."

"I know. But he jumped into a creek to save another logger from drowning, and he's taken a very bad cold. Dr. Palmer is afraid it will turn into pneumonia."

"Pneumonia?" Something hard and unforgiving wrapped itself around her throat and chest in tight bands. Willa's hands closed on her shoulders, gave her a little shake.

"Are you all right, Ellen?"

She nodded, tried to hold at bay all the dire thoughts rushing into her head.

"Ellen, look at me."

She opened her eyes, gazed into Willa's blue-green ones.

"I'm sorry to have to rush, but I need to take this hot broth upstairs. Dr. Palmer wants Daniel to have something to warm him after the cold ride in from camp. You go home and I will keep you informed on Daniel's condition." Willa turned and picked up the bowl.

"No." She could hardly get the word past the fear squeezing her throat. She yanked the ties and pulled off her bonnet, hung it on a peg with her muff before she could change her mind.

Willa gaped. "What do you mean, no? What are you doing?"

"I mean I'm not going home." She removed her cloak, hung it on the peg with her muff and bonnet. "You have a husband, two children and a new baby. What will they do if you take ill?" She reached out and took the bowl from Willa. "I will take care of Daniel. You need to stay out of his room lest you take his cold."

"Ellen!" Willa stared, shock written all over her face. She narrowed her eyes and peered closely at her. "Are you certain?"

"Yes." The odd thing was, now that she'd made the declaration, she truly was certain it was what she wanted to do. But that didn't take away the fear. "You take care of your family. I will take care of Daniel." She lifted her hems with her free hand and started up the stairs, her shaking making the soup quiver in the bowl.

"Ellen, wait!" Willa rushed up the stairs, reached in her pocket and pulled out a small piece of folded cheese-cloth. "There are pieces of gingerroot in here. Chew on them while you tend Daniel. It will help to keep you from taking the cold." Willa tucked the small packet into her hand holding her skirt and gave it a squeeze. "Thank you for what you are doing, Ellen. Turn right at the top of the stairs. Daniel is in the bedroom on the left of the hall."

There was the warmth of old friendship, gratitude and a new look of respect in Willa's eyes. It fueled her determination. She nodded, finished climbing the stairs and walked down the hall.

The knock drew his gaze. Daniel watched Matthew walk to the door and pull it open. He dreaded facing Willa. She'd—

"Why, Ellen!" Matthew took a step back.

He caught a glimpse of blond curls above a pale face. *"Ellen?"* Shock brought her name bursting from his mouth. A cough took him. He hunched forward, unable to quell the spasm.

"Well, young lady, I'm surprised to see you here." Dr. Palmer turned to face the doorway. "Where's Willa?"

That's what he wanted to know. He tried to stop coughing in order to hear Ellen's answer to the question. His heart all but stopped when she stepped into the bedroom, her long skirts whispering against the floor.

"Willa is downstairs, Doctor. I've brought the broth. I am going to care for Daniel."

What? He was so startled he stopped coughing. "No!"

She lifted her chin, looked at him. "I've never known you to be selfish, Daniel. Willa has a family to care for. It would not do for her to take your cold and become ill."

She'd left him no argument. He stared at her, noted the slight quiver at the corner of her lips. She might fool the others, but he knew she was afraid. He nodded. "N-nor y-you." He pushed himself into a sitting position, angered by how much effort it took. Chills coursed up and down his spine at the movement. He looked at Matthew. "Take me h-home."

Matthew shook his head. "I can't do that, Daniel. There's no one to care for you there." He turned toward Ellen. "Thank you for your offer to care for Daniel in Willa's stead, Ellen. It's most generous and kind of you. I will, of course, be here to help Daniel with his personal needs."

"That's settled then."

He glared at the doctor. He might as well not even be in the room! He scowled, wanting to protest, to get up and walk out, but he was too weak. He'd needed Matthew's help to climb the stairs, and he'd never make it out of the house by himself. And he for sure didn't want to fall on his face in front of Ellen.

"All right, Ellen. Here are your instructions." Dr. Palmer nodded toward the bowl she held. "Get that broth down him while it's hot. I've got Bertha boiling water for him to drink. He'll need lots of fluids should he get fevered. Get as much water in him as you can. He's to stay in bed and remain well covered. I don't want him to get chilled. If his head hurts or he gets fevered, put cold cloths on his forehead. That's about it. I'll leave instructions for his meals with Willa. Oh, yes, pneumonia is a chancy thing. I don't want him left alone." The doctor picked up his black bag and headed for the door. "I'll drop by tomorrow to see how he's doing."

"Thank you again for taking over the nursing chores for Willa, Ellen. I'll come back later and help settle Daniel for the night." Matthew smiled and followed the doctor from the room.

Silence.

He leaned back against the headboard, shivering and aching and wishing he were anywhere but here alone with Ellen. Even in his weak, sick condition the sight of her made his heart pound and his pulse race. He had the irrational wish that it was the sickness causing those things. He set his mind not to cough and cleared his throat. "I know h-how—" he frowned and tried to stop the chills that made his teeth chatter "—frightened you are of b-being around sickness. I'm s-sorry—"

She stiffened and moved toward the bed. "I don't want to discuss Walker or my fear, Daniel. I've made my decision. Now, you need to eat this broth while it's hot."

He gathered his will and reached for the bowl. His hands shook in spite of his best effort to stop them.

She shook her head and picked up the spoon, leaned toward him.

He couldn't even look away. He opened his mouth and accepted the broth.

"Well, *this* is different. It's always been you taking care of me."

His heart jolted when she smiled. Memories swarmed. He stopped worrying about getting pneumonia. Her presence would probably be the end of him.

Chapter Seventeen

"This is utter foolishness! Your father and I forbid it!"

Ellen looked up as her mother swept through the bedroom door, then returned to her task. She'd witnessed the look that had flashed between her parents downstairs and had been sure her mother would follow her to try and talk her out of her plans. Still, she had hoped she was wrong. "I'm sorry you and Father disapprove, Mother." She added her soap and cream to the other items already in her small toiletry box and fastened the latch. "I dislike going against your wishes, but Daniel is ill, and Willa needs my help. I'm going."

"Bertha can—"

"Bertha has her hands full already. And she will be even busier preparing special meals for Daniel." *And Daniel is too ill to be left alone.* The fear gripped her anew. She set the small box on her bed, folded her dressing gown and laid it on top of the clothes she'd packed inside of the large bag already there. *Her slippers.* She grabbed them off the floor, placed them in the bag and snapped the latch shut.

"Ellen, think of what you are doing. What you are

risking! All that you have dreamed of for so long is at stake. What if Mr. Cuthbert arrives while you are at Willa's caring for another man?"

"A *friend,* Mother. Daniel is a friend." *At least, he was until you and Father put a stop to our friendship.*

"He's still a man, Ellen. Think of your reputation!"

"My *reputation,* Mother?" She straightened, looked her mother in the eyes and took a deep breath. "Of all the people in Pinewood, only you and Father will look askance at what I am doing, Mother. And for reasons that have nothing to do with any impropriety on my part. I am going to a home, a *parsonage,* where I will be well chaperoned by my friend and her *reverend* husband while I care for another old friend. Everyone in Pinewood will know that, Mother. And they will all heartily approve of my actions, because the people of Pinewood take care of their own."

Her mother gasped, narrowed her eyes. "What has come over you, Ellen? You never have spoken to me in such a disrespectful manner."

"I'm not being disrespectful, Mother. I'm being honest. Now, if you will excuse me, Reverend Calvert is waiting to escort me back to the parsonage." She picked up her things and headed for the door.

"What if you take ill?"

The quiet words stabbed to the core of her being. She froze, fought back tears that her mother would say such a thing to her when she knew of her terror of sickness. She drew in a breath to quell her trembling and steady her voice. "Then I shall have to get better." She hurried out the door to the stairs and started down before the fear overwhelmed and imprisoned her.

"And if Mr. Cuthbert comes while you're gone?"

She glanced over her shoulder at her mother standing at the top of the stairs. "Send him to the parsonage, Mother. I'll receive him there."

The chills were better, fewer and of shorter duration, as long as he didn't move. Daniel lay like a stone, his eyes closed, taking short, shallow breaths. He couldn't feign sleep when Ellen was around, because of the coughing, but he didn't have to look at her. It was difficult enough knowing she was in the room. The soft swish of her long skirts as she moved around drove him crazy! But he'd be able to relax now that she'd gone home for the night.

Bumps and thumps mixed with footsteps came from the hallway. He frowned and opened his eyes.

Ellen entered carrying a large bag and a small box. Willa stepped into the open doorway holding a blanket and pillow. "Where do you want Matthew to put the rocker, Ellen?"

He jerked to a sitting position, broke into a coughing fit. Chills chased each other up and down his spine, branched off into his arms and legs for fun.

"A moment, Willa...." Ellen put down the box and bag and rushed to the nightstand, poured water from the pitcher into a glass and held it out to him. "This may help."

He waved the water away, strained against the urge to cough again.

"Don't be stubborn, Daniel. Ellen is only following Dr. Palmer's instructions. He said you were to drink as much water as possible."

He looked at Willa's concerned expression and forced

his lips into a grin. "Come to b-bully me into behaving, h-have you, Pest?"

Relief washed over her face. She gave him a cheeky smile. "Someone has to. And Ellen is too much of a lady."

He could read the desire to come in and help take care of him in Willa's eyes. He took the glass from Ellen, being careful not to touch her hand, took a few swallows and handed it back. The cool water increased the chills. He pulled up another smile, aimed it at Willa. "Satisfied?"

"It will do, for now."

He turned the smile into a mock scowl. "I th-thought you were supposed to s-stay away from here."

"She's not coming in." Ellen hurried to the doorway, came back carrying the blanket and pillow.

He'd never felt so helpless. Or so trapped. "Th-there's no n-need for—" Ellen paid him no mind. She dropped the blanket and pillow onto a chair, picked up the box and bag and carried them into the dressing room. He stopped forcing out words and leaned back against the pillow to conserve his strength for a battle he might actually have a chance of winning. He had a feeling there would be more than a few ahead.

"Put the rocker by the hearth, please, Matthew. I don't want Ellen to get chilled."

"I'll be fine, Willa. There is plenty of wood for the fire." Ellen emerged, rubbing cream into her hands.

Willa turned into the hallway, listened and turned back. "The baby is crying. I have to go. Bertha is preparing your supper, Daniel. Please eat as much as you can. You must keep up your strength. And you as well, Ellen. Let me know if you need anything more." Willa hurried away.

"And me." Matthew stepped to the bed, looked down at him. "Is there anything you need before I go down to my study, Daniel?"

"No. You've d-done more than enough." The words came out a raspy growl, without much power.

Matthew clapped him on the shoulder and left the room.

He gave serious consideration to crawling after him. He would have if not for his pride and the fact that he was garbed in a suit of Matthew's flannel nightclothes. No, that wouldn't do. His ego had taken enough of a beating for one day. He took the only other route of escape open to him. He closed his eyes and pretended to be asleep.

The quiet pressed in upon her. Ellen wandered about the room, looked at the books on the shelves, ran her fingertip over the chalk figures of a man and woman dressed in Elizabethan clothes.

How could her mother have said such a thing to her, when she knew she had lived in terror of becoming sick ever since Walker had died when she was four years old? Walker. Her older brother and only sibling. Daniel's friend.

She glanced at Daniel, remembering that dark time. He had been devastated by the loss of his closest friend. But still he had tried to make her feel better—less fearful. He was there to comfort her when no one else seemed to understand. He was only nine years old then, but his age hadn't mattered. Daniel had always understood her. And even now, when he had withdrawn his friendship and looked at her with disdain, he was still kind. He'd been patient with her while she learned to make the decorations. And he'd said she made nice bows. What if—

Fear clutched at her heart. But it was no longer for herself. Tears stung her eyes. *Please heal Daniel, Lord. Please don't take him from me.*

She moved to the window and stood staring out into the darkness, fighting the fear. It wasn't as if Daniel were a part of her life anymore, and yet…he was always there in her heart. The residue of her childhood admiration, no doubt, though one would think she would be over that at her age.

She glanced again toward the bed. A smile grew inside her, buried the fear beneath a surge of memories. His hair, dark in the dim lantern light, was tousled from sleep, the curls springy and free the way they had been when he was young. She lowered her gaze to his chin and her smile widened. When she had first noticed the hint of a cleft and asked him had he hurt himself, he'd told her that God made man of clay, and that the small indentation was the mark left by God's finger when God had tested him to see if he was done yet. Laughter bubbled up her throat. For days she had studied people's faces to see if they had any test marks made by God's finger on them.

The laughter turned to an ache, a longing to know again the closeness, the special friendship that had once been hers with Daniel. A coughing spasm took him and the fear pounced. She turned from the window to pour him some water, but he was still asleep.

A log on the fire burned through, bits of it dropping between the iron bars of the grate to the ashes below and bursting into flames. She started toward the woodbox to get another log and stopped short. "Oh!"

Joshua and Sally stood in the open doorway, the boy's brute of a dog at his side, the girl's cat curled in her arms.

She cast a wary look at the dog and moved as close as she dared. "Is there something you wanted?"

Their heads nodded in unison; their blond curls bobbed. Joshua looked toward the bed. "Mama said we could come see Uncle Daniel if we were real quiet and stayed out here in the hall. She said he has to rest to get better. Like we did." He spoke softly, earnestly.

"That's true." It *was* true. The children had recovered when they'd had the measles. Hope rose.

"I brought Tickles so Uncle Daniel could hold him." The little girl held out her cat. "It makes me feel better to hold him when I'm sick."

"I see. That's very thoughtful of you, Sally." She smiled, went a step closer, glanced at the dog and stopped. "But Daniel is asleep right now."

The little girl's face lit up with a sweet smile. "That's all right. That's 'cause Jesus is making him better." Sally pulled her cat back into her arms, tucked her little chin into his fur. "When Mama told us Uncle Daniel has to rest to get better, me and Joshua prayed and asked Jesus to make Uncle Daniel sleep a lot. Didn't we, Josh?"

Joshua nodded, stole another look at Daniel and turned into the hall. "C'mon, Happy. C'mon, Sally. Mama said not to stay too long." He dipped his head in her direction. "Bye, Miss Ellen. We'll come back tomorrow."

"Goodbye." She stepped to the door and watched them walk to the stairs. *Uncle Daniel.* They had prayed for him. What adorable children. How blessed Willa was to have them. And Matthew. And the baby. Her throat tightened. How empty her own life was. She pressed her hand against a swelling pressure in her chest, turned back into the bedroom.

Daniel was watching her. The intensity of his gaze brought warmth rushing into her cheeks. "You're awake." An inane statement. "Would you like some water, or—"

"Supper?"

"Bertha!" She turned back to the doorway, took the tray from Willa's housekeeper and took a delicate sniff of the steam rising from the two bowls. "This smells delicious."

"It's only stew. But it's nourishing for sure. There's bread and butter 'neath that towel. And a bit of jam, too. I figured something sweet might coax him to eat a mite more. He's always helping himself to cookies and such."

"That's b-because they're so good."

"As good an excuse as any, I'd suppose." The housekeeper leaned in the door and gave Daniel a stern look. "I expect that bowl to be empty when I come for the dishes. You can't get better without nourishment." Bertha turned and hurried off.

"Sorry c-can't help—" A fit of coughing stopped Daniel's words.

"I can manage." She caught her lower lip in her teeth and moved toward the nightstand, stared down at the bowls to be sure she didn't spill the stew. "There!" She set the tray on the table and heaved a sigh of relief. "I don't know how Bertha carried that stew up the stairs without spilling any."

"Practice."

Terse and to the point. An indictment of her incompetence. "Yes. Something I'm woefully lacking in."

He shoved to a sitting position. "I didn't—" The coughing convulsed him. When it passed, he leaned back shivering.

"The chills have returned?"

"When I m-move."

She nodded, removed the towel from the tray and spread it over his chest. "Some hot food in you should help stop the shivering." She picked up the bowl and a fork, stabbed a piece of beef, swiped it through the gravy and held it out to him.

He took the fork from her hand and grabbed hold of the bowl. "I can d-do it. You e-eat."

He didn't want her help. She swallowed hard, turned to the tray and buttered a piece of bread, added some jam and set the plate on his lap where he could reach it. "I once asked Mother if I could help Isobel cook."

She looked up, saw the surprise in his eyes. "She said no, of course. And I was made to practice reciting verses. Which was too bad, because otherwise I would know how to carry a tray of food."

"I—"

She shook her head and gestured toward his bowl. "Don't talk or you'll start to cough again." She looked into those green eyes she knew so well and forced her lips to smile. "And I suggest you eat your stew before it gets cold, else both Dr. Palmer and Bertha will be annoyed with you. And me."

She brought a chair from the corner to the nightstand, pulled her bowl close and forced herself to eat. Daniel might want no part of her, not even her help when he was sick and needed care. But she had told him something he didn't know about her—something that had surprised him. Perhaps it would help change his opinion of her. At least it was a start.

The chills shook him awake. Daniel drifted his gaze over the strange room, frowned. His mind refused to work, his thoughts no more substantial than the wisps of smoke floating off the logs and up the chimney.

A fireplace. That was a clue. Was he at the cabin? No. Then where? He closed his eyes, tried to remember, to piece the bits of information together. He was in a bed. His head ached and he had chills. He was ill.

The frown turned into a scowl. He was never sick, so what—

The spinner! Yes. Joe was pinned in the creek, and he went in to get him out. He must have taken ill from the cold— Willa. He was at Willa's. And she— No, Ellen. His heart jolted. Ellen had come to care for him. Ellen, who was so terrified of becoming sick she refused to enter a house where anyone was ill. What had brought her here? Or had he dreamed it all? No, she had come because of Willa.

He opened his eyes and turned his head to look on the other side of the room. The rocker was empty. A coughing fit took him. He wrapped his arms about his chest, held it tight to ease the pain that slashed across it. Footsteps hurried from the direction of the dressing room. Glass clinked on glass.

"Drink this, Daniel. It will help."

He opened his eyes and looked up. Ellen stood beside the bed, a graceful silhouette against the dim light spilling through the open door from the hallway. Firelight flickered, enhancing her long curving eyelashes and delicate cheekbones, her finely molded nose and soft full lips. Curls fell in disarray about her face, caught in a ribbon at the nape of her neck, then cascaded down her back. Her beauty stole what remained of his breath.

He pushed to a sitting position and reached for the glass she offered. The soft warmth of her fingertips touched his, and he hadn't the strength to draw his away. He tucked away the memory of the feel of them in his heart, the beauty of her in his mind and prayed God would heal him quickly so he could return to work and earn the money to leave Pinewood.

Chapter Eighteen

His coughing woke her again. Ellen threw off the blanket, rose from the rocker and poured a glass of water. "I have your drink ready, Daniel."

"L-later."

She looked down at him, the dim lantern light flowing in the open door at the other end of the bedroom of little help. All she could see was his huddled form shaking in spite of the blanket and quilt covering him. "Please, Daniel. You need the water."

She watched him roll onto his back, brace his arms and shove himself upright. The quilt and blanket fell off his shoulders. He coughed, hunched forward, his body shaking. She felt like a beast for making him move.

"Take the glass." She pushed it into his hands, grabbed the blanket and lifted it to cover his shoulders.

He jerked back and looked up at her, his green eyes reflecting the flickering flames of the fire. "Don't d-do that." He swallowed some water, leaned back against the headboard and closed his eyes.

He didn't even want her to touch him. She blinked back a rush of tears, swallowed hard and lifted the glass from his trembling hand. "When you are settled again, I'll straighten the covers over you."

She set the glass on the nightstand, waited. He didn't move, only leaned against the cold wood headboard and shivered. "You need to get under the covers, Daniel. You're not supposed to get chilled."

"I c-can breathe b-better this way."

He was having trouble breathing! The fear took her by the throat, squeezed. *Please help him, Lord! I don't know what to do!* She whipped around to go call for Willa and spotted the rocker. She ran to it, snatched up the pillow and blanket and ran back to the bed. "Lean forward." It was a command, not a request. She was too frightened to care about being polite.

He opened his eyes, looked at her, then leaned forward, his shoulders hunched.

She snatched up his pillow, fluffed it, placed it behind his back, added her own and covered them with the folded blanket, leaving the ends free on each side. "All right, lean back."

He pushed up, straightened his shoulders and rested back against the blanket covering the pillows. "F-feels good. W-warm from f-fire."

"I'm going to cover you now."

His brows rose. He opened his eyes, looked at her. "You're g-getting as b-bossy as Pest."

"I'll consider that a compliment." She grabbed the ends of the blanket and pulled them forward over his arms and shoulders, then overlapped them in front of him. Her hands trembled as she snatched hold of the edges of the blanket and quilt jumbled in his lap, yanked them up over his blanket-covered chest, slid them beneath his chin and tucked them down between his back and the pillows. "There."

He'd gone rigid. She placed her hands against the headboard above his shoulders and pushed herself erect. His eyes were closed, but he wasn't sleeping. That little muscle along his jaw was twitching. He was angry with her for touching him. Well, he could be mad! She wasn't going to let him make his illness worse simply because he didn't like her!

The surge of unaccustomed resolve carried her over to the fireplace. She added wood to the fire and looked around for something else she could do to help Daniel. No idea came to her. She thought back to conversations her elite friends had about ill family members, hoping to glean some wisdom. But, again, there was nothing. Her wealthy friends didn't interrupt their lives. They had their servants care for the person who was ill.

She tiptoed back to the bed and looked at Daniel. She'd swaddled him like a baby in blankets, but he was still Daniel. He was still her hero. And nobody was going to take care of him but her! Whether he liked it or not. *Please make him well, Almighty God. Please make him well!*

Tears threatened. Sobs welled into her throat. She clasped her hands over her mouth and ran for the dressing room, closed the door, leaned back against it and let the tears flow.

"All right, your personal needs have been taken care of, and my examination is over. There's no one else in the room. I expect some honest answers, son." Dr. Palmer looked down at him, worry lines etching his forehead. "How's your strength?"

He gathered what little he had. "I'm—"

"The truth, Daniel."

He leaned back and closed his eyes. "Weak as a n-newborn babe." The coughing took him again. He winced, pressed his hands to his chest.

"Chest hurt when you cough?"

He opened his eyes and looked at him.

The doctor nodded, frowned. "All right, foolish question. How's your head?"

"Hurts."

"Hard to breathe?"

"Yes."

"Keep drinking lots of water—that's important. And rest. I'll be back to check on you tomorrow."

"When w-will I be b-better, Doc?"

Dr. Palmer picked up his bag and looked him in the eye. "I can't say, son. Depends on too many things. But you're a strong, healthy young man. It shouldn't be too long."

He didn't like that little word *too*. He nodded, watched the doctor walk from the room and closed his eyes. *I need Your help, Lord. Seems like I'm getting weaker instead of stronger. I need You, Lord....*

A coughing spasm convulsed his throat, clutched his chest and took his strength. He sagged into the pillows and closed his eyes.

Daniel has pneumonia....

The fear was there, waiting outside the limits of her determination. Ellen clasped the extra pillow Willa had given her to her chest and hurried to the bed.

Keep him propped up—it will help him breathe...

watch for fever...cold cloths on his forehead...don't let him get chilled...no one to go in the room...

Dr. Palmer's instructions repeated over and over in her head. She cast a glance at the hearth to be sure the fire was going well, hurried on toward the bed.

"Is Uncle Daniel sleeping? Is he getting better?"

Joshua's whisper came from over her shoulder. She laid the pillow on the bed and walked toward the doorway, paused. "Will you hold your dog, please?"

Joshua put his hand on his dog, looked up at her. "Mama said you're scared of dogs because you was—were—attacked by a dog when you was—were—little like Sally." He frowned and shook his head, his blond curls bobbing. "That's scary, all right. But you don't have to be afraid of all dogs. Dogs are like people—a few are mean, but most of them are nice and friendly."

Joshua looked toward the bed, his handsome little face sober. "Mama said Uncle Daniel saved you from that mean dog. And now he's saved that logger by jumping in that cold water to help him. Uncle Daniel's a brave man. I like him lots." Joshua's lower lip trembled; he blinked his eyes and turned away. "C'mon, Happy. Let's go get a cookie."

He's afraid for Daniel. She stared after Joshua and his dog, her heart hurting for the little boy, then took a deep breath and turned back into the bedroom.

—he's saved that logger by jumping in that cold water to help him. Uncle Daniel's a brave man.

Her mind flashed back twelve years to a worn-smooth log that spanned Stony Creek and the rushing floodwater beneath it. She recalled the feel of the soles of her new shoes slipping on the damp wood and the cold, muddy water closing over her head, of being swept downstream while her sodden skirts dragged her deeper....

She shook her head, crossed to the bed and looked down at Daniel. Willa and the others had told her how they had turned at her scream and witnessed her fall into the water. How Daniel had run out on the log and dove into that roaring floodwater to save her.

She remembered the fear, the choking sensation as the water filled her nose and throat, the tug when Daniel had grabbed her collar. She'd never forget the gleam of the sunshine on her eyelids as he lifted her head above the suffocating water and dragged her to shore. Daniel. Her hero. She still had—

"Ellen."

She blinked the tears from her eyes and hurried over to the doorway. "What is it, Willa?"

"You have a caller. Mr. Cuthbert is downstairs."

"Mr. Cuthbert?" The name sounded from a different world.

"Yes. And you needn't worry about privacy. The children have been told not to go near the sitting room until your caller leaves."

"But...no. I can't, Willa." She glanced toward the bed. "You'll have to make my excuses to Mr. Cuthbert. I have to stay with Daniel."

Willa stared at her a moment, then peeked around the doorframe. "Daniel is sleeping. I'll stay here in the hall and watch. If he wakes, I'll come get you. Give me a minute to get Mary."

She stared after Willa, trying to find some enthusiasm, some excitement at the news that her beau was here. There was none. Perhaps the excitement would come when she saw Mr. Cuthbert.

She crossed to the mirror and fluffed her curls, smoothed the bodice of her old blue gown. How shocked he would be to see her dressed so out of fashion. But there was no time to change.

Willa's footsteps sounded in the hallway.

She turned, bumped a chair and lost her balance. She put out her hand to steady herself and brushed against Daniel's jacket hanging on a peg. A faint smell of horses and pine trees and the out-of-doors released at the contact. She clasped his jacket in her hands, buried her face in its folds and breathed in the scent of Daniel. Her heart swelled, filled with memories of him.

"Ellen, I'm back."

The whisper drew her out of her thoughts. She hung Daniel's jacket on the peg and walked to the door, looked at baby Mary asleep in Willa's arms and sighed. Mr. Cuthbert was waiting downstairs. The choice was before her. What was it that she wanted?

"Willa, do you have a warmed soapstone in your bed when you retire?"

Willa looked up at her with a question in her eyes, then shook her head. "No, Ellen. I don't."

She nodded, turned toward the stairway.

"I don't need a soapstone. I have Matthew to warm me. And I wouldn't trade his love for all the luxuries and riches in the world."

The answer followed her downstairs.

Earl Cuthbert stood by the fireplace, his black suit of the finest wool, tucked-front shirt and snowy-white cravat with its diamond stickpin announcing his importance. There was a look of distaste on his face as he gazed at the Christmas tree in the corner. She looked at the apple-and-cranberry garlands draping the tree, the white paper angels and stars with red and green ribbon loops that adorned its branches, the brown paper dog and cat with bright red bows Joshua and Sally had made. She'd loved every minute of decorating that tree with— She caught her breath, looked up at the white paper star, then stepped into the sitting room.

Earl Cuthbert looked up at her entrance, smiled and came toward her, made a polite bow. "My dear Miss Hall, how good to see you again. I've been most eager for this visit." He swept his gaze over her gown and raised a brow but made no comment. "I called at your home as arranged, but your parents informed me that you are visiting an ill friend and wished me to call on you here at her home. I hope her condition is improving?"

"I am sorry for the inconvenience of this visit to you, Mr. Cuthbert. Had there been time, I would have written telling you not to come." She smiled and gestured toward the chairs by the hearth. "Shall we have a seat while I explain?"

She led the way to the chairs, sat and waited for him to take the opposite chair before she continued. "I am afraid there has been a misunderstanding, Mr. Cuthbert." She took a breath, spoke the truth. "I am not visiting my ill friend. I am caring for him."

"Him? This friend of yours is a man?"

He did not look pleased. "Yes."

"And you are overseeing his care?"

Should she let his misconception stand? She glanced at the Bible resting on the lamp stand beside his chair. "No, Mr. Cuthbert. I am caring for him myself."

"My dear Miss Hall!" He rose, looked down at her. "That must cease at once."

Indeed. She took a calming breath. "I'm afraid that's not possible. My friend's condition has grown worse."

"Then hire someone to care for him." He smiled, resumed his seat. "Surely you see the impropriety of your actions?"

"No, I do not, Mr. Cuthbert." She squared her shoulders and lifted her chin. "Daniel is an old friend. He is sick and needs care and has no one to tend him. I am doing so in a most proper way, well chaperoned by my friend Willa and her husband, Reverend Calvert."

"I believe you, my dear Miss Hall." Earl Cuthbert's boot heel tapped against the floor; his fingers drummed on his jiggling knee. "Nonetheless, the very idea of an unmarried woman tending to an ill man is unseemly. I'm afraid I must insist that you stop this inappropriate behavior immediately."

Inappropriate behavior? She shot to her feet. "And by what authority do you make such a demand, sir?"

He rose, his face flushed. "No wife of a man in my position can conduct herself in such a manner."

"Then it is most fortunate I am not your wife, sir."

"Well, you will be."

It was the moment she had worked toward, waited for. And now… She turned toward the corner, looked at the Christmas tree Daniel had cut and helped decorate and shook her head. "No, Mr. Cuthbert, I will not."

He scowled, strode to the center of the room, turned and came back. "You refuse my hand?"

"I would were I *asked.*"

"But you refused Lodge."

"Yes, I did."

"I don't understand, Miss Hall. Why would you refuse me, also?"

"Because I find I am no longer interested in warmed soapstones, Mr. Cuthbert." She smiled at his puzzled expression and led the way to the entrance hall. "Thank you for coming, sir. I'm sorry your journey was for naught."

Daniel frowned, watched Ellen through his slitted eyelids. Why did she keep looking out the window? Waiting to see her beau appear? What was his name? Dodge? Hodge? Lodge! That was it, Lodge. He smiled inwardly, inordinately pleased with himself for thinking of the man's name.

He was hot. Too hot. He scowled, shoved the blankets down off his shoulders and rested his arms on top of them. Chills shook him. That woman by the window should put more wood on the fire. It wasn't right to make a man so cold he got sick. He'd tell her as soon as he remembered her name. Willa? No. *Musquash.* Hah! He remembered!

"Daniel, you need to stay covered."

Who was Daniel? Why was that woman putting a blanket on him? He didn't want a blanket on. He didn't like…what? The man. There was something about the man he didn't like. His looks! He didn't like his looks. All pinched and…pinched…and—

Her hands were soft. Softer than his ma's. But he didn't want her to touch him. He frowned, turned onto his side…coughed. Somebody drove an ax into his chest. He felt around but couldn't find it. There were only blankets, but he needed to pull the ax out….

"Daniel, please…you need to stay covered."

A tree broke free, twisted on the stump. "It's a spinner!" He threw himself to the side, coughed and shivered. The woman lifted his head, tucked a pillow beneath, then pulled the covers over him up to his neck. He fought against the darkness that was dragging at him. There was something he had to tell her. Something he had to do...

He rolled onto his side and looked up at her. She was crying. Maybe she knew already. He struggled to get enough air to speak. "Pa's dead. I've got to bury my dream." There—it was done.

He closed his eyes and let the darkness take him.

Chapter Nineteen

"He has a fever, Willa. I'm certain Daniel has a fever."
Ellen looked at Willa, wished she could step into the hall
and fall into her arms. But that was not allowed. She
had to find the courage to fight her fear within herself.

"Are you all right, Ellen? Oh, I so wish I could come
in and see Daniel and help you care for him!"

She stared at Willa, at her clenched hands and the
shadows in her blue-green eyes—competent, strong
Willa was afraid, too. And she couldn't come in and
see Daniel for herself. Willa needed her reassurance.
She took a breath to steady her voice.

"I know it's hard for you not to see Daniel, Willa.
But you *do* help me by giving me advice. Now, about
Daniel's condition. He is as Dr. Palmer described. He
is flushed, his forehead is hot beneath my hand and his
eyes—" she choked, went on "—his eyes when he opens
them are bright and shiny like glass." She pressed her
lips together to hold back all of the things begging to
be said.

Willa nodded, straightened. "You're right, Ellen. He
is fevered. Do as Dr. Palmer said—get him to drink lots

of water. Bully him into it if you must! Daniel can be very stubborn."

"I know. Remember the bee tree?" She met Willa's watery gaze, and they stood looking at one another over the threshold, assailed by memories of strong, adventurous Daniel—and of Walker. She caught a shuddering breath and smiled. "He's our hero, Willa. We'll take good care of him together—you with your knowledge and skill, and me with…my hands." *She had nothing of substance to offer, nothing of worth to give.* "Now, if you'll excuse me, I've some bullying to do."

She wanted to cry. Oh, how she wanted to cry. But she wouldn't. Daniel needed her to be strong. And she would be. For him.

It was snowing again. The large fluffy flakes that had been falling all day had covered the world outside the bedroom window with a fresh white blanket. She shivered in the cold coming off the snow-framed glass panes and listened to Daniel's unintelligible muttering. The instances were becoming fewer and the time between them was lengthening.

Should she try giving him water again? He had turned away from the glass the last time. A spoon! Perhaps a spoon would work.

"Ellen."

Relief shot through her. She spun toward the door. "Is Dr. Palmer on his way?" The look in Willa's eyes was answer enough. Her stomach sank.

"Dr. Palmer can't come. He's attending Phylinda Arden. She's having difficulty birthing the baby." Willa stepped closer, looked toward the bed where Daniel lay quiet except for the wheezing of his hard-won breaths and blinked away tears. "He said there is nothing he could do if he could come. That there is nothing anyone can do for him now. Daniel has—has reached a crisis." Willa blinked, straightened her shoulders, jutted her chin. "He will be better in the morning."

The unspoken alternative hung in the air between them. She couldn't speak, merely nodded.

"I have other...distressing news." Ellen reached her hand out toward her, drew it back. "Oh, Ellen, I'm so sorry, but Mary is fretful and will not be comforted or settle down to sleep. And there is no one here to help with her. Matthew and the children are at church. And Bertha has gone to spend Christmas with her daughter. I can't bring Mary here to the hallway and have her cries disturb Daniel."

"No, of course not." She tried to keep her fear from creeping into her voice. "But there's no reason for you to do so, Willa. All we can do is wait. And I will be staying at Daniel's bedside to make certain he stays...covered."

"Matthew had to go, Ellen." Willa's shoulders sagged. "It's Christmas Eve."

"Christmas Eve... I'd forgotten."

Willa tilted her head, listened. "Mary is crying."

"And I need to tend to Daniel."

They looked at one another.

Willa reached in her pocket and pulled out a small packet. "Here is more ginger for you. I'll be back whenever I'm able."

She nodded and watched Willa walk away, then crossed the room to the nightstand, poured some water into the glass and picked up the spoon from the supper tray. *There is nothing anyone can do for him now.* Something inside her rebelled at the thought. She glanced up at the plastered ceiling. "I'm not giving up, Lord. I'm not giving up."

The spoon clinked against the glass. She turned to the bed, the water in the spoon quivering in her trembling hand. "It's time for some water, Daniel." She reached down and drew the fingertip of her free hand lightly across his mouth. His lips moved, parted. She slipped the spoon into the slight opening and dribbled the life-giving liquid into his mouth.

"Angels we have heard on high…"

Singing floated into the room, muted by distance.

"Do you hear the carolers, Daniel?" There was no sign that he heard them, or her.

She walked to the window. Dozens of lanterns gleamed against the darkness, encircled the gazebo, shone on the carolers. Their blended light bathed the snow-covered railing and the pine-bough swags and red bows in a golden glow. An image of Daniel leaning back to pound in a nail, one leg wrapped around a post and one foot braced against the railing, filled her mind. Tears poured from her eyes.

She rested her fingertips on the horizontal bars of the wood grids framing the small glass panes of the window and cleared the lump from her throat. "They're gathered at the gazebo, Daniel. I can't even count the lanterns. Half of Pinewood must be there." She turned from the window, gazed at Daniel struggling to breathe, to *live*. A constricting tightness gripped her own chest.

"Silent night, holy night…"

The voices grew louder. Light flowed into the dark room. She looked out, caught her breath at the sight of the carolers gathering below, the light of their lanterns driving back the darkness of the night. "Daniel, they're here! They're singing for you, Daniel." *Thank You, Lord. Thank You for all of these good people who love and care about Daniel.*

The singing stopped. She wiped the tears from her cheeks and opened her eyes. The parsonage yard was filled with people kneeling in the snow, their lanterns casting small circles of golden light on them as they prayed.

Every minute seemed like an hour. An hour became an eternity. Her thoughts tortured her. She'd been blind. So blind. And now it was too late. Daniel felt nothing but the remnant of childhood affection tinged with disdain for her. A disdain she deserved.

Be not high-minded... That was exactly what she'd been, high-minded—looking down on others, on these good people who had shown her nothing but kindness and care all of her life. How could she ever have thought herself better than them because she lived in a larger, finely furnished house and had fashionable clothes? Tears stung her eyes.

Trust not in the riches of this world... But she had. Until she'd come home, that was all she had sought, all she had trusted in. Blind, blind, blind!

Love...honesty...peace...joy...whatever has virtue, is pure or lovely, these are the things we are to think on and value... Truly, her beauty was all on the outside. And Daniel, who always understood her, knew it.

Trust not in uncertain riches, but in the living God, who giveth us richly all things to enjoy...

"Forgive me, Lord. Please forgive me. I've been so wrong. So very, very wrong."

Daniel coughed, moaned. She reached into the bowl

of water on the nightstand for the cloth, twisted it and turned to the bed. Fear clutched at her again. He was so flushed. His face so hot against her hands. She replaced the cloth on his forehead with the cool one, tossed the other into the bowl.

He was so quiet, so weak it was unnerving. Daniel, her hero. Her love in her romantic childhood dreams. And in her heart. She knew that now. She'd fooled herself for so long, thinking it was Daniel's friendship she missed, longed for. It wasn't his friendship. It was *him.* She loved him. And somewhere deep inside her heart she'd always known she loved him. From the day he'd pulled her gasping and struggling to breathe from that flood—

She whirled about and ran to the dressing room, dug to the bottom of her toiletry box. It was in here somewhere. She'd never thrown it away. She found it beneath a scented sachet.

She closed her trembling fingers around the flat stone shaped like a lopsided heart and went back to Daniel. His breathing was labored, his face below the cold cloth on his forehead flushed, taut with his effort to draw breath.

"I have the stone, Daniel." She uncurled her fingers to show it resting on her palm. Tears spilled down her cheeks. "Do you remember? It's the stone you gave me to stop me from crying the day you dove into Stony Creek and pulled me from those raging floodwaters. You saved my life, Daniel." She wiped the tears from her cheeks, took a steadying breath. "You're my hero, Daniel. You've *always* been my hero. Please, *please,* don't leave me. I know you don't want me as a friend anymore, and I deserve that. But please, *please,* don't leave me. *Fight,* Daniel. Fight to live! I need you here. I need to know you're here, even if I never see you again."

She sank to her knees by the bed, the fear rending her heart, the rock clutched in her folded hands.

"I know it's too late for my dreams to come true, Lord. I know how Daniel feels about me, and he's right. I see now the shallow woman I've become, and I don't blame him for distancing himself from me. But please spare him." Her voice broke on a sob. She took a ragged breath. "I can't bear to lose Daniel, Lord. I need to know he's here, even if he never again calls me friend. But, oh, how I long to hear him call me Musquash again."

The sobs lessened. Her tears stopped. She slipped the stone in her pocket and rose from her knees shaking and spent, ashamed of breaking down when Daniel needed her to be strong. But it was so hard to face the long hours of fear all alone.

She splashed cold water on her puffy, burning eyes, squeezed out the cloth in the bowl and replaced the one turned warm on Daniel's forehead. She hated the sound of his tortured breathing yet listened for it, held to it as the one assurance he was still with her. He was still fighting.

She rubbed at the ache in her temples and walked to the woodbox. Matthew would have to bring in more wood in the morning. She added two pieces of split log to the fire, straightened and rubbed her upper arms. How many more hours to this endless night? She walked to the window but there was only darkness, and she had no way to tell how long it would be until the dawn.

She returned to the chair by the bed and seated herself.

The fire crackled.

Daniel breathed.
She prayed.

She'd dozed off. How could she? What if— She held
her breath, listened. There was something— Daniel
wasn't wheezing. *No! Lord, please, no!* Fear chased
down her spine, turned her weak. She forced breath into
her lungs, commanded her legs to work and started to
rise, wobbled. She tried again and made it.

A slight wheeze brought a surge of relief so strong it
left her light-headed. His breathing might have gotten
less strong, but he was still alive.

She stepped to the head of the bed to change the cloth
on his forehead, then drew back. The cloth already there
wasn't hot. It wasn't even warm. Either she'd slept only a
few minutes or... She removed the cloth and placed her
trembling hand on Daniel's forehead, her heart pounding out hope. He was cool. The fever was gone! Was
that good? Or—

"Mouth's dry."

"Oh!" She jerked back, stared at Daniel's opened eyes.
"You're awake!"

"Thirsty."

It was a raspy croak, followed by a cough.

She whirled to the nightstand, tossed the cloth in the
bowl and poured him some water. "Here." She held the
glass to his mouth willing her hand to stop shaking.

He took a few swallows. "Enough." He stared up at
her. "What are you—" he dragged in a breath "—doing
here?"

"You've been very sick." She brushed back a curl,
flushed when his gaze followed her movement. He was
probably thinking how vain she was. Her cheeks warmed

beneath his steady gaze. "Would you like more water? Dr. Palmer said—"

He nodded. "I'm beginning to…remember." He drank the rest of the water when she held it to his mouth. Coughed again. "How long have I—" another breath "—been here?"

She tried to think back but her mind wouldn't cooperate. All she could think of was that he was better. "I've lost track of the days. It's only a few."

He nodded. His eyelids slid closed…opened again.

"I think perhaps it would be best if you try to rest, Daniel. You can ask questions later."

His gaze met hers. "If you rest, too. You look…tired."

His concern for her while he was so ill brought the tears surging. She turned around and set the glass back on the nightstand. "All right. I'll be right here in the chair, if you need me."

"No. Rocker." His eyelids drifted closed. "I can… call…"

She looked down at him sleeping. His face was peaceful, not taut and tense like before. He still had a bit of a wheeze when he breathed but, oh, he was so much better. Joy welled, filled her heart. *Thank You, Lord. Thank You for sparing Daniel.*

Exhaustion hit. It took concentration to walk to the hearth and add wood to the fire. She glanced at the window. Dawn was breaking. It had been a long, long night. She swayed, grabbed hold of the rocker, rubbed her tired eyes and patted her cheeks. She couldn't sleep yet. She had to…to tell Willa…what?

Soft footsteps sounded in the hall. Willa was…coming.... She struggled to capture the elusive thought. Daniel. Daniel was better.... Yes, that was it. She looked toward the door, saw Willa and smiled.

Chapter Twenty

She'd fallen asleep! Ellen jerked to a sitting position. The room spun. "Oh!" She grabbed her head, sank back against the pillow. *Daniel!*

She struggled to rise. Hands gripped her shoulders, pushed gently. She fell back, forced her eyes to open and blinked to clear her blurred vision. "Willa!" There was something wrong. She frowned, searched through the fog in her mind and found what she was seeking. "You're not supposed to be in here. The doctor—"

"It's all right, Ellen. Dr. Palmer said Daniel has passed the crisis. I can—"

"Daniel is—" It all came rushing back. Tears stung her eyes. She sat up and grabbed Willa's hands, smiled her joy. "Daniel is *better*, Willa. He truly is! He doesn't have a fever, and he isn't wheezing so much, and he *talked* to me! He did. He asked for water and—"

She stopped, blinked and shook her head. "Dr. Palmer was here?"

"Yes."

"When?"

"Yesterday."

She frowned, rubbed her temples. "I can't remember...."

"That's because you were sleeping."

"Sleeping!" She shot Willa an accusing look. "Why didn't you wake me? I need to take care of— *Yesterday?*"

Willa nodded, smiled. "Yes, yesterday. And I didn't wake you because Dr. Palmer told me not to. He said you were exhausted and needed to sleep and get your strength back as much as Daniel did. So Matthew carried you in here to sleep in Sally's bed." She gave a soft laugh. "I must say, you and Daniel are both very easy to care for. You have slept the entire time. And so has Daniel, except for waking to drink or eat. Dr. Palmer says Daniel will be as good as new after a couple more days of rest."

Willa smiled, her blue-green eyes shining down at her. "It wasn't the way I had planned for our Christmas to be with Matthew at the church preaching and supervising the children's speaking roles while I stayed here to care for Mary and watch over Daniel and you. But it was the best Christmas ever!"

"I slept through Christmas?"

Willa nodded and wrapped her in a warm, fierce hug. "Thank you, Ellen, for all you've done. Dr. Palmer said strong and healthy as Daniel is, he probably wouldn't have...gotten better without your excellent care. Now—" Willa straightened, pulled in a breath "—you rest, my dear friend. And when you wake, I'm going to fix you and Daniel the best breakfast you've ever had!"

She watched Willa rush out the door, threw the blanket off of her legs and staggered across the hall. She had to look at Daniel, to see for herself that he was all right. The room swayed. She grabbed for the doorframe.

"I've discovered if you don't move fast, you don't get dizzy."

Daniel. She looked over at him, caught her breath. He *was* better. He was sitting with his back against the headboard, his arms resting on the blanket that covered him to the waist. The color was back in his face, the alert look in his eyes. He looked…normal—only tired. And handsome. Someone had shaved him and combed his hair. She liked it better with his curls all mussed. She flushed at the thought, looked down and frowned at her wrinkled skirts. She must look a sight. She held to the door and glanced toward the dressing room. It was so far….

"You look b—worn out."

She met his gaze. He looked away, scrubbed his hand over the back of his neck. "I'm sorry to have been a b—"

"Don't you say *burden,* Daniel. Don't you dare!" The flash of anger brought a surge of energy along with it that allowed her to meet his startled gaze without bursting into tears. She ached to tell him all she'd discovered about herself while she waited through those long, fear-filled days. To tell him she loved him, had always loved him and would love only him forever. But the set look on his face buried the words deep within her. "Willa needed help and I gave it. As for caring for you—it's the least I could do after all the times you've watched over me. Including pulling me from Stony Creek and saving my life." She curled her fingers around the stone in her pocket.

He gave a curt nod. "I guess we're even now."

She looked at his shadowed eyes, his firmly pressed lips, the twitching of the little muscle along his jaw. *How little he thought of her.* The hurt squeezed her heart, left her breathless. "I guess we are." She clenched her teeth to hold back the sobs rising into her throat, crossed to the dressing room, closed the door and collapsed against it.

Daniel didn't want her near him. It was in his voice, his posture, the way he refused to look at her. He would never believe she had changed. She had realized her love for him too late.

The pain was unbearable. She had to go away. She couldn't bear to stay here. She would go somewhere she wouldn't have to face Daniel's disdain and her friends' pity. Somewhere she could keep safe the memory of the way it was when he had been her friend and hero and love. Her world. And she would leave with her head high.

She poured water into the bowl and began to wash, shivers rising at the touch of the cold water. Her new velvet gown dangled from the peg where she'd hung it the day she'd come. How ironic that she had taken it off because she'd thought, *hoped,* seeing her wearing her old gowns might make Daniel realize she had changed, that she didn't care about having fashionable clothes anymore. Now it would be the gown she wore as she walked away. The one he would remember her in.

A few quick strokes of the brush brought her flyaway curls under control. She bunched them, used the gown's matching velvet ribbon to hold them in place, gathered her toiletries and fastened the box. She picked up the gown she'd stepped out of and folded it to fit in her bag. A hard lump bumped against her fingers. Her throat closed. She drew a long breath to control the tears welling into her eyes, took hold of the stone, slipped it into her pocket and closed the bag.

Daniel was sleeping. *Thank You, Lord. I won't have to say goodbye—to pretend.* She grabbed her toiletry box and the bag and tiptoed across the room and out into the hallway, stopped and looked back over her shoulder. She couldn't leave…not this way. Compelled by an urging she couldn't deny, she set down her things and walked back into the room.

A few steps took her to where Daniel's jacket hung on a peg. She breathed in the scent of it, pulled the stone from her pocket. *He had always understood her. Perhaps he would know…*. She took a breath to ease the ache in her heart, slipped the stone in his jacket pocket and walked from the room.

Willa was in her bedroom changing Mary. The sight of her friend deepened the pain in her heart. It was good Willa was busy. She hadn't the strength for a long goodbye. She fastened her old, polite smile on her face and lifted her chin. "Willa, I'm sorry to disturb you while you're tending Mary, but I wanted to say goodbye."

"Goodbye?" Willa turned, swept her gaze over her new velvet gown. "You're going home."

"Yes, you are able to care for Daniel now. There's no reason for me to stay." She put on another phony smile. "Tell Joshua he may have my breakfast to share with his dog. And please tell Sally and Matthew I said goodbye."

She made an elegant turn, the rich velvet of her gown whispering softly, picked up her things and walked down the stairs, her heart breaking. If she hurried, she would have time to visit Sadie before dinner. She'd plan what to say while Asa hitched up the sleigh.

Daniel forked up another bite of stew and chewed. It tasted like sawdust. And he should know. He'd probably swallowed a bucketful of the stuff hanging around the mill while they unloaded the logs he hauled in. It wasn't the food. Willa was an excellent cook. Right up there with his ma. It was his sour mood.

"You don't seem to have much appetite, Daniel. Is there something wrong?"

He looked up at Willa, noted the speculative look in her eye. He might have known she'd start thinking about his change of mood. He couldn't deny the lack of appetite, or she'd really get suspicious. He shook his head and forked up another mouthful with more enthusiasm. "I guess it's from being sick."

"Hmm, that's possible."

She didn't sound convinced.

"And a man doesn't get that hungry when he's sitting around doing nothing."

"I suppose."

He was of no mind-set to spar. He scowled up at her. "Have you got something to say, Pest?"

"No. I'm sorry if I seem distracted." She smiled. "I was thinking about Ellen refusing Mr. Cuthbert's proposal the other day. Oh, but you didn't know about that, did you?"

He gritted his teeth, put down his fork.

"Are you through with that?" She took the plate and put it back on his supper tray, then poured a cup of coffee. "It happened while she was caring for you. She wasn't even going to see him, but I arranged to sit in the hall and keep watch over you so she could. She sent him and his proposal back to Buffalo in short order. The same as she did Mr. Lodge. Be careful—this is very hot." Willa handed him the coffee, smiled down at him. "Did you know she refused Mr. Lodge's hand? Or were you back at camp before the news spread around town? I can't remem—"

"Willa, *stop*. Or I will get out of this bed and carry you bodily from this room, sick or not." He met her gaze full on. "I'm in no temper to talk about this, Pest. If Ellen refused those men, it's because she has a dozen more wealthier or more prestigious beaux waiting to court her. And even if she doesn't, it's nothing to do with me. I've told you before—I have nothing of worth to offer her. Now, go tend to your family and let me drink my coffee in peace."

"Daniel—"

He looked at her.

"Oh, very well! But you, Daniel Braynard, are too *stubborn* for your own good!"

He acknowledged the truth of the statement with a dip of his head.

Willa snatched up his tray and flounced from the room.

"What do you mean, you're not going back to Buffalo, Ellen?" Her father frowned, set his pipe in its holder. "You're not thinking clearly. You may have erred in refusing Mr. Lodge's and Mr. Cuthbert's offers of marriage, but there are other men—perhaps not quite as wealthy or prestigious as they—who are worthy of consideration. And where else would you go?"

"Rochester."

"Rochester?" Her mother frowned. "We have no connections to the elite in Rochester, Ellen. How will you meet eligible men?"

She took a breath, braced herself for the coming battle. "I'm not going there to search for a husband, Mother. I'm going there to teach school."

"Teach school?" Her mother and father looked at her as if she'd lost her mind.

"Yes. At the young ladies' seminary where Sadie taught. I'm certain I will be able to obtain a teaching position there. I went to see Sadie this morning, and she gave me a letter of recommendation." *After a good deal of persuasion.*

"Utter nonsense." Her father gave her a reproving look. "We have not raised you to waste your time in such profitless pursuits, Ellen. Things can still be salvaged. You will go back to your aunt in Buffalo. My plans—"

"Have come to naught." She straightened her back, lifted her chin. "I'm sorry to disappoint you, Father. But I am going to Rochester."

His eyes narrowed on her. "I think not. I'll not pay for something that has no expectation of gain."

Was that all she meant to him? A means of obtaining wealth? "There are things other than money to be gained, Father."

"Don't be impertinent, young woman!"

"I'm not. I'm being honest, Father." She lifted her chin another notch. "And I'm going to Rochester. Tomorrow." She looked at her parents' faces, shock and anger warring for expression on their features. "Now, if you will excuse me, I have my packing to do."

Daniel stared at the chair in the corner, the one Ellen had brought to his bedside. Whenever he'd opened his eyes, she'd been there. And the sight of her had given him strength, made him fight harder to breathe, to live.

He frowned, stared at the flickering fire. All day long bits and pieces of memories had been stealing into his thoughts. The way she looked tending the fire. The feel of her hand on his forehead as she checked for fever and changed the cloths that had helped the pain in his head.

The featherlight touch of her fingertips against his lips. The fear in her eyes. The sound of her crying.

The room was unbearably empty without her.

He clenched his hands, drew in a breath, blew it out, then drew in another. The terrible pressure was gone. His lungs expanded without pain.

He swung his legs over the side of the bed, touched his feet to the floor and shifted his weight onto them. His first step was a little shaky but nothing alarming. He took another, then another and another, leaned against the mantel to rest, then did it again.

How would he ever get the vision out of his head of her standing looking down at him with her blue eyes swimming with tears, her face warm and flushed from the fire, and her blond curls tumbling every which way against her face and onto her shoulders? He knew he'd never get it out of his heart.

He had to get out of this room. He had to get out of Pinewood.

He made two full circuits, stepped into the dimly lit hall and walked up and down, up and down, his stocking-clad feet noiseless against the floorboards. He could do it. He wasn't ready to fell a tree, but he could make the walk to the Townsend sawmill. He'd leave first thing in the morning.

Chapter Twenty-One

It felt good to be dressed in his own clothes again. Daniel glanced up at the window. He'd overslept. It was full dawn. He folded his thick wool socks down over the tops of his calf-high boots, stood and shrugged into his jacket.

He could hear Willa and Matthew stirring around downstairs, hoped Joshua and Sally were still asleep. This was going to be hard enough without having to say goodbye to them. But Willa would explain to them. And make a better job of it than he could.

His face tightened. It was time to go. He reached into his pocket and tugged out his hat, something thudded against the floor. He looked down. Pain slashed through his heart, stole his breath. He bent and took the rock into his hand, straightened with the stone shaped like a lopsided heart resting on his palm. His pulse drummed in his ears. It was the same stone. It had been over twelve years, but he'd know it anywhere. It was the one he'd found in the muddy grass where he'd laid Ellen after he'd pulled her from Stony Creek. He'd picked the stone up, wiped the mud off on his pants and given it to her to stop her from being so afraid. How had it come to be in his pocket?

His heart lurched. There was only one answer. Ellen had kept the stone all of these years. And she had put it in his jacket pocket. But why? The truth slipped into his heart, nestled there as if it had finally found its home.

He closed his eyes and shook his head, denying what he knew was true. He clenched his fingers around the stone, his heart pounding. Ellen loved him. That was the message she'd sent by leaving him the stone. He wanted to be wrong. But he wasn't. He'd read the same message of love in her eyes and in the touch of her hands while she'd been caring for him. He'd simply refused to acknowledge it, hadn't want it to be true, because it made what he had to do so much harder. And more necessary. *Why now, Lord? Why now? It would have been better to have never known.*

"No, Daniel, you can't go. I won't let you. I can't bear it! And, anyway, it's foolishness for you to go out in this weather before you're fully well."

Daniel's chest tightened. Willa's pleading was another wound to his already-bleeding heart. "Look, Pest. I'm thankful for all you've done for me, and I know you're likely right." He slipped his hand into his pocket, closed his fingers around the stone. "But I have to do this. I'll be back to visit—someday."

"Daniel, please—" Willa's voice broke on a sob. She whirled about, looked up at her husband. "Matthew, *do* something."

"I'm going to."

Daniel shot a look at Matthew Calvert, waited. He sure didn't want to have to fight with the man who had come to be his friend. But he was leaving Pinewood this morning one way or the other.

"Willa, I've been an ordained minister for several years." Matthew leaned over his wife's shoulder, lifted his coat from its peg and shrugged into it. "And there are a lot of things I don't know or understand." He grabbed his hat and put it on. "But one thing I *have* learned is that when God is working in someone's life, it's best for men to keep their hands off the situation." Matthew planted a kiss on his wife's cheek, clasped her chin in his hand and looked into her eyes. "It's time for you to let go, Willa. Now, tell Daniel goodbye, while I go hitch up the sleigh. I'm going to take him to the sawmill."

The heart-wrenching business of saying goodbye had become a little easier. Daniel looked at Matthew over the top of Willa's head and sent him a silent message of thanks.

She should have packed last night, but she'd been too…undone. Ellen looked at the array of fancy, stylish gowns spread over her bed and heaved a sigh. None of them were appropriate for a teacher in a young ladies' seminary, but she had to choose. Asa said they had to leave for Olville directly after dinner if she was to be at the station in time to catch the stage. *As if she could eat.* She eyed the gowns again and turned away in disgust. She would leave them all here and pack the old gowns she'd been wearing since she started helping Willa. The new velvet she was wearing would serve for any important occasions.

Her stomach churned. *Was Daniel further improved this morning? Was he getting stronger?* The ache in her heart became unbearable. She folded the petticoat she held, put it in the smaller trunk and crossed to the window. She'd promised herself she wouldn't look at the parsonage again, but she couldn't stop herself. All that she wanted was within its walls. Oh, why had it taken her so long to realize what was truly in her heart? Her parents' dreams were not hers. She didn't need or want fancy gowns or jewels or any of the other trappings of wealth. She wanted Daniel. To marry Daniel had been her childhood dream. And now she knew that dream had never died. It had only been buried beneath the pursuit of *things*.

The tears started again. She arched her neck and placed her forehead against the cold glass to ease the throb in her head. She wanted to be Daniel's wife and bear his children. And for them to have a dog and a cat and…and she wanted to cook for him and mend his clothes the way his mother had mended his torn jacket.

She could learn. She was certain she could. She had learned to make the decorations. But it was too late. She had come to her senses too late. Daniel had lost all regard and respect for her. And it was her fault. It was all her fault! She had acted so haughty and superior to everyone—how was he to know she would rather live with him in a company-owned log cabin than in the grandest mansion with any other man?

Oh, why had she ever listened to her mother and father? She whirled from the window, swept aside the gowns and threw herself on the bed, sobbing into her pillow.

Daniel watched Matthew enter the Townsend house, wrapped the scarf his mother had made him more closely around his neck to ward off the chills that seemed to come easily and headed down the wooded path that led to the sawmill. It was a cowardly thing, putting off saying goodbye to Sadie, but he was still shaken from his leave-taking from Willa. He'd been friends with them for so long, they were more like sisters to him really.

He jerked his mind back from that path. There was business to take care of. He emerged from the path, glanced around and shook his head. He couldn't even imagine not coming to this sawmill again. It had been a part of his life as long as he could remember. He took a breath, climbed the steps to the office, knocked and stepped inside.

"Daniel!" Cole Aylward came around his desk and shook his hand, clapped him on the shoulder. "It's good to see you out and about again. You went through a tough time there." He waved him to a chair and sat down on the corner of his desk. "I thought Sadie was going to wear herself out praying for you. She would have come to see you and help with your care, but Doc Palmer told her no."

He nodded, tugged off his hat and gloves but remained standing. *Irish could take over his place as teamster. He was good with the horses.* "I need to talk to you, Cole."

"All right. But before you begin, I have something I want to discuss with you, Daniel. I'd planned on talking with you about it when the camps started operating again after the blizzard. Then the accident happened and I've had no chance." Cole lifted a small piece of smooth wood off the desk and turned it over in his hand. "I've got a problem, Daniel."

He stiffened, his instinct to offer help squelched by the knowledge that he wouldn't be around after tomorrow.

"My problem is this. I've become so busy with my

'rolling chair' business, I haven't the time to manage the lumber camps, this—" Cole waved a hand toward the sawmill "—or my shingle mill any longer."

"Not to be rude, Cole—" he shivered in the cold air coming in the cracks around the door and moved closer to the woodstove "—but I don't see what any of this has to do with me. And—"

"I want to know if you'd be interested in taking over my place as manager of the Townsend Timber businesses."

"What? *Me?*" The shock went clear to his toes.

"Yes." Cole rose, stood in front of him. "I've watched the way you conduct yourself with the loggers and the workers here in the mill. You have a way of handling men that draws their respect and cooperation. And your ability to think quick and do the right thing in an emergency situation has been amply proven." Cole grinned. "And it won't hurt to have a man running things who the loggers consider a hero. They're a tough bunch to control. So—Manning and I have discussed all of this and feel you're the man we'd like to take over as manager. What do you say?"

He stared at Cole, his mind reeling. *Manning Townsend's business manager! Him?*

"Oh, before you answer, consider that the job would include you running my shingle mill. The wage for that will be separate from the Townsend compensation." Cole frowned, tossed the chunk of wood into the air and caught it. "There will be ample salary commensurate with both positions, of course. And one other thing for you to consider before you make your decision. The manager must live close to the businesses. So Townsend Timber will cede you a few acres of land and build you a fine house, large enough for raising a family, on the far end of the property. What do you say? Shall we discuss wages?"

A home of his own... The means to support a wife and children... Ellen... He slipped his hand into his pocket, gripped the rock and grinned. "I say yes."

There was nothing to delay her further. Her farewells to her parents had been made. Ellen frowned and swirled her blue cloak around her shoulders, shook out its hem and fastened the loop closures. They were unyielding in their opposition to her plans. And her father had firmly refused to pay for her journey, insisting the cost must be paid from her own limited funds. All she could do now was hope that one day they would understand and forgive her for disappointing them.

She stepped to the mirror and put on her bonnet, pulled on her gloves and picked up her muff. She would have little money left when she reached Rochester, but she was determined that her parents would not again dictate the direction of her life. She was through living their dreams. It had cost her her own. Oh, if she had only realized.... But she had been too young. She had simply, obediently followed where her parents led.

She took a breath to quell another onslaught of tears and stepped to the bottom of the stairs. "Hurry with those trunks, Asa. I will be waiting in the sleigh."

She stepped outside and closed the door on what might have been. It was snowing again. Large fluffy flakes like the day she and Daniel— No, she wouldn't think of that. She ducked her head and walked down the steps and out to the carriageway. No more memories to crush her heart. From now on she must—

She stopped, stared at the scarred leather logger boots with red wool socks folded down over their tops. Her heart skipped, took up a staggered beat. She drew on her years of practice and arranged her features in a polite smile, raised her head. "What are you doing outside, Daniel? It's cold." She couldn't quite hide her concern for him. "You should go back in before you take another chill."

He pushed away from the sleigh and took a step toward her. "I came to see you. Are you going somewhere?"

His voice... She made the mistake of looking into his eyes. Her knees went weak. She cleared her throat, lifted her chin and prayed he would leave before she was struck with another uncontrollable crying spell. "I'm going to Rochester. Not that it's any concern of yours." She upped her chin another notch.

"No, you're not. You're not going anywhere."

"I beg your pardon."

He took another step, stopped in front of her and raised his hand. "I got your Christmas gift."

She looked down at the lopsided heart stone on his palm. *He didn't want it. He was giving it back.* The rejection tore at her heart. She blinked hard, didn't dare speak.

"I hope this means you've given me your heart, because I gave you mine the day I gave this stone to you, and I've never taken it back."

She heard the words, the beautiful, heart-stopping words. She simply couldn't believe them. She lifted her gaze to his. "Wh-what?"

"I've loved you since that day, Ellen. I tried to talk myself out of it. Tried to believe it was only a foolish childhood crush, but my heart knew all along that I want you to be mine forever." He dropped the stone in his pocket, gently tugged the ties on her bonnet and slipped his hands beneath the fur-trimmed brim to cup her face. Her bonnet fell away. He lowered his head, touched his lips to hers. She went on tiptoe answering the wonder of his love, and all her silly young-girl dreams came true.

He raised his head, drew in a shaky breath and brushed the tears from her cheeks with his thumbs. "I'm not a teamster anymore, Ellen. I have a new job as manager of the Townsend Timber businesses. And I'm going to manage Cole's shingle mill, as well. I'll earn a good wage, and they've given me land and are going to build me a nice house. A house suitable for raising a family. I won't be rich, Ellen, but I'll be able to provide you with all you need. I want to share that house and raise a family with you." His voice was low and husky. His eyes smoky with green flames in their depths. They took her breath away. She'd already lost her heart.

She lifted her hand and touched the cleft in his chin, more certain than she had ever been of anything in her life that Daniel was the perfect, the *only,* man for her. "I wouldn't care if you were still a teamster, Daniel." Tears choked her voice. "When I thought I might lose you, I realized I don't care about earthly riches anymore. I love you, Daniel. I've always loved you. All I want or need is your love."

"It's yours forever." He slid his hands inside her cloak and pulled her close into his arms. "Will you marry me, Ellen Hall?"

She slipped her arms around his neck and whispered her answer against his soft, warm lips. "Yes, oh, yes, Daniel…and—" His kiss stole her strength. His arms tightened, held her safe against him. Daniel always kept her safe.

"And…"

She sighed, looked up at him and smiled. "Call me Musquash."

Epilogue

~∾~

Ellen smiled and touched the small mother-of-pearl buttons that started at the high collar of her pearl-blue velvet gown and continued down the bodice to the wide band at her narrow waist. The garment was elegant. And warm. An important plus on this cold February day.

She turned her head and looked through the snow falling outside the parsonage window to the blanket-covered bay gelding harnessed to Daniel's new cutter waiting in front of the church to carry them to their new home. Her stomach fluttered. She took a deep breath.

"Hold still, Ellen." Her mother settled the strip of pearl-blue velvet that matched her gown around the base of the curls piled at her crown, tied it in place and stepped back. "Let me see the front."

The long skirt of her gown whispered softly as she turned. Her mother nodded. "You were right about not adding flowers to the band or gown, Ellen. The elegance suits you. You look beautiful. And…happy."

"I am happy, Mother. I never knew I could *be* this happy! I only wish Father—" She stopped, determined not to let her father's rigid refusal to accept and bless her marriage to Daniel spoil her wedding day. "Thank you for my gown, Mother. I'm sorry that making it for me caused dissension between you and Father."

"You're my daughter. It's my place, my privilege and my joy to make your wedding dress. If your father cannot see that, well…then he is more blind than I have been." Her mother drew a breath, released it. "I've been wrong, Ellen. I can see that when I look at your happiness. And I'm thankful you spurned our advice and followed your heart." Her mother's eyes shimmered with tears. "Daniel is a fine man, Ellen. I see that now. And I hope, one day, you will both find it in your hearts to forgive your father and me for the years of happiness we stole from you." The tears overflowed. Her mother took a hesitant step forward and pulled her into her arms. "I love you, Ellen."

She couldn't remember ever being in her mother's arms or hearing those words. Her mind grappled with the unfamiliar, accepted it. "I love you, too, Mother." The words were foreign to her tongue, but they tasted wonderful.

"Now—" her mother released her, stepped back, blinked her eyes and lifted her chin "—there is still a little time. I'm going home and have a talk with your father."

She stared, stunned speechless as her mother picked up her coat and bonnet and marched out the door.

The church bells rang.

Cole Aylward smiled, crooked his arm. "Ready?"

She took a breath and nodded, slipped her gloved hand through his arm and walked with him down the parsonage walkway to Main Street. "Thank you for escorting me, Cole."

"It's my pleasure." He took her elbow, helped her up the church steps and opened the door. "This is fine practice for when I will escort Sadie's and my daughters down the aisle."

"Daughters?" She gasped and looked over her shoulder as Cole removed her cloak. "You mean— Is Sadie—" His grin was all the answer she needed. "She didn't tell me."

"She hasn't seen you since she found out." He hung her cloak on a peg, opened the door to the sanctuary and waved his arm. The hum of voices stopped. He came back and offered his arm again.

She slipped her hand through it and squeezed. "I'm so happy for you both!"

He grinned and nodded and they stepped through the door into the sanctuary. She paused, stared. There wasn't an empty spot in the church. The pews were filled with villagers and townspeople pressed shoulder to shoulder. The aisles along the outside walls were packed full of the overflow, along with loggers and teamsters and their families. Her heart swelled with pride. They were all here for Daniel. Everyone loved Daniel. But not as much as she did. No one could.

Callie and Ezra sat with Sophia Sheffield, all of them smiling at her. A radiant Sadie was beside Grandmother Townsend, who sat at the end of the pew holding hands with Grandfather Townsend, seated in his rolling chair in the aisle. He grinned up at her as they neared, lifted his good hand to touch hers and whispered, "I pray you will be as happy as Rachel and I have always been."

Tears welled. She leaned down and kissed his cheek

above his gray beard, straightened and looked at Willa holding baby Mary and smiling, her green-blue eyes sparkling. She mouthed a silent "Thank you" to her, received a cheeky grin and a silent "You're welcome" in reply.

"She's gonna be our aunt Ellen now."

"How come?"

"Because she's marrying Uncle Daniel."

"Oh. I'm glad."

Joshua's and Sally's whispers, loud in the silence, brought grins and chuckles from those around them.

She leaned down and whispered, "I'm glad, too."

"So am I."

Mrs. Braynard! She glanced at the other side of the aisle and caught her breath. Daniel's mother was sitting beside her mother in her parents' pew. Her father sat rigid and facing straight ahead beside them. But at least he was there. It was a start. She smiled at her mother, let go of Cole's arm and stretched her hands out toward Daniel's mother. "I'm so glad you're here, Mrs. Braynard. I thought you were in Syracuse."

"I'll be goin' back to care for Ruth. But I've been prayin' for this for twelve years. I couldn't miss it." Mrs. Braynard's soft, warm hand closed around hers, squeezed. A smile curved her lips, warmed her green eyes. She went on tiptoe and whispered, "You can let go of that now—you have the real one."

She smiled and opened her hand, looked down at the lopsided heart-shaped stone on her palm. They had been so young then.... She heard a footstep and looked up. Daniel took her hand in his, his long, strong fingers folding over the stone. Her heart trembled at the love in his eyes. He tightened his grip and drew her close.

"Twelve years is a long time to wait. Let's get married, Musquash." His lips brushed her cheek, a promise of forever in their tender touch.

With the stone clasped between their joined hands, they stepped to the altar.

* * * * *

Dear Reader,

I hope you enjoyed reading *A Season of the Heart.* Ellen and Daniel's story ends the Pinewood Weddings series, though I hadn't intended it to be that way. You see, authors can be…well…*hijacked* by their characters. That is what happened to me.

The Pinewood Weddings series was supposed to be three books about three young ladies, lifelong friends in a small town. I added a gentleman friend—Daniel— for these young women because I've always wanted a brother. With his addition my cast of main characters was set. And then Ellen sneaked in there. In the first book, mind you!

I paid Daniel and Ellen little attention. Daniel was there to give brotherly support to my main characters when needed. And Ellen…well, I wasn't sure *why* Ellen was there. And then I wrote a scene in the first book, *Wooing the Schoolmarm,* that the charming Daniel and the audacious Ellen simply stole from me. Cheeky pair! That scene came out nothing like I had intended when I started writing it. And when it was finished, I knew Daniel and Ellen had to have their own story. Thus *A Season of the Heart* was birthed, the fourth and final book in the series.

I hope you have enjoyed getting to know Willa and Matthew, Callie and Ezra, Sadie and Cole, and Daniel and Ellen, along with the village of Pinewood and its residents. It's a bit sad for me to leave them. But I have recently made the acquaintance of some young ladies who are accepting teaching and lecturing positions for a summer course at Fair Point on Chautauqua Lake in

New York. I fully expect there will be clashes with handsome young students and even professors, for these feisty young women number a temperance advocate and a suffragette among them.

I do enjoy hearing from my readers. If you would care to share your thoughts about Ellen and Daniel's story or about Pinewood Village with me, I may be contacted at dorothyjclark@hotmail.com or www.dorothyjclark.com.

Until the summer session at Fair Point begins,

Dorothy Clark

Questions for Discussion

1. Ellen and Daniel decorated the church and the gazebo with materials available to them. Have you ever made Christmas decorations? What is your favorite?

2. Daniel saved Ellen from drowning when he was twelve years old. He told Willa that he knew that day he never wanted to live without Ellen in his life. Do you believe young people can fall in love? Do you think such a love can last a lifetime? Have you any examples to support your opinion?

3. When Daniel realized he loved Ellen, he also realized they were on different levels socially and financially and that her parents would never approve of him as a suitor for Ellen when they were grown. What did he do?

4. Ellen was a normal, happy young girl with friends she loved. What changed her?

5. Daniel made a plan so he would be accepted by Ellen's parents when they grew to a courting age. What changed his plan? Why did it change it?

6. Why did Ellen's parents forbid her to see her friends? Did they succeed in their purpose?

7. Do you think you can "brainwash" a person to the degree that you change their very nature? Explain your opinion.

8. When Ellen's beaux came to Pinewood to ask for her hand in marriage, she suddenly saw them in a different light? Why? Was there more than one reason? Name them.

9. Jesus said, "It is easier for a camel to go through the eye of a needle than for a rich man to enter into the kingdom of God." Why did Jesus say that? Is being wealthy a sin? What is sinful about wealth?

10. When Ellen returned to Pinewood, she slowly changed from the haughty fortune seeker her parents had raised her to be back to the person she truly was in her heart. What was the first thing that happened to her that instigated that change?

11. Why was Daniel so adamant about keeping his feelings hidden from Ellen? Was his motive an admirable one? Do you agree or disagree with him?

12. Why did Willa's *needing* her have such a profound effect upon Ellen? Do you like to feel needed? Do you like to feel you have value in the eyes of others?

WOLF CREEK FATHER
by Penny Richards

As a widower, sheriff Colt Garrett has his hands full with a rambunctious son and daughter. Could a feisty schoolteacher fill the missing piece to their motherless family?

COWBOY SEEKS A BRIDE
Four Stones Ranch
by Louise M. Gouge

Marybeth O'Brien moves west, promised in marriage to a rancher but determined to find her long-lost brother first. Along with the rancher's offer of help, she discovers a feeling of home and family she never knew possible.

FALLING FOR THE ENEMY
by Naomi Rawlings

Lord Gregory Halston is a proper British aristocrat, yet to rescue his brother he needs guidance from a spirited Frenchwoman with a grudge against England—and a heart he has no right to claim.

ACCIDENTAL FIANCÉE
by Mary Moore

Fabricating an engagement is the only way to save the reputations of Lord Weston and Lady Grace Endicott after a misunderstanding. Falling for their betrothed is far from their intentions.

LIHCNM1214

REQUEST YOUR FREE BOOKS!

2 FREE INSPIRATIONAL NOVELS
PLUS 2
FREE
MYSTERY GIFTS

Love Inspired
HISTORICAL
INSPIRATIONAL HISTORICAL ROMANCE

YES! Please send me 2 FREE Love Inspired® Historical novels and my 2 FREE mystery gifts (gifts are worth about $10). After receiving them, if I don't wish to receive any more books, I can return the shipping statement marked "cancel." If I don't cancel, I will receive 4 brand-new novels every month and be billed just $4.74 per book in the U.S. or $5.24 per book in Canada. That's a saving of at least 21% off the cover price. It's quite a bargain! Shipping and handling is just 50¢ per book in the U.S. and 75¢ per book in Canada.* I understand that accepting the 2 free books and gifts places me under no obligation to buy anything. I can always return a shipment and cancel at any time. Even if I never buy another book, the two free books and gifts are mine to keep forever.

102/302 IDN F5CN

Name	(PLEASE PRINT)	

Address		Apt. #

City	State/Prov.	Zip/Postal Code

Signature (if under 18, a parent or guardian must sign)

Mail to the Harlequin® Reader Service:
IN U.S.A.: P.O. Box 1867, Buffalo, NY 14240-1867
IN CANADA: P.O. Box 609, Fort Erie, Ontario L2A 5X3

Want to try two free books from another series?
Call 1-800-873-8635 or visit www.ReaderService.com.

* Terms and prices subject to change without notice. Prices do not include applicable taxes. Sales tax applicable in N.Y. Canadian residents will be charged applicable taxes. Offer not valid in Quebec. This offer is limited to one order per household. Not valid for current subscribers to Love Inspired Historical books. All orders subject to credit approval. Credit or debit balances in a customer's account(s) may be offset by any other outstanding balance owed by or to the customer. Please allow 4 to 6 weeks for delivery. Offer available while quantities last.

Your Privacy—The Harlequin® Reader Service is committed to protecting your privacy. Our Privacy Policy is available online at www.ReaderService.com or upon request from the Harlequin Reader Service.

We make a portion of our mailing list available to reputable third parties that offer products we believe may interest you. If you prefer that we not exchange your name with third parties, or if you wish to clarify or modify your communication preferences, please visit us at www.ReaderService.com/consumerchoice or write to us at Harlequin Reader Service Preference Service, P.O. Box 9062, Buffalo, NY 14269. Include your complete name and address.

LIH13R

"I think she likes you," Brady offered.

Really? Colt thought with a start. Brady thought Allie
liked him? "I like her, too." And he did, despite their on-
again, off-again sparring the past year.

"Are you taking her some ice for her ice cream?" Cilla
asked.

"I don't know. It depends." On the one hand, after not
seeing her all week, he was anxious to see her; on the other,
he wasn't certain what he would say or do when he did.

"On what?"

"A lot of things."

"But we will see her at the ice cream social, won't we?"

Fed up with the game of Twenty Questions, Colt, fork in
one hand, knife in the other, rested his forearms on the edge
of the table and looked from one of his children to the other.
The innocence on their faces didn't fool him for a minute.
What was this all about, anyway?

The answer came out of nowhere, slamming into him
with the force of Ed Rawlings's angry bull when he'd
pinned Colt against a fence. He knew exactly what was up.

"The two of you wouldn't be trying to push me and

Allison into spending more time together, would you?"

Brady looked at Cilla, the expression in his eyes begging her to spit it out. "Well, actually," she said, "Brady and I have talked about it, and we think it would be swell if you started courting her."

Glowering at his sister, and swinging that frowning gaze to Colt, Brady said, "What she really means is that since we have to have a stepmother, we'd like her."

"What did you say?" Colt asked, uncertain that he'd heard correctly.

"Cilla and I want Miss Grainger to be our ma."

Don't miss WOLF CREEK FATHER
by Penny Richards,
available January 2015 wherever
Love Inspired® Historical books and ebooks are sold.